Praise for Barbara Seranella and her newest Munch Mancini mystery

NO MAN STANDING

"Barbara Seranella continues to make everything in [Munch] Mancini's life so believably fragile and difficult to achieve. . . . We gasp and curse as Mancini appears to deliberately court disaster by defending not only her own turf but that of those she loves, and then watch in helpless awe as Seranella steers her and us through to safety one more time."

—*Chicago Tribune*

"Seranella's strong suit is her ability to view life in an unconventional, believably streetwise manner. A bristling attitude of unrelenting suspicion permeates the novels."

—*Los Angeles Times*

"Established fans will lap this one up as eagerly as earlier books in the series."

—*Publishers Weekly*

"Munch proves herself again to be a likable and earnest character with a tough side that is explained by glimpses into her dark past. Her romantic entanglement with a police officer promises interesting times ahead. This story should send some readers back to the first books in the series to catch up on what they've missed."

—*Booklist*

"With each successive book, [Seranella's] storytelling abilities improve, and this one is no exception. . . . Seranella does an excellent job in weaving her characters into her story line and producing a novel that will grab readers and glue them to the page."

—*Easy Reader* (Manhattan Beach, CA)

"A tightly-plotted mystery, characters and dialogue that ring with truth, and most of all, Munch herself—wry, funny, and loving, but nobody's fool—make *NO MAN STANDING* a riveting read. I didn't want this book to end!"

—*Romantic Times* (Top Pick)

UNFINISHED BUSINESS

Los Angeles Times "Best Book of 2001"

"Creepy, funny . . . surprising. . . . Munch Mancini is one of the most interesting investigators prowling the streets these days, a woman who brings to mind the phrase 'true grit' and appears to have the staying power to claim that place for some time."

—*The Houston Chronicle*

"[Mancini is] adroit, resourceful, smart."

—*Los Angeles Times*

"Munch is a likable protagonist, and Seranella's twenty years as a mechanic puts an unusual spin on this series."

—*Publishers Weekly*

"Munch is an original character with plenty of flaws but blessed with a sense of humor about herself. Ms. Seranella has made her into a detective of considerable charm and complexity. The story line is complicated, the characters are intelligent, and the conclusion is surprising and scary."

—*The Dallas Morning News*

UNWANTED COMPANY

"The ensuing mayhem would be hilarious if it weren't so creepy and scary—a combination of emotions that Seranella handles with the same kind of no-sweat skill that Munch applies to her automotive repairs."

—*The New York Times Book Review*

"A page-turner."

—*Los Angeles Times*

NO OFFENSE INTENDED

"Seranella more than makes the point that anything an antihero can do, an antiheroine can do better. . . . [Her] prose is lean and mean."

—*Los Angeles Times*

"Seranella . . . keeps the story line moving at a brisk pace, with surprises around every corner."

—*Chicago Tribune*

"A wonderful book . . . the real truth and the real story here is Munch Mancini's noble struggle for survival in a harsh world. You can't help but take this woman—and this book—to heart."

—Michael Connelly

NO HUMAN INVOLVED

"Scenes pulse with such startling immediacy."

—*Kirkus Reviews*

"A gripping, high-tension ballad of lowlife in L.A."

—*L.A. Buzz*

Also by Barbara Seranella

No Human Involved
No Offense Intended
Unwanted Company
Unfinished Business

BARBARA SERANELLA

NO MAN STANDING

A MUNCH MANCINI CRIME NOVEL

POCKET BOOKS
New York London Toronto Sydney Singapore

This book is a work of fiction. Names, characters, places and incidents are products of the author's imagination or are used fictitiously. Any resemblance to actual events or locales or persons, living or dead, is entirely coincidental.

POCKET BOOKS, a division of Simon & Schuster, Inc.
1230 Avenue of the Americas, New York, NY 10020

Originally published in hardcover in 2002 by Scribner

ISBN: 0-7434-2033-0

First Pocket Books printing April 2003

10 9 8 7 6 5 4 3 2 1

For information regarding special discounts for bulk purchases, please contact Simon & Schuster Special Sales at 1-800-456-6798 or business@simonandschuster.com

Front cover photo credits: Sean Murphy/Getty Images, Siede Preis/Getty Images

Printed in the U.S.A.

For Nicky,
forever in our hearts

Chapter 1

Los Angeles Homicide Detective Art Becker studied the trail of ants streaming into the open mouth of the dead man. After a minute he hefted his portly frame upright and waved to his new partner, Rico Chacón.

Chacón's athletic younger body moved effortlessly toward him. "We've got one more in the house," Chacón said, staring down at the first victim. Even on this overcast morning, he wore sunglasses—Carreras, the kind that adjusted to the light.

The two detectives belonged to a team of robbery/homicide investigators that worked out of the Pacific Division station on Culver and Centinela. Homicide was not unheard of in these parts. The projects up on Slauson were usually good for at least a stabbing on a Saturday night. There was a block on Short Avenue where every other graffiti-covered house was for sale, the signs riddled with bullet holes. But this street was more your working-class residential—a lot of Hispanics, a few blacks, but mainly Midwest transplants.

The two victims had been tentatively identified by the first unit on the scene as Dwayne and Lila Mae Summers. Approximate ages: mid-fifties. Becker made a note of the date, Thursday, January 17, 1985, on a fresh page of his notebook and next to that he wrote, *Cloudy, 50°*. In cross-examination, a criminal-defense attorney had once asked him what the weather had been like the day of the crime. It had looked bad to the jury when he had to admit he didn't remember. That was the last time he was going to get caught like that, he thought, as he continued his inspection of the corpse.

Cause of death for the guy was probably going to be related to the hole in his head. It looked like a bullet wound, but Becker knew better than to assume. He had seen enough tools, kitchen and garden implements, and scraps of hardware stuck in bodies to know how deceptive entry wounds could be. Skin stretched and hair made scalp wounds even more difficult to reckon. Size and shape of the projectile would be determined later by the coroner. However, judging from the scuff marks in the dirt, it was safe to say the vic had died on the run. Becker looked for scorch marks from muzzle flash but found none.

The two uniformed officers who had first responded to the call and now had the duty of guarding the bodies had made a game of picking an ant in line and wagering on the number of seconds it would take it to reach the guy's mouth.

"Just to the lips?" Becker asked. "Or all the way inside?"

"Inside," the taller of the two uniforms said.

Becker noticed a little piece of machinery sticking up out of the dirt. He kicked at it with his toe, and it came loose from the ground. The piece of black metal was an inch long, cast in a figure-eight pattern. Not a tool, he decided as he stooped and picked it up, but some sort of hardware. Two round half-inch stainless-steel prongs, their ends grooved, connected to the figure-eight-shaped flange. He turned it back and forth in his hand and showed it to Chacón. "Know what this is?"

"No, maybe a car part."

"Let's bag it," Becker said.

Chacón put the piece in a little plastic evidence bag on which he recorded the date and location.

"Who's the mope?" Becker asked, indicating the middle-aged white man sitting within the outside layer of yellow tape. Two perimeters had been erected. Tape one protected the interior scene. The second, encompassing driveways on either side of the house and part of the street, formed a staging area where the officers, witnesses, and forensics people could operate and be separated from the public and media.

"Neighbor," the second uniformed cop answered. "He's the guy who found the DBs and called it in."

"What's his name?" Chacón asked.

"Johnson. Cal Johnson."

Becker nodded toward the house. As primary officer assigned to this case, he made the call on how they would proceed. Before speaking to Johnson, he wanted to familiarize himself with the entire crime scene. He walked around an anemic flower bed of mostly dirt and dying daisies and stepped up the single wooden stair leading to the front door. To the right of the door a rusted hibachi sat in cement. The woman's body was just inside. From the neck down, her body faced the ceiling. It took him a second to realize that he was looking at the back of her head. Her face lay buried in the blood-soaked gray carpet. The torque that had snapped her neck had exposed white vertebrae. The fingers on both hands were bruised a deep purple and twisted at unnatural angles.

Chacón came up behind him. He was one of those tall, quiet types who observed everything but said little. Now he made a small grunt of shock.

Becker closed his eyes and took a deep breath through his mouth, giving his senses a break. He had seen death before, but this one made him check his gag reflex. Murder was one thing. People get mad, lose control, snap or whatever, and kill someone. It happened every day, every minute of the day somewhere, probably. But what kind of a human was capable of committing such extreme torture? That he would never fathom. Maybe he was old-fashioned, but the fact that the victim was a woman made this cruelty even worse. He flexed his own undamaged hands, unwillingly imagining the ache of having his fingers cracked like wishbones.

"Let's get to work," he said.

He opened his eyes and looked around the room. The table in front of the couch had been upended and several pictures torn from the wall. Rectangular patches of unfaded paint testified to their previous locations. From the doorway he could also see that drawers in the bedroom dresser had been pulled out and dumped on the floor. The two men toured the rest of the house. The first police on the scene had done this also, making sure no other victims had been overlooked. Becker and Chacón took care to travel in pathways already used by those officers. The kitchen appeared undisturbed as did the bathroom. They returned to the front room where the body was and tried to reconstruct what had happened.

It seemed that either the unknown subject(s) had found what they were looking for or something had interrupted them. A mass of aged papers was on the floor of the bedroom closet. The cardboard box that had apparently held the papers sat upright beside them. ELLEN was written in Marks-A-Lot across the front. Clearly a parent's collection of mementos. They were arranged in chronological order, starting with grammar school report cards and childish drawings rendered in happy colors—a girl and her mom and dad holding hands in the sun with flowers growing at their feet. Becker thought of the abused flower bed out front.

The artwork turned more sophisticated. Pencil sketches of horses and dogs. His own preteen girls were nuts for horses and dogs. Directly to the right of the sketches was a 1971 junior high school yearbook opened to the *S*'s. He looked for and found a Summers. Ellen Summers. If she was in ninth grade fourteen years ago, that would put her age at about twenty-nine now.

The documentation that was fanned across the floor filled in those missing years. Release forms from county jail, bail receipts, and probation reports. There was also a flyer from a club called the Spearmint Rhino. It advertised itself as an adult cabaret. The picture of the sultry blonde on all fours and clad only in a

G-string filled in the subtext. The face of the girl on the flyer matched the ninth-grade black-and-white photo of Ellen Summers given a few trips around a rough block. The flyer had crease marks in it, as if it had been folded in thirds and fitted inside an envelope.

An uneven spray of blood over the papers told him that they had been arranged here prior to at least some of the carnage.

"Time to talk to the neighbor," Becker said. The two detectives left the house and approached Cal Johnson, who was still sitting between the tapes.

"I couldn't figure it out," Johnson said. A black cap with SIR MIX CONCRETE PRODUCTS written in white letters above the brim shaded the top half of his face. The stub of an unlit cigar was wedged between his fingers.

He sat on a frayed lawn chair. It sagged under his weight. He was in his mid-fifties and had the milky eyes of a serious drinker. Broken capillaries flecked his nose and cheeks. His jowls wobbled as he shook his head, too overwhelmed to go on.

Becker waited patiently for the guy to continue. He'd seen this before. People needed to pick their own way to explain horror.

"I thought maybe her hair was covering her face. I even tried to push it aside so she could breathe but her face wasn't where it was supposed to be. Then I saw all the blood." Johnson stopped to spit.

Becker nodded, feeling the bile in his own throat. And then there were the fingers, he wouldn't have missed those. Judging from the darkness of the bruising, the damage to them had happened prior to death. Becker wondered again if the killer(s) had gotten what they wanted.

"Did you touch anything else?"

Johnson shook his head. "I just wanted out of there."

"Where did you call from?"

"My house," he said, nodding toward next door. "There's a daughter, I think."

"Yes, sir," Becker said. "I believe you're right."

"Dwayne wasn't the daddy," Johnson added, indicating the male victim. "Second marriage."

The rest of the forensic team arrived, and the next four hours were spent going over the crime scene and taking statements. One woman was almost certain she had heard a car speeding away, but she could offer no description.

It was midday when Becker and Chacón drove back to the station. They ran the daughter's name through the Criminal Justice Information System and were soon rewarded with an abundance of data. They cleared their intentions with the coroner's office. Death notifications usually fell to the medical examiner or at least were done in conjunction with the ME's office. This one Becker wanted to handle personally.

The two cops drove to the daughter's current known address: the California Institution for Women at Frontera. Becker had made many visits to closest of kin in his twenty-year career. Delivered horrible news—a fifteen-year-old struck down on his bike in a straight-up hit-and-run. Spouses killed in freak accidents. An elderly relative not heard from in a while—found dead a week and God forbid if a hungry Fido had been locked alone in the house with the dearly departed. It always surprised him how calmly most people took the news. Shock, probably. They'd shift into host mode, invite him in, make coffee, ask their questions politely, and he'd always put on his best I-give-a-shit face. There was the one time a guy acted differently. His father had been killed in a home-invasion robbery. The guy ranted and railed, got hysterical. Later it turned out the son had contracted the hit. Becker never forgot that.

Two things were on his mind as he headed east to San Bernardino County. He wondered how Ellen Summers was going to take the news and if his stomach would settle in time to enjoy Flo's daily special at the restaurant on the grounds of the nearby Chino Airport.

Chapter 2

Munch saw the cops approaching, but she wasn't quick enough.

"Nicky, Sam," she yelled to the two dogs frolicking in the surf. Nicky, the border collie mix, could always be depended on to heed her summons, but Sam, the lab/husky, had developed her usual case of deafness. Munch faced the cops and grinned. "I know, I know," she said, trying to ward off their lecture. "No dogs on the beach. We were just leaving."

They weren't even real cops, but city-employed Beach Patrol with the authority to write tickets. The first officer, a somewhat pudgy unsmiling white guy in a blue windbreaker, hung back. His partner, a blond woman with her hair tied into a ponytail, pulled out her citation book. A gust of cold wind blew sand over them.

The dogs' choke chains and leashes hung heavily in Munch's hand. She rattled them at the dogs and made a last attempt to mollify the pseudo-cops.

"Nobody else was down here, and they love the water so much . . ." She left it up to them to fill in the rest and to maybe have a heart.

Nicky came bounding up to them. Her mouth hung open in a dog smile. She accepted the chain that Munch dropped around her neck.

"C'mon, Sam," Munch yelled again.

The cop opened her ticket book and poised her pen to write. "I'm issuing you a citation for failure to observe the posted signs and violation of Health and Safety Code—"

"Spare me," Munch said, cutting her off. No point in being friendly now, the bitch was obviously going to write her a ticket. There was no law saying Munch had to listen to this junior cop's justifications. Instead, she clamped her thin lips tightly together and searched her mind for the words that would wound the deepest.

Keeping Santa Monica safe, are we? she wanted to ask. *Solving major crimes? Is this how cops grow up to be bigger assholes, starting out by harassing tax-paying citizens for letting their dogs play? Are you proud of yourself, you glorified Meter Maid, with your walkie-talkie and your little rule book?* She realized her inner tirade had taken on a sexist slant. Gender wasn't the issue. This junior cop was being a jerk regardless of her personal plumbing.

Munch wanted to point out that even the cop's own partner was keeping his distance, standing twenty yards away and not looking at them.

"Your name?" the blond cop asked.

The rookie was not going to ask to see any ID and why should she? It wasn't like Munch was driving, and it wasn't like the old days in Venice. In Venice Beach the real cops, the kind who carried guns and drove black-and-whites, would pull over and harass her for just standing on the street corner. They would ask her not just for her ID, but also to roll up her sleeves. The act of unbuttoning her shirt cuffs and pushing them up past her elbows always made her feel like a rape victim who removed her own clothes. *If I go along, if I make this easier, will you please not hurt me as much?* There was always a good chance that they wouldn't bust her, although they would have that right. Especially when she exposed her recent needle marks, still red and freshly scabbed. Internal possession of a controlled substance, they called it. A felony. But the whole exercise was not about what she was guilty of. It was more of a power thing, daring you to commit the worst offense: Contempt of Cop.

And yet . . .

Those were the kinds of cops she loved. Getting busted had rescued her from her life on the street. Going to jail had interrupted the savage spiral of her existence and had given her a chance to come out from under the fog of addiction.

"Your name, ma'am?" the cop asked again, her tone peevish now. They hated it when you made them wait.

"Miranda," Munch said, hearing her own voice tight with anger for being busted for something as stupid as walking two dogs on a deserted beach in the middle of winter. "Miranda Mancini." Even as she said the words, she couldn't believe it. Why was she giving this broad her real name? Times sure had changed.

While the cop wrote, Munch remembered another ticket she'd gotten with her old running partner, Ellen.

The two of them had been stopped for jaywalking of all things. This was ten years ago. They'd been in downtown Los Angeles and dressed in their full biker regalia. Munch in grungy jeans so thick with grease that they looked like leather. Ellen in tight bell bottoms and one of her big floozy wigs. The cop riding shotgun had said, "Don't get much cooler than you two." And despite herself Munch had felt a thrill of pride, even though she didn't miss the sarcastic tone of his voice.

Ellen. Or as she was referred to in Munch's private lexicon, *Fucking Ellen.*

She was thinking about her friend a lot lately. Ellen was getting out of prison soon. Again. Munch had recently resumed a relationship with Ellen's mom, Lila Mae. Now that Munch was a mom herself, her sympathies for Lila Mae had undergone a huge overhaul.

When Munch got sober eight years ago, she soon realized that there were many persons she had hurt besides herself. Her influence on Ellen, and by extension, Ellen's long-suffering family, was a prime example. It was curious, this role reversal of hers and Ellen's. Ellen had always been the more controlled of the two, keeping her shit a little better together, usually with the aid of some man. Munch had taken her craziness to the brink of destruction. Ellen had the fatal flaw of continuously rallying from her various misadventures, never quite being beaten. She landed on her feet, usually with someone else's money or husband, but on her feet just the same.

Crashing and burning, hitting bottom, had ultimately saved Munch. As with most of her fellow members in AA and Narcotics Anonymous, she had had to find her way to salvation through a journey to the very depths of hell. It was only then, with no other options left, that she was ready to try something as radical as complete sobriety.

Munch tried to explain all this to Lila Mae, that she would do her best for Ellen, but that they could only hope that Ellen had suffered enough. Lila Mae had thought that odd, to wish enough suffering on anybody. Munch had shrugged and said that was only one of a long line of paradoxes in this life. Lila Mae had said, "I expect so."

Munch slipped the chain over Sam's head and casually positioned the wet canine, dripping with sea water, between herself and the cop. Sam shook herself, spraying cold water on both of them.

"Sorry," Munch said. Sure.

The cop looked annoyed, which helped ease Munch's irritation. The real irony was that the dogs belonged to LAPD Homicide Detective Mace St. John, the man who had also had a huge hand in Munch's current state of salvation. She was watching Sam and Nicky while Mace and his wife, Caroline, were up in Big Bear on their second, or maybe it was their third, honeymoon. Munch tried not to keep count.

The detective was also still recovering from a heart attack. St. John would have a fit if he learned she was letting his precious dogs run around without their leashes. He was protective of those he loved, to the point of paranoia. Mace St. John was the kind of guy who looked at the beach and saw only riptides.

Munch recited the rest of her information in response to Officer Ponytail's questions. She fudged a little on the height and weight, building herself up to five foot two and one hundred and five pounds.

"Occupation?"

Now she's really going to think I'm lying, Munch thought. "Auto mechanic," she said.

To the cop's credit, she didn't blink. Munch was glad. She was in no mood for the inevitable questions that followed and the too-long answer to *How'd you get into that?*

The cop handed her the ticket to sign. Munch took her time, reading every word of the small print. The cop shifted feet and Munch smiled inwardly. Finally, she signed her name on the bottom line, keeping her lips pressed together to express her annoyance.

The cop ripped the ticket loose and handed it over.

Munch didn't say thank you. Some small part in her brain congratulated her for being in touch with her feelings.

The Beach Patrol waited while she stuck the ticket in her pocket and walked the dogs through the tunnel running under the Pacific Coast Highway. She toweled the dogs dry as best she could, then had them jump into the backseat of her GTO. The bumper sticker on the rear window proclaimed: *Reality is for people who can't handle drugs.*

"I hope you're happy," she said to the panting dogs. So much for their little excursion to relieve the drudgery of moving.

Chapter 3

Munch was still in a dark mood when she arrived home. Her now legally adopted daughter, Asia, was in school. After raising the child from infancy, Munch had finally completed the arduous process of gaining legal sanction of their relationship. Asia had hoped to play hooky for the day. To help Munch pack, she said, but Munch knew the eight-year-old's true motives were to stay home with the dogs.

"You need to honor your commitment," she had told her daughter.

"What's a commitment?" Asia asked.

"A promise. A duty. You have a commitment to go to school like I have a commitment to go to work."

"But you're not going to work today."

"But I arranged this week off ahead of time so I wouldn't let Lou down. Besides, you need to go to school today because you're bringing the cupcakes for

Lindsey." Lindsey Ramsey was Asia's best friend of the moment. Today was her ninth birthday, which meant a little in-class party. Asia was going to Lindsey's house after school to continue the celebration. "You don't just get to keep the promises that are fun."

"All right," Asia had said, but with reluctance. Playing with the dogs was more fun. She was at that age when she wanted a dog. She wanted a daddy too, but Munch explained they would take things one at a time.

When Ellen Summers's name was called over the loudspeaker, announcing that she had visitors, she turned off her sewing machine. The job in the clothing factory making Nomex outerware for the Forest Service was a plum assignment. It paid ninety-five cents an hour, and every day spent working took a day off her sentence. She turned in her scissors to the Correctional Officer, the CO in charge of the tools, and received her picture ID card in return. No doors in this place opened for you without your ID card.

"Mrs. Walker, do I have time to freshen up?" she asked her escort.

Mrs. Walker rolled her eyes. "Yeah, okay. But make it quick."

They stopped at Ellen's room, a six-by-nine cell she shared with a forger from Cincinnati. There wasn't much she could do to spiff up the prison-issued baseball jersey and blue jeans. She brushed her hair, retied her ponytail, and applied a few touch-up strokes to her makeup. She always liked to look her best. So much in this world was judged on appearances, a girl did well to keep her weapons honed.

As they walked across the yard Ellen wondered if Munch had made the long trip out here. Had she decided to brave the smells of cow manure and the arrogant attitudes of the staff? Bless her little heart. Maybe Munch was going to offer her a job driving her limo. She'd already said she didn't blame Ellen for what happened that first time. Friends that good only came along once in a lifetime.

Mrs. Walker directed Ellen toward the administration building. The visitor yard was in the other direction.

CiCi, the lifer clerking in reception looked up. "Uh uh," she said in that deep melodic tone that only black women seemed able to hit. "What you do now?"

"One more day and I'm out of here," Ellen said, looking up to the second floor at the grated windows of the warden's office. "They probably want to thank me for all my good work."

CiCi cackled, exposing toothless gums. "Don't be sticking your nose up," she said. "You just like me. You'll be back. You just doing your time on the installment plan."

CiCi had been crazier when Ellen first met her. That was eight years ago, when Ellen was beginning her first stretch in CIW. They met in Graystone, the two-tiered building at the southern end of the facility, so called because it was built of gray stone, like some medieval castle, and looked much different from the other redbrick buildings.

The first thing Ellen had seen as she was herded through the double-locked steel gates of Graystone were the words NO WARNING SHOTS FIRED. Women screamed all day there. Discipline problems were locked down in Graystone's single cells, also inmates on medication and lifers adjusting to their first year. After those first few years, they tended to settle down and accept their fate. Graystone also served as a holding facility for all the new prisoners awaiting processing. CiCi qualified to be there three different ways. Yet despite her desperate anger, she'd helped Ellen through the orientation process, and had given her the heads-up about the job in the clothing factory. That was eight years ago, and since then Ellen had been back in the system twice more, each instance vowing that this time would be her last.

"C'mon," Mrs. Walker said and led her up the stairs, to the offices of the Institution Investigator.

Here we go again, Ellen thought.

Her visitors, two guys she didn't recognize, were already there waiting. One was sitting on the couch. His face was craggy; his eyes small and flat. She guessed his age at fiftyish. The other guy, younger, taller, much cuter, and Hispanic, remained standing.

"Well, now," she said in her heaviest Deep South drawl, taking a seat beside the older one, sitting so that her breasts jutted toward him, "who do we have here?"

"Detective Becker," the older cop answered, handing her a business card that identified him as being an LAPD detective with the Pacific Division.

She waited. He had come to see her, which meant he wanted something.

"Ellen," he said, regarding her with his cold dull eyes, "I have some bad news."

She almost laughed. Since when had a cop brought her anything but.

"I was at your mother's house earlier today. She was the victim of an apparent robbery."

Ellen remained silent, feeling the blood draining from her face. Why was he telling her this? He could see she was in custody. They couldn't pin this on her.

"The house had been ransacked," he continued. "Any idea what your mother had that was so valuable?"

She breathed then. Slowly, so this guy wouldn't notice she'd forgotten to for a minute. So that was it. They were trying to find out about the money again. Only this time they were backing into it through the mama angle. "You guys don't quit," she said, playing with the low-slung collar of her shirt, drawing his eyes to the movement. "I haven't seen or heard from my mama in months. Did she send you here?"

"No, Ellen." He looked into her eyes then. His pockmarked face rigid, eyes expressionless, telling her nothing. Still, she watched his lips move. Instinct told her that the next thing he said was going to change her life forever. "Your mother didn't send me. She was apparently home when the robbery took place. There was a struggle. Your mother received injuries. Injuries she didn't survive."

"What?" She felt her eyes blinking, closing and opening, quickly, repeatedly. Was this guy telling her Lila Mae was dead?

"I'm sorry," he said.

"What about Dwayne? Her husband? Where was he when all this was going on?"

"We think he may have surprised the suspects. Officers found him in the side yard with a puncture wound to the head."

"He's dead too?" she asked, wishing this guy would just come out and say it.

"Yes, I'm afraid so."

She felt tears running down her cheeks. They surprised her. Not because they were inappropriate. This was horrible news. Terrible. She just didn't feel anything. It was as if her body was reacting for her. "How did my mom die?"

The cop handed her a box of Kleenex. "At this point we believe she was beaten to death. Autopsies in a couple of days will reveal more. Any idea who would do such a thing? Your mom have any enemies?"

"I don't know what she had," Ellen said. She tried to force herself to look in his eyes—to convince him of her sincerity—but she couldn't. "She was just an old woman. She didn't do anything."

When she looked back up, Becker was watching her steadily, that way cops do when they're waiting for you to trip yourself up. "One more thing," he said, "before they killed her they broke her fingers."

"Oh my God."

"Can you think of anything that mi—"

"Hell." She slammed her palm on the cushion between them. The action made him jump, reach for something on his belt. "What are you doing wasting your time here? Go find the sons of bitches!"

"We're going to do our best, Ellen."

He acted like he might have another question or two, but she waved him away. She didn't have anything more to say to him, not until she had a chance to think this through.

He rose to leave. The other cop—the quiet, good-looking one—was already at the door. She buried her face in her hands. This time her sobs were for real.

Becker watched the Correctional Officer lead Ellen Summers away. The bit about the fingers had been a calculated risk on his part, but he'd gotten his payoff. The look on her face before she went into her righteous indignation mode was pure terror. He requested and received Ellen Summers's case file. It took a few minutes to locate.

"Sorry for the wait," the flushed inmate serving as clerk said when she handed it over. "I'm still new at this job and someone misfiled this."

Among other things, the folder had a record of all of Ellen Summers's visitors and a list of all persons who had sent her mail.

"Can you run me a copy of this?" Becker asked.

The woman smiled and said, "Sure."

"I'll wait." He studied a vase full of flowers on the desk and the framed Sears studio photo of a little boy in his Sunday suit. Women's prisons were notably more laid back than men's. Becker considered how easy it was to forget some of these inmates weren't regular people.

When he got to his car he cross-referenced the sign-in sheet against Ellen's court documents, paying particular attention to codefendants. Career criminals were not great innovators. They tended to caper with the same people over and over. With the advent of computer recordkeeping, crooks left cyber-fingerprints everywhere they went.

Ellen hadn't had many visitors in the past six months. She was telling the truth about her mama not seeing her in a long time. The last and only visit from Lila Mae had been in September. Two agents from Secret Service named Carter and Long had spent twenty-eight minutes with the prisoner in December. Other than that, the ledger was blank except for the name Miranda Mancini, which appeared several times. Mancini hadn't been back in two months.

Chacón took his turn with the paperwork, grunting when he got to the list of visitors.

"What is it?" Becker asked.

Chacón pointed to Miranda Mancini's name. "I'll interview her. We've met before."

"Yeah, okay," Becker said. He copied a few more names from the list, dividing the workload, and handed them to Chacón. "These too. We're going to pull out all the stops on this one."

"You got it," the younger man said, slipping the list into his own notebook.

Becker nodded toward the prison. "What did you think?"

"She's dirty," Chacón said.

"She's also one day short," Becker said, pointing out Ellen's scheduled release date.

"Just in time for the funerals."

Chapter 4

Late Thursday afternoon, Munch drove up Chautauqua Boulevard in Pacific Palisades to retrieve Asia from Lindsey Ramsey's birthday party. The steep four-lane street wound past large homes with circular driveways and ocean views. Nicky and Sam balanced in the backseat, whining with longing at all the greenery. A few of the estates even had tennis courts, although Munch never saw anybody actually using one of them. After the party, Lindsey was coming home with Asia to spend the night.

Munch caught a red light on Sunset Boulevard. Sitting there, she thought of the awkward business ahead. Lindsey had a daddy named Alex. Munch had made a big mistake with the guy a month back. She had seen his long hair, his pro-ecology, anti-nuke bumper stickers, and pegged him for a harmless hippie type. It wasn't long before she discovered that Alex had a knack for always turning the conversation back to himself. Unfortunately, she hadn't realized how annoyingly self-involved he was until after she had gone ahead and done the deed with him.

Asia was all for the two parents hooking up and had been disappointed when Munch told her that she didn't like Alex Ramsey "that way." How do you explain to an eight-year-old about the type of man her best friend's father really was? That he was just another one of those pretty boys walking around with an open umbilical cord looking for a place to plug in?

Alex also liked to complain about how obsessed his soon-to-be ex was with him. They had been separated six months with a divorce pending. *She* had left *him,* he said. Now that he was seeing other people, she wanted him back. His mouth said it like it was a problem, but his facial expressions declared a twisted sort of pride—like who could blame her?

Munch had reached the conclusion that both husband and wife were infatuated with the same person. The fiasco with Alex had come on the heels of yet another failed relationship, although it hadn't really felt like a failure as much as an escape. Munch had been in a serious courtship with Garret Dimond. They had even started talking about moving in together. Then Munch had done some earnest soul-searching and arrived at the inescapable realization that she wasn't in love with Garret and never would be.

This personal epiphany had been painful for all concerned. Garret was a good guy; it was never his goodness that was in question. Good didn't always get it. He was a hardworking, considerate man who was going to make somebody a fine husband someday, but that somebody was not going to be Munch.

Garret insisted on remaining friends. He also said

he was willing to wait. She tried to tell him as nicely as possible not to bother. He wasn't taking a hint.

"Does he have a brother you can sleep with?" Ellen had asked from jail.

"I'm not even sure that would do it," Munch had replied with a laugh, remembering how much simpler life had been in the bad old days. Ellen and she had had answers for everything back then. *Live hard, ride fast, die young, and leave a beautiful corpse* was their credo followed by *Fuck 'em if they can't take a joke.* Those two sentiments covered most of the ground they traveled.

Of course, they hadn't died young and most of the old rules had changed.

Ellen. Ellen hadn't changed. There was a lot to be said for friendships that stretched back to puberty. To date, Munch had been unable to cultivate a new woman friend with whom she felt totally free to be herself. Besides, who she was was constantly evolving. That fact was even part of Garret's argument for sticking around, as if she might one day wake up and love him.

Asia had already picked out a flower-girl dress from one of her bride catalogs.

"Garret's not the one," Munch told her. She explained that love between a man and woman wasn't something that could be wished into existence. It just had to be there. She didn't feel it for Garret, and she hadn't achieved sobriety in order to make herself the prisoner of a one-sided love relationship.

"You're not too upset, are you?"

"Nah, I saw it coming."

"Remember," Munch had said, taking the opportunity to give a life lesson, "honesty is always the best policy."

"In my experience, too," Asia replied.

Eight years old, Munch often had to remind herself.

She watched the traffic whiz along Sunset Boulevard and shook her head. If only interpersonal relationships were as easy to fathom as the workings of the four-stroke internal combustion engine. Tina Turner sang, *What's love got to do with it?* on the radio. Munch turned up the volume and sang along. The light changed and she gunned the motor to get into the right lane for the immediate turn onto the tree-lined street of the Ramseys' upscale suburban neighborhood.

The dogs shifted in the backseat, and she put a hand behind her to pat them.

Lindsey lived on one of Palisades' alphabet streets. Highly prized real estate, each street in the residential grid started with a successive letter of the alphabet beginning with Albright and ending with Kagawa. The Ramseys lived on Galloway, between Fiske and Hartzell. Total yuppie land.

Practically every driveway sported a BMW or one of those four-wheel drive vehicles that ate through brakes like candy. Munch worked on a lot of those at her shop in Brentwood and had even invested in the special tools necessary to remove the hubs. She didn't understand the attraction of Chevy Blazers, Jeep Cherokees, Land Rovers, and those monstrous ten-passenger Suburbans that the sushi-eaters drove. It wasn't like they ever went off-road, and trucks were much more expensive to keep up. Maybe that was the point.

By contrast, her seventies-vintage Pontiac GTO,

though immaculately maintained, looked like something one of the maids or gardeners drove. But it wouldn't go out of style every other year, and she could fix or replace practically everything under the hood with a 9/16 wrench and a screwdriver. That made a hell of a lot more sense than impressing the other mothers at ballet recitals.

Munch got in sight of the Ramseys' house and knew immediately that something was wrong in storybook land. The front door of the Spanish-style two-story home was open. Alex and some redheaded woman were on the front lawn arguing. This had to be the infamous ex, Noreen. The side of Alex's face bore four fresh red scratches that stretched from below his eye to the base of his jaw. Their width suggested fingernails.

Noreen's shoulder-length hair was frizzy and dry-looking. She wore wire-rimmed, expensive-looking glasses. Her voice was pitched loud enough to carry through Munch's rolled-up windows. It was a superior-sounding voice. Her tone reminded Munch of some of her least-favorite gas station customers, the kind who were always busy and irritated and talked at you as if you were dense and barely worth their breath. Noreen looked at least a decade older than Alex, who would turn twenty-nine this year, the same as Munch.

Munch waited a moment before getting out of her car, hoping that this domestic battle would cease. Alex and Noreen were screaming and showing no class at all. Alex was dressed in his usual casual chic: jeans and sweatshirt. Noreen wore a fitted skirt, silk blouse, and heels.

How could they fight like this in front of the kid?

Munch wondered. And at the child's birthday party? Some things should be sacred.

A group of maybe ten kids in party hats huddled together in one corner of the lawn. Some were sucking their thumbs. Others looked like they'd been crying. The large, colorful plastic Playskool jungle gym had been tipped over. Munch got out of her car and hopped the low white picket fence. She bypassed the adults and went straight for the group of children. They flocked to Munch, leaning in to her, clutching at her jacket hem. She collected as many as she could in her arms, starting with Asia.

Next to the kids, the tattered half of a Pin-the-Tail-on-the-Donkey game fluttered against the garage door. The front half of the smiling donkey was still held by thumbtacks, but the image was marred now by a spray of something red and fresh.

Munch ran her hands over every inch of her daughter's body, making reassuring noises and checking for blood or any other signs of damage. Asia submitted without protest. "Are you all right?"

Asia nodded bravely.

"You want to go home? I've got Sam and Nicky in the car."

This announcement didn't even bring a smile to Asia's face. The little girl stared at something over Munch's shoulder. Munch turned in time to see Noreen point an accusing finger at her.

"I've heard *all* about *you,*" the witch said.

"I've heard about you too." Munch was not in a mood to let the veiled insult go unchallenged. Alex had told Munch that his estranged wife had some composure issues. Munch would have called it something else.

Other parents had begun to arrive.

"Lindsey said they always yell at each other," Asia confided with a knowing look. Too knowing for an eight-year-old. "But they usually don't hit."

Munch looked around. "Where is Lindsey? She still spending the night?"

"She's inside," Asia said. "I'll show you."

Asia led Munch to the side entrance. They found Lindsey sitting by herself in the kitchen. Two untouched pieces of birthday cake sat before her on the table. The scoops of vanilla ice cream had melted and were dripping over the edges of the Winnie-the-Pooh paper plates.

"Lindsey?" Munch said.

The little girl turned dull eyes to Munch and hiccuped once. She opened her mouth to say something. No words came out. Her jaw quivered.

Munch smoothed back the child's hair. Lindsey and Asia liked to dress alike, even after shedding their matching school uniforms. Today they had gone for the *Flashdance* look: black leg warmers, sweatshirts with the bands cut out, Nike tennis shoes. They even wore their brown hair the same way—tying fluorescent pink Madonna-inspired bandannas under their natural brown curls, with the knotted ends at the side of their heads. A teacher at the school once confided that if it wasn't for Asia's Latina skin tone contrasted against Lindsey's bone whiteness, she wouldn't be able to tell them apart half the time.

"I'm taking you to my house," Munch said, speaking in an adult tone—the only kind she ever used with anyone.

Lindsey nodded, her expression woeful, resigned.

She was even paler than usual with dark circles under her eyes. Munch felt a weird sense of déjà vu, as if this same conversation had taken place before, only now her part of the dialogue was different.

She took Lindsey's hand and led her outside. The child's flesh was cold. A tremble telegraphed across their fingertips.

"We're getting out of here," Munch said. "This is bullshit."

Lindsey stared at her wide-eyed, and Munch felt a guilty twinge for the swearing. The kid had no doubt heard much worse, not that that was any excuse.

"I'm going to take care of you." When Lindsey didn't answer, Munch stopped and knelt down so that they were eye level. She made sure those haunted little eyes were focused on her own.

"Do you hear me?" Munch said. "I promise to take care of you. I mean it."

The street was congested now with station wagons, SUVs, anxious parents, and curious neighbors.

Munch secured Asia and Lindsey in individual seat belts in the backseat. As if sensing their distress, the two dogs curbed their usual enthusiasm. Munch watched as they gently nudged at the little girls' necks and ears with their noses.

"Where's your overnight bag?" Munch asked.

"Oh," Asia said, theatrically amazed. "We forgot to pack."

Lindsey looked almost fearfully back at her house.

"Don't worry," Munch said. "I'll get your stuff and tell your daddy we're leaving."

Lindsey nodded.

Munch went back in the house through the kitchen,

grabbed a paper grocery sack from the stack beside the refrigerator, then started up the stairs. The first door she opened was not a child's room. It was filled with clothes on standing racks, lots of jeans and sweatshirts and tennis shoes.

Lindsey's room, at the end of the hall, revealed a chaotic jumble of too much furniture and not enough light. Dark curtains covered the windows. Shelves were packed with toys that should have been discarded years ago—baby rattles, building blocks, felt books. Glossy photographs of Madonna and Michael Jackson, cut from the pages of *Teen Beat Magazine,* hung over the bed.

Munch opened the closet. She pushed aside little down jackets that would have been tight on a three-year-old, toddler-size jumpers and sun dresses. Ballet slippers, go-go boots, and a rainbow selection of tennis shoes were heaped in a pile beneath them. She stuffed a pair of pajamas and a change of clothes into the paper bag and went in search of the bathroom to collect the kid's toothbrush.

The bathroom was across the hall from the jeans and sweatshirt room. The mirrored cabinet door above the sink hung open. The top shelves were filled with prescription pill bottles. Feeling a semiprofessional interest, she turned them to read the labels: Ritalin, Seconal, Valium, Elavil, Halcion, Compazine. All the flavors of the psychotropic rainbow—uppers, downers, inners and outers, and each one prescribed for Noreen Ramsey.

Apparently Ms. Noreen here had chosen to ignore Nancy Reagan's plea to just say no. As if those billboards worked for anyone. If a person had the ability to say no in the first place, then he or she probably wasn't the type who got addicted. But this was the age of sound bites, and the movie-star president's neat little wife had found a catchy phrase of her own. *Just Say No.* Munch shook her head; diseases were not conquered by clever slogans.

She was reminded of a George Carlin comedy bit. He had come up with a sure-fire criminal defense tactic: "I forgot." As in, "I'm sorry, Your Honor, I forgot armed robbery was against the law." At least he knew he was being ridiculous.

Munch's intestines clenched as another thought occurred to her. If Noreen had moved out, why had she left her pills behind? They would have been the first thing Munch would have packed. Munch checked the dates of the prescriptions. Most of them were current.

Great, Munch thought, now she had not only slept with an idiot, but he apparently wasn't as unattached as he claimed.

She closed the cabinet and picked up the toothbrush perched on the sink's edge. The handle was pink and shaped into a smiling mermaid. She jammed it into the bag of clothes and headed back down the stairs.

Noreen confronted her on the lawn.

"What do you think you're doing?"

"I was just picking up Lindsey's clothes," Munch said, trying not to hate this woman, not to waste any emotion on her. "You remember the kid, don't you? She's spending the night."

"I'm not sure you're the type of person I want my child around."

Munch took a deep breath and let it out through her mouth.

Noreen ripped the bag from Munch's hands. The clothes spilled out. "Haven't you stolen enough from me?"

"I haven't ripped you off for anything," Munch said, taking the woman's measure, knowing how hard it was to keep your balance in high heels on grass. Munch's first impulse had always been to deal with interpersonal disputes in the most direct manner possible. Her fists clenched as she imagined herself knocking Noreen to the ground, taking a fistful of the woman's red hair in one hand, and using it to hold her head still while she beat her—

Munch stopped herself midfantasy, restraining her thoughts as well as her impulses. She was hoping to set a good example for her kid. Mature adults chose their actions rather than reacting.

"Whore," Noreen said, really pushing her luck.

The image of a bloodied Noreen persisted in Munch's mind. She didn't know if Noreen was trying to be literal, but *whore* was about the worst insult she could have chosen. In the bad old days, it was a term Munch often applied to herself with varying degrees of brass and boldness. Now the word conjured feelings of shame.

"Get out of my way," Munch said, her voice low, adrenaline constricting her throat.

"You weren't the first," Noreen said. "He didn't tell you that, did he? You won't win."

"I'm not even playing."

Alex came up behind his wife and said, "It's better if they go."

Munch picked up Lindsey's toothbrush, but left the rest of the clothes where they had fallen.

"We discussed you," Noreen said in that college-educated voice of hers. "Alex told me everything."

"I hope he remembered to include the part where I said I didn't want to see him anymore."

"And yet here you are."

Munch looked at Alex for support. He made an expression as if to say, *There's no reasoning with her.*

"Oh, God, Alex," Noreen said, pointing, her pencil-drawn eyebrows arched high. "Look at her hands."

Munch clenched her fists, instinctively hiding her grease-stained fingernails. Then she caught herself, angry that this woman had made her feel less-than for this evidence of her perfectly honorable profession.

"C'mon, Noreen, give it a rest," Alex said, turning to the front window and checking his face in the reflection. "Lins has been looking forward to this."

Munch bit back the words she would have liked to have said. She was pretty sure Alex's evening plans were dependent on his being sans any extraneous company such as a daughter. "That's right, this is just about the kids." She turned to Alex, letting her contempt for him show in her voice. "Now be a good adult and wave good-bye to your daughter."

Chapter 5

What was it about making a big change in your life that seemed to attract chaos? Munch wondered as she cleared Asia's and Lindsey's plates from the kitchen counter. Moving was difficult enough, but then the universe threw you six other curves. There was probably a scientific explanation. Maybe the concentration of extra activity created some sort of an energy magnet—and not necessarily for positive energy.

As if to emphasize her point, the dogs jumped up and ran to the door. Ten seconds later, somebody knocked. The dogs didn't bark, but they weren't wagging their tails either. Ears pricked forward, they focused with every muscle of their bodies on whatever or whoever was outside.

She stepped between the packing crates stacked waist-high throughout the room. Black Marks-A-Lot printing identified the contents: BOOKS, SUMMER CLOTHES, LIMO RECORDS.

She glanced through the peephole and saw an attractive man. Maybe the day was going to end on a positive note after all. The guy was Chicano, her age or maybe a few years older, and wearing a slightly rumpled suit.

"Wait here," she told the dogs, and they both sat.

She opened the door and stood facing the man. It was a moment before either spoke. His nose angled to one side, as if it had been broken at one time and not set. He wore a musky cologne. He flipped his wallet open to show her a shiny new-looking LAPD detective's badge.

Now what? "Can I help you?"

"Miranda Mancini?"

"Who is it, Mom?" Asia came to stand beside her.

Crouching down so that he was eye level with Asia he said, "I'm Enrique Chacón." When he said his name—*Cha-cone*—it was as if a whip cracked the air and filled it with a static charge. Munch felt something inside her brain shift sharply to attention. He looked up with a friendly, surprisingly open smile.

"Actually," he said, "we've met before."

"Oh?" He did seem vaguely familiar.

"I used to work narcotics."

Munch's hands instinctively moved to cover Asia's ears.

"You're the mechanic, right?"

She nodded carefully, still trying to place the guy.

"In San Diego, about six months ago. You were with Mace St. John, looking for your limo and that friend of yours. You thought she'd gone to Mexico."

"Oh yeah, right." He was referring to Ellen, who

had managed to land a killer as her very first and unauthorized charter in Munch's limousine. "We found her back in L.A."

"I heard all about it. Didn't the two of you help St. John catch a murderer and break up some big weapons deal?"

"I didn't know about the plutonium until later. We were just trying to stop the guy." In addition to committing murder and rape, the two men who had booked her limo during the Olympics last summer had been auctioning a cache of stolen plutonium to some Mideast fanatics. Munch and Ellen had had their hands full just trying to stay alive. After the dust settled, Munch had gone on with her life, and Ellen, true to form, had returned to prison on a parole violation.

"Is this your daughter?"

"Yes, this is Asia. Asia, this is Detective Chacón."

"Hi, honey. Call me Rico." He looked again at Munch, then at the boxes.

"Are you moving?"

"We bought a new house," Asia announced.

"Good for you," Rico said. "I'm not interrupting anything, am I?"

"No, we've eaten." The dogs were still sitting tensely at her side. "He's okay," she told them. They responded by wagging their tails. Rico reached over and gave their heads a pat.

"St. John said your limo got pretty thrashed in TJ."

"It's all put back together. I was back in business within a few weeks." The gift of hundred-dollar bills from Ellen had facilitated the speed of the repairs.

Munch hadn't questioned Ellen too closely on the source of the cash. Where Ellen was concerned, it was sometimes best not to know the details.

"How do you know Mace St. John?" Rico asked.

"He's my godfather," Asia said, as if the question had been directed at her. "I don't have a regular daddy."

"Thank you, honey," Munch said. This was not the first time Asia had volunteered that information to a good-looking man. Knowing Asia, it wouldn't be the last either. "I don't think Detective Chacón cares about that."

"Actually," he said, "that was going to be one of my next questions, and it's Rico." Again the smile. He reached into his pants pocket and removed a roll of LifeSavers. "Do you mind?" he asked Munch, motioning toward Asia.

"No," she said, as if he had given her a choice.

He handed the candies to Asia, who took them and sneaked a look at her mother. "My friend Lindsey likes LifeSavers too."

Rico produced a second roll. Did he realize he'd just been hustled by a third-grader?

Asia ran off to share her new treasure.

He glanced at his watch. "Can you step outside for a minute?"

"Well . . ." She looked behind her nervously.

"We'll just be right out here."

"Let me grab a coat, and tell Asia what's going on."

"I'll wait."

The girls were in Asia's room, sitting cross-legged on the floor and facing each other. Munch watched from the doorway, wanting nothing but to let these kids float unharmed in their cocoon of innocence. She hadn't pressed Lindsey about what went on at the party. At this point she felt the kid's well-being was better served by providing a calm and normal home.

"You know what?" Asia said, her face only inches away from her friend. "If you go like this real hard for a long time . . ." She rubbed her knuckles into her shut eyes, elbows extended, then stopped and said, "It makes it look like you've been crying."

"Hey," Munch said, slipping into her coat. "I'll just be right outside if you need me."

"Okay," Asia said, making a so-go-already gesture with her hand.

Munch stepped outside and felt the first heavy drops of the night's threatened downpour.

"Let's sit in my car," Rico said.

His car was a metallic-green '66 Chevrolet Impala. Two-door. Tinted windows. Low-profile tires mounted on shiny mag rims. Munch half-expected to see some of those chrome organ pipes in the rear window and fuzzy dice hanging from the rearview mirror.

She let herself into the passenger side, noticing the tuck-and-roll upholstery, and the aftermarket stereo system—an expensive Blaupunkt.

"So," Rico said, sliding in on the driver's side. He let his arm drape across the top of the seat. His fingers were long, she noticed. No ring. "Auto mechanic, limo owner and operator, mother. All that keeps you pretty busy, huh?"

"The limo business is off and on," she said. *Mostly off*, she thought, looking at the big car depreciating in her driveway.

"Give me one of your cards," he said. "I might be able to throw you some business."

She reached in her coat pocket and pulled out three. The streetlight illuminated his face as he read the card. His cheekbones were high, giving his face a lean chiseled aspect, which would have been severe if not for the unexpected gentleness reflected in his soft brown eyes.

Rain pelted the windshield. The world outside the steamy windows seemed to have faded away.

"Where's your new house?"

"Santa Monica." She wondered when he was going to get down to business.

"Not far."

"Just a few miles."

"Your first time?"

"First time?"

"As a homeowner."

"Oh yeah, yeah. We're pretty excited about it. Nice not to have that rent money just go down the drain each month."

"I bet. So are you and St. John . . ."

"Friends," she said, almost too quickly, "His wife too. I knew her first."

He nodded as if that was the answer he wanted and then reached across her to put the business cards in his glove compartment with more arm than was necessary. His elbow rested lightly on her knee as he rummaged for something.

A quiver ran up her thigh and stopped in her belly. She tried to keep her leg very still, holding her breath even. She didn't want to jerk away from his touch. Overreactions were as telling as underreactions.

"Cold?" he asked. He pulled out the pen he'd been searching for and shut the glove box.

She brought her hand down to her knee to hold it still, then crossed her legs. He watched her with a look that seemed to say, *You're not fooling me.* She couldn't imagine what he was thinking . . . well, maybe she could. Either way, she had to do something to get the twitch under control.

He leaned back, lifting his butt off the seat, his pelvis pushing against the steering wheel as he reached into his pocket and pulled out a plastic bag. He shook the bag so that what was inside of it dropped to one corner and then held it up for her to inspect. "You know what this is?"

"It's a center link, for a motorcycle chain." She pointed to the grooves on the ends of the pegs. "There's a special clip that fits here. Bikers wear them on their belt loops, in case their chains break." She didn't add that she had carried one on her key ring when she used to ride, ashamed now at the lengths she used to go to be those assholes' all-purpose woman.

Rico nodded thoughtfully and put the piece back in his pocket. She did her best not to watch the place where his steering wheel rubbed. The phrase "Where's the beef?" came to her mind. She quashed the impulse to say it.

"What's all this about?" she asked.

The look he gave her before he spoke was full of sympathy. "Your friend Ellen."

Ellen. She should have known.

"How well did she get along with her mother?" Rico asked, pulling out a notepad from his suit pocket.

"Lila Mae? Okay, I guess. What do you mean 'did'? Something happen?"

"How well did you know Mrs. Summers?"

Again with the past tense. Munch felt her body go still. "Is she . . . dead?"

"I'm afraid so."

His words ricocheted through her brain, connecting the image of Lila Mae Summers to the concept that she was gone forever. "Oh no," she said with a gulping sob. "Does Ellen know?"

"Yes. We notified her."

"In jail?" she asked, the tears flowing freely now.

He nodded.

"Was she murdered?" Her voice came out high.

"Lila Mae and Dwayne Summers were victims of a double homicide this morning. Seeing how you and Ellen were friends, I thought you might want to know."

"How was she? God, she must have flipped out," Munch said, too stunned to think clearly. Mrs. Summers was dead. Ellen would never see her mother again.

"She was upset."

"I hope she calls me. God. What a shock."

"These kinds of things usually are. Tough on everybody. Did you know them well?"

"Yeah, I spent more time at their house than my own when I was a teenager."

"When was the last time you spoke to either Lila Mae or Dwayne Summers?"

"Dwayne and I hardly ever talked unless he

answered the phone. But Mrs. Summers?" She thought a moment. "I sent her a Christmas card and she called me about a month ago when she got it, around the middle of December."

"Do you remember what else you talked about?"

"You know, how we were doing. Ellen mostly." Munch thought of the last words she had said to Lila Mae Summers. About her promise to the old woman that she would try to steer Ellen toward the sane and sober life. A promise that had now taken on extra weight. Thank God she had made her peace with the woman. Then another thought occurred to her, one that compounded this tragedy. Even if Ellen was finally ready to grasp sobriety, she would never be able to make things right face-to-face with her mom.

"Ellen couldn't think of any reason someone might want to harm her mother or stepfather. Did Mrs. Summers mention to you any threats to her person? Any enemies? Arguments with neighbors? Anything like that?"

"No, no. Just chitchat kind of stuff."

Munch was only vaguely aware of him opening his door.

In her mind she was sixteen again. Lila Mae was picking her and Ellen up from the police station. The charge was only drunk in public. Lila Mae signed them both out. Munch's dad had been too loaded to come to the station himself. Afterward Lila Mae had taken them home and fed them hot soup. Campbell's cream of asparagus, of all things. Munch hadn't minded the accompanying lecture. Being around Lila Mae was the closest she'd ever come to a normal family life, to an adult not wanting something from her other than for her to straighten out. Even now she always kept a can of cream of asparagus soup in her pantry.

"Are you going to be all right?" Rico had come around to her side of the car and opened her door. One hand rested on the roof trim, the other gripped the window frame.

Munch blinked before answering. She realized she had zoned out. Almost like a freeway fugue when she would suddenly find herself at her off ramp with no recollection of the last ten minutes of commute. She wondered if that happened to everybody or if it was some residual drug thing.

"Sure," she said, also noticing that the rain had stopped. "I'm just, uh . . ."

"In shock?"

"Yeah, but thanks for coming by. It was nice of you."

"Hey, any friend of St. John's . . ."

As she got out of the car, she had to pass beneath the bridge of his body. He didn't move back when her shoulder grazed against him.

"Will you do something for me, Munch?" His tone was confidential, personal.

"What's that?"

He handed her a business card with a Los Angeles city logo on it and the words LOS ANGELES POLICE DEPARTMENT. His name and phone number were written in blue ink in the spaces provided.

"Will you call me if you think of something that might help the investigation?"

"Sure," she said. What other answer was there?

"Nice seeing you again. Are you sure you're going to be all right?"

"No. Yeah, uh, you too." She looked at her house, her cars, her life, and they all looked different.

"I'd better be going." His feet stayed firmly planted. One on the street, one on the curb.

"I'll call you," she said, but only because he seemed to be waiting for those words.

"Good." He shut the car door gently.

She returned to the house and put the kids to bed. Once they were asleep, she sat out on the back porch and had a good cry. Then she attacked the hall storage closet, carefully lifting out dusty boxes. One at a time, she carried them to the middle of the living room floor. There were four. She opened the first and went through the contents, finding little OshKosh overalls that had been way too cute to throw away and a pair of Mary Jane tap shoes she had foolishly spent fifty bucks on only to have Asia outgrow them in a month. They both had value, but were they worth carting to another closet so they could sit and gather the new house's dust?

"Mmm, nah," she said out loud. She started to drop the overalls in a box of stuff to take to Goodwill, hesitating only a moment longer to bury her face in the denim, yearning for any lingering scents of Asia's kindergarten years. Then she got ruthless. One memento after another went to trash or Goodwill. In the fourth box she came across a file that was labeled JAIL POETRY.

She opened the manila file that was filled with folded sheets of yellow legal pad paper. They used to call her "The Poet" in her cellblock. When the prisoners lined up outside their cells before being marched to their meals, they would have Munch read her latest creation. Even the guards went along, breaking their own rule about not opening the gates to take them all to the cafeteria until the girls were quiet.

Munch unfolded the first sheet of paper. The poem was untitled, but had obviously been inspired by her cohabitees at dear old Sybil Brand Institute for Women.

I once knew a broad who thought she was slick
Till she propped a dude she thought was a trick
Now the bitch is walking Sybil's stroll
Where there ain't much money, but a lot of soul

Munch smiled, thinking how all the black girls must have hooted at that line.

There once was a fiend who loved her drugs
She preferred her dope to any man's hugs
When she pulled her last deal, the room was quite dark
"You know I would have froze," she said, "if I knew he was a narc."
Ninety days she's been down on that house on the hill
She's been sick ever since, and she's kicking still

Munch paused for a moment to remember how it felt to be dope sick in jail. How they'd given her nothing but a thin wool blanket that didn't ward off the chills or block out the fluorescent lights that stayed on around the clock. She continued reading.

I asked my cellie why she'd been picked up
She said she had been broke and a little down
on her luck
The liquor store seemed cool when she cased
the joint
Then she recalled with a smile how she'd over-
looked one point
Seems the Venice Jail sat just two blocks away
That's how I got here, says she, and looks like
I'll stay

A little rough, Munch thought, but not bad. Under the poem, she found a letter she had written to Sleaze John, but had apparently never sent. The part that bothered her the most was her description of the other women in Sybil Brand. Most addict and alcoholic women came into the program hating women. Munch had been no exception.

"These women are starting to get to me," she wrote. *"What do you expect, though, when you lock a bunch of cunts up together? They all started bitching and yelling the other night in the dayroom—over a motherfucking candy bar! Ain't that about some petty bullshit? Just like a bitch, too. I ain't like that."*

Did she really use to believe all that? Munch wondered. Or was she just saying what she thought he would want to hear? Either way, it was disturbing.

At last she came to the heroin ballads, and it was an hour before she was through reading. There was one titled "Thou Shall Not Shoot Dope" that she found especially powerful. Each stanza but the last began with the line "Thou shall not shoot dope," and then went on to list the downsides of being a junkie: the consequences, the jail, the soul damage. She had even gotten biblical, likened sticking the needle in her vein to the bite of the serpent from the Garden of Eden.

Thou shall not shoot dope, I'll spit in the
devil's face
I'll look at the bars and remember, his tempta-
tions put me in this place
I met him in his serpent's form, his "apple"
wrapped in a balloon
I sank his fangs into my arm and let his poison
work its ruin
Thou shall not cop, I tell myself as I walk out
the door
I clutch my money in my hand, the payment of
a whore
Just one more time, I promise me, but He
knows my true heart
God, why'd you ever make dope at all and
why'd you let me start?

She read the ending of the poem twice, remembering all too well how she felt when she wrote it, the despair of knowing it was killing her and knowing she couldn't quit.

She folded the yellow sheet carefully and put it back in the manila folder, then she placed the file with the box of stuff she was keeping. Posting all that on a billboard probably wouldn't help anyone either, but it beat the hell out of *Just Say No.*

Munch put on an oversized T-shirt and climbed into bed, saying silent prayers of gratitude. With all she had to think about, Lila Mae and Dwayne murdered, Ellen getting the news in jail, even Lindsey's bad day, Munch was ashamed to notice that her thoughts as she waited to fall asleep were of Rico Chacón's chest against her shoulder.

Chapter 6

The following morning, the news of Dwayne and Lila Mae's murders was in the Metro section of the *L.A. Times.* Munch found it on page three in a little box with the headline COUPLE FOUND MURDERED. The article was brief and uninformative, reporting only that the police were investigating and that the exact causes of death were as yet undetermined pending autopsies scheduled for later in the week.

After depositing the kids at school and stopping at the market to pick up more packing boxes, Munch returned home. She took a break midmorning and attempted getting through to the prison one more time. She was finally rewarded with ringing instead of a busy signal.

"Yes," she said, sitting straighter in her chair when a live human voice answered. "I have a friend who's being released today, and I was wondering if you could tell me when that would be."

"You're not family?" the male voice asked.

"No."

"Then I'm sorry. That information is confidential."

"Can I get a message to her?"

"No, it doesn't work that way. You should have made arrangements earlier."

"Well, I would have," Munch said, "but there are extenuating circumstances. You see, her mom was killed yesterday and since we had no way of knowing that was going to happen there was no way we could have planned for it."

"I'm sorry," the voice said, although Munch didn't think he was being completely honest about his feelings. "We have procedures and there are no exceptions."

"Even when someone's mom dies?"

"What do you think would happen if we bent the rules every time someone's mom died?" he asked. "Moms would be dropping right and left." He laughed.

"This is funny to you?" she said, knowing her rage was futile.

"That's all I can tell you, ma'am," he said and hung up.

She slammed her own phone down. The dogs ran to her with bright eyes and pricked ears.

"That guy was a jerk," she told them.

Sam cocked her head sideways, but didn't seem surprised.

"Who wants to go for a walk?"

Nicky barked. Sam pranced to the front door and nuzzled the leashes on top of the television. Munch laughed. "All right. Once around the block and then back to work. Maybe Ellen will call us."

At two o'clock the phone rang, but it wasn't Ellen. It was Alex Ramsey.

"Can Lins stay with you again tonight?" he asked.

She looked around at the mayhem of her home. "Sure, why not?" The two kids were good at entertaining each other.

"Thanks," he said.

"Did you get Noreen straightened out?"

"She bought plane tickets to Hawaii. Can you believe it? As if she could just buy me like that?"

"Are you holding out for Europe?" Munch asked.

"You're kidding, right?"

"I think so. When will you pick up Lindsey?"

"I'm not sure yet. Maybe not till Sunday. Can I call you?"

"Sure. Leave a message if I'm out."

At three o'clock, Munch gave up on hearing from Ellen and went to the school to pick up the kids.

Ellen walked home from the corner liquor store. Her destination was a ground-floor apartment in the Culver City projects off Braddock. She knew the manager there, and he had been more than happy to rent her one of his empty units.

It was late in the afternoon and some of her new neighbors were getting home from work. Kids played in the dirt yards of their apartment complexes. It was weird to see kids playing. Weird to be wearing her own clothes again. Weird to know she couldn't call her mother. Ellen wasn't ready for her to be gone. There were so many words she was still waiting for Lila Mae to say.

At least the warden had had the decency to let her make a phone call to her daddy in North Carolina without having to go through the customary request-and-twenty-four-hour-wait procedure.

Upon her release from CIW that morning, the deputies had driven her to the bus station where she'd retrieved her clothes from the locker she'd left them in six months earlier. Agents Long and Carter were also there. Their presence wasn't a big surprise. Being on parole meant she had signed off on all her search-and-seizure rights. All any cop needed was the okeydoke from her PO to riffle through any places under her control or that she occupied. Like she would ever be so stupid as to hide some big cache of money in a public bus locker. She wasn't sure which ticked her off worse, the intrusion on her privacy or the insult to her intelligence. Finding only clothes and beauty accessories, they let her go on her way.

She had twenty-four hours to report to her parole officer and begin the next round of repression. She decided to get it out of the way as soon as possible.

She stopped only long enough to change into clothes more her style and put on one of her beloved wigs—the long, blond curly one. There was nothing like a short skirt and big hair to give a girl confidence. Even so, she was wrung out from crying and no amount of makeup was going to mask that.

Her new PO, Mr. Sinatra, worked out of the Inglewood office on La Brea. The Inglewood parole office was the nearest to her county of commitment. As luck would have it, when Ellen was sitting in the lobby waiting for her name to be called, she saw a few other familiar faces, one of these being Patrice, an old running partner who had up-to-date connections.

Ellen wasn't interested in buying dope. The last thing she needed right now was a dirty test. Even pot showed up in those urine analyses. They were that chickenshit about it. When Ellen told Patrice what she *was* in the market for, Patrice gave her an address in Venice and said to ask for Lenny, he would be expecting her.

A bored, overweight black woman entered the reception room. She was holding a clipboard. "Ellen Summers," she called out in an impassive voice.

Ellen straightened the hem of her miniskirt. The black woman looked her up and down, eyes at half mast. She shook her head like she was tired of her job. "This way."

Mr. Sinatra was bald and fat and looked like the kind of guy who sweated a lot. He stood when she entered his office and started the interview by offering her his condolences.

"I don't know how you feel," he said, "but I'm doing my best to put myself in your shoes. Let the police investigate the murder. You just worry about completing this parole. If you think you know something, tell the police."

Ellen struggled to maintain a pleasant expression. He was right about one thing. There was no fucking way he knew how she felt.

"I can be your best friend or your worst enemy," he said. "But *I* will never lie to you."

The way he put his emphasis on his last *I* suggested that he didn't expect the same from her. He'd obviously been at this job awhile.

She listened as politely as any hostage could be expected to as he went into a twenty-minute speech laying down his rules.

The diatribe concluded with, "If you want to play games just remember, when all is said and done, I'll be the one holding the aces and you'll always be the one with the deuces. I'll win every time."

She said all the appropriate "yes, sir's" and "no, sir's." They'd parted with her promising to let him know as soon as she found work or made any other major changes in her life.

The brown sack she carried now, two hours later, did little to conceal the shape of the bottle within. Change from her dollar bill rattled around the bottom of the sack as she walked. She held the bottle by its neck. The brass-colored twist-top cap poked out the top.

"What's the word?" she asked, singing to herself in a soft voice. She held the bag up and answered, "Thunderbird." The jingle wasn't nearly as fun sung solo.

She turned into the courtyard of the complex, unlatched the chain-link gate, and took a good long look at her new home. Throw rugs hung drying on the banisters next to wilted house plants in green plastic pots. Both served to symbolize once good intentions gone unremembered. Sheets substituted for curtains in half the apartments. A cat with no collar scooted past her and up one of the shaggy palm trees lining the back alley.

"What's the price?" she asked, hoping the familiar cadence would put her more in the party spirit. "Thirty-two twice." She unlocked the door to the apartment, using the single key in her pocket. Life had gotten simple again, but that wouldn't last long. She pulled the bright green bottle from the bag and ran her finger over the label and its familiar logo. Recommended by winos everywhere and probably not the juice of one grape in it.

She walked over to the refrigerator and stuck the bottle into the empty freezer. Thunderbird was best drunk ice cold, a good chug at a time. By the time you got a third of the way through the bottle, the taste didn't bother you anymore. Halfway through and nothing bothered you. Right about now that sounded like a hell of a plan.

"Who drinks it the most?" Her voice was barely a whisper. "Us crazy folks."

She opened the larger, lower compartment of the refrigerator and stared at the empty racks. Later she'd buy some eggs, butter, and a loaf of bread. But for now, what she felt in her gut wasn't hunger and she took her needs one at a time.

God, they'd killed her mama. It didn't make any sense. Ellen's throat and chest ached, felt as if they were tied in knots and being squeezed shut, as if she were being murdered slowly herself. She felt an overwhelming exhaustion, and for a moment considered climbing into her bed and pulling the covers over her head, but she really didn't have the luxury of time. The irony of her situation wasn't lost on her. For the previous six months, time had been all she had. Now it conspired against her.

Under the raw sadness she felt an odd sense of relief. Some sort of pressure was off her back. Munch had told her she'd felt like that when her house burnt down that time. She said it was like the line in that Janis Joplin song: *Freedom's just another word for nothing left to lose.* But Munch took it a step farther. She said that when something devastating and unforeseen happens, and when you get over the first shock, you look around and realize you're still intact. Your existence, who you are, isn't dependent on any thing or person. Munch's words hadn't made much sense to Ellen then. She was getting them now. She opened the bottle and took a long hit.

Goddamn, she thought, *but this is some nasty shit.* It was especially cloying warm. She shuddered and put the wine back in the freezer.

She and Munch had discovered Thunderbird years earlier, when they shared an apartment in Venice Beach. *Lord,* she remembered, *what a great location that place had been—within easy walking distance of the connection, a good working corner, and the free clinic.*

Randy had turned them on to the stuff. Good old Randy, also affectionately referred to as "Rough and Ready." He came over for an afternoon and stayed a week, chaining his scooter to the stairwell, and stretching those long limbs of his all over the house. He'd brought with him three quart bottles of T-bird and new meaning to the term *double dating.*

Most of the guys she and Munch partied with back then were beer drinkers. But beer had its drawbacks. A person could drink beer all night, spending half of that time in the bathroom, and not get the same buzz that a pint bottle of T-bird delivered. Not to mention all those calories. There were those who argued that their daily nutritional needs were fulfilled by the mix of malt and barley. Such horseshit. Thunderbird did nothing but get you drunk. She and Munch were always honest about what they were after—the twelve daily essential vitamins and minerals weren't on their short list.

She stepped over to the curtains and pulled them slightly ajar. The apartment came furnished with a hard couch, a few rusty floor lamps, and a kitchen table accompanied by two mismatched chairs. The small, single bedroom had a twin bed, dresser, and nightstand. She provided her own linens, such as it was. Previous tenants had left behind cutlery and some chipped dimestore dishes. Living in the lap of luxury all right. She pulled up one of the chairs to the bay window and set an ashtray on the sill. It was just about show time.

She went into the bathroom, stuck the hard rubber stopper into the bathtub drain, and turned on the water. There had been a distinct lack of privacy at CIW. The sounds of girls having sex with each other carried through the night. Some were gay when they arrived, even more were just gay for the stay. Then there were the militant Aryan Sisterhood members with lightning bolts tattooed to the sides of their necks, strutting like their shit really meant something. The blacks and Latinas were always looking for a fight, and there were the guards who liked to watch. But she knew how to play the game, she knew how to wait, to hold on to herself.

Munch had visited a couple of times. It was almost easier when she didn't. Those brief respites in the company of one of her few true friends had only served to stir up feelings better left suppressed. She never told Munch about the other visits. She'd brought enough trouble to her friend, and besides, what was there to talk about? Like she told the guys from the government, she didn't know anything about any money. The end.

She went into the bedroom. Her jeans, purchased from CIW's own factory, were still fairly clean, as was her blouse. She hung up both in the closet with her other clothes. One of the first things she had done upon arriving at her new home was unload the large suitcase that held her densely packed wardrobe. Then she'd removed her wigs and their forms from the red I. Magnin shopping bag and lined them up on the pressed-wood dresser. She put her makeup case full of all her beauty aids on the bathroom counter. The act of unpacking had felt good to her, claiming this space, sorting out her new life.

She listened with half an ear to the bathwater filling. It was almost time. Funny how a person can tell without seeing when a tub is almost full.

Thirty minutes later, Ellen finished with her bath. She wrapped the towel turban-style over her wet hair and slipped into her robe, loving the smooth feel of it on her skin. She took her time, savoring the sensations she had been denied for all of 1983, and then after only a short few weeks of freedom in the summer, most of '84 as well. The last had been all about some bogus parole violation. Well, okay, maybe not entirely bogus, but certainly chickenshit. And now they wanted her cooperation. The bastards.

She went into the kitchen and retrieved her bottle. The sun had set while she had been taking her bath. She turned on the floor lamp in the corner of the living room, then took her bottle, nail polish, and cigarettes over to the chair by the window.

She stared out into the night sky. After half a year of no stars, even storm clouds were a welcome relief. She lit a cigarette and cracked open the bottle. With her heel on the windowsill, she tilted back in her chair and took a good long hit. The robe fell away from her freshly shaved leg.

The wine hit her tongue and, with a will of its own, her face contorted in a wince. She wondered if they were watching her, waiting for her to make a move. They could wait.

Or maybe they'd be wondering if they were on the wrong track. Would they be starting to think that she couldn't possibly have all that money? If she had hundreds of thousands of dollars, would she still be drinking cheap wine and staying in some roach-infested apartment in one of the worst sections of West Los Angeles?

She took another swig just in case they had binoculars trained on her through the window. This was going to be the role of her life, and she damn sure was going to make it convincing.

Chapter 7

The morning sun cut through the curtains, casting just enough light to make Ellen squint. She grabbed her sunglasses from the nightstand, then lay back down on the pillows. While waiting for the thrumming in her temples to subside, she contemplated her next move. She knew she couldn't just go running over to Munch's house the moment she felt like it, not that Munch would appreciate seeing her so obviously hungover. No, she'd wait a few days and go visit her casual-like. The last thing she wanted was to appear anxious.

She thought of her mother, wondering if she had died cursing the daughter who'd brought her nothing but trouble. "You always back the wrong horse," Lila Mae used to say. Lila Mae had gone to great lengths to avoid trouble. Or at the very least, to keep her eyes closed.

The last communication Ellen received from her mom had been an article about vitamins with no attached note. And before that Lila Mae had written that she had told the men from the government who'd come to see her that her daughter had not left any packages with her. She was only telling the truth, she said. Lila Mae was nothing if not consistent, which was precisely why she would be the last person Ellen would have entrusted with any contraband. Anybody with half a brain could have figured that out. But instead they had tortured and beat her. An old woman. Beat her to bloody death. While that pig she'd married had probably been hauling ass to save himself. He got off easy with just the one wound to the head, according to that cop.

A knock on her apartment door interrupted her thoughts. She picked up her watch from the nightstand but had to take off the shades to see it clearly. It read a little after nine. *They weren't wasting any time.*

She got up and reached for her bathrobe. "I'm coming," she called out as she headed for the door. "You just hold on a moment."

"Ellen Summers?" a man's voice asked.

She didn't ask, "Who is it?" The fact that he had asked for her by her first and last name obviously meant trouble. But it was a male voice, she thought while fumbling to unbutton the top two buttons of her nightshirt, and that gave her a definite advantage. Munch had told her once that when she was feeling nervous she just reminded herself that fear and excitement felt the same. Ellen used that philosophy now to explain the spiders doing cartwheels in her stomach. She wet a finger and rubbed it beneath each eye to clean up any residual mascara smudges.

She peeked out the kitchen window before opening the door.

The guy standing on the stoop was in his mid-thirties, sort of scrawny, nothing to write home about, but not repulsive either. Clean cut, cheap suit. If she'd met him under other circumstances she would have pegged him for one of those sidewalk missionaries who wants you to read one of his pamphlets and change your life.

You can do this, she told herself.

When she opened the door he had his knuckles poised to rap again. On seeing her, he lowered his hand and smiled weakly.

She waited a beat, giving him a long look, and making her expression brighten as if the sight of him on her threshold was making her day. "Well, now," she said, a slow smile curling her lips, and her Southern drawl giving each word its own weight, "what do we have here?"

He handed her a business card. "My name is Fred Purcell," he said. "I'm with Universal Security." When he spoke, his large Adam's apple traveled the length of his throat.

She scrutinized his card, bending forward slightly to do so. Her robe fell open. She caught the sides of it and folded them around herself as if the peek he'd just been given had been an accident. "How do you do, Mr. Fred Purcell." She knotted the sash around her waist. He worked hard to avert his eyes. His face showed the strain of it. "This must be about the money," she said, looking past his shoulder at the cars in the street. The morning dew glinted off all but one, a gray Ford Mustang. Had to be Mr. Boney Maroney's here.

His face went through a quick transition of expressions: interest, surprise, hope, suspicion. To his credit, he recovered quickly and asked, "So you were expecting me?"

"Not you exactly. Who all did you say you worked for?" She kept her tone light, even playful, but inside she was screaming, *Are you the one, motherfucker?* He might be skinny, but sometimes the skinny guys were deceptively strong.

"Can I come in?"

"Whatever for?" Ellen said, but even as she spoke, she opened the door a little wider. She knew she could take him if she had to. Before going to bed last night she had hidden knives under every couch cushion. He wouldn't be expecting that. But besides that, it was broad daylight in a crowded apartment complex. He wasn't there to do violence. She'd have smelled it by now. "I can't tell you anymore than I told everybody else," she said, giving him her best little-ol'-me voice.

"How about we have a cup of coffee and talk about what you can and can't do?"

"Now you sound like my parole officer," she said.

"Except I'm on your side."

"Yeah," she said, laughing. "That's what they all say."

He craned his neck forward and looked inside her apartment, obviously hoping for an invitation. Let him look, she thought. Let him see the stains on the wall, the crack radiating from an old bullet hole in the front window, and how the linoleum on the kitchen floor curls up at the edges. She really didn't have anything more to tell him, but she needed answers. Who hired him? The feds had their own people. This guy was obviously an independent. How good he was remained to be seen. And as far as being on her side, well, she'd be the judge of that. Ellen was a lot of things, trusting wasn't one of them.

She made no move to allow him entry. "If you want coffee, we'll have to go out. I don't have a lick of food in the house."

"Sure, that would be fine," he said.

"I'll just be a minute," she said, closing the door in his face. She went back into the bedroom and went about selecting this morning's costume. She decided on a pair of black jeans, the kidskin boots with the stiletto heels, and a big fluffy sweater that stopped short of her butt and showed her navel when she stretched. She went with the red wig. The blond one needed combing out and the black one was just too dark for this hour of the morning. The last thing she did before leaving the bedroom was to position strands of blond hair over the corners of each dresser drawer. Then she went into the bathroom to put her face on and give herself a pep talk.

Making what you had to say believable was an art. Like any sales job, you had to know how thick to lay it on and when to just shut up. There had to be the proper amount of fire behind your convictions, without giving too many over-the-top details. That's where a lot of people failed in their bullshit.

Like this one guy she used to hang with, Mot. His real name was Tom, but he was forever getting things backward. One time they were having too much fun for him to go to work, so he called his boss and said he had to take a few days off. She sat on the bed and listened to his half of the conversation.

His brother had been killed, he said. She rolled her eyes, but he paid her no mind. He told his employer that this dead brother of his had worked on an offshore oil rig up by Santa Barbara. She drew a finger across her throat, desperately trying to get Mot to quit while he was ahead. But no, he wasn't done. He went on to describe in great detail how a large anchor chain had accidentally wrapped itself around this hapless brother's legs and pulled him under. Ellen wondered then why Mot didn't go all the way and describe the large squid that swallowed his sibling whole. Needless to say, when Mot returned to work the next week, he was out of a job.

She had a lot more at stake than a job.

Ten minutes later, she was ready to face Mr. Fred Purcell again, her transformation complete. She opened the front door and asked, "Are you ready?" Judging by his startled reaction, he wasn't. They should never have sent a man, especially a young one with active hormones. But of course, that hadn't been their first mistake.

Ellen locked the door behind her. No sense in making anyone's job easier.

They walked a short way to a dingy little coffee shop. After seating them in a corner booth, the waitress handed them menus, filled their coffee cups, and left them alone.

"What looks good?" Purcell asked.

Ellen answered with her eyes first, peeking over the top of her menu. "Mmmm," she said. "Can't say I've made up my mind yet. I am hungry for just about everything these days." She was gratified to see that knob in his throat jerk like a piñata on Cinco de Mayo.

A man's body was always the first thing to betray him.

The waitress returned. Purcell ordered scrambled eggs and dry toast. Ellen asked for a short stack of pancakes, then rearranged her flatware and appreciated the fact that she'd been given three utensils and there would be no trustee standing at the end of the chow line taking inventory after the meal.

When they were alone again, Purcell folded his hands in front of him on the table. "My clients are offering a ten percent finder's fee for the return of their money."

Her forehead furrowed in honest perplexity. "I never understood that finder's fee business," she said. "Now don't take this the wrong way"—she reached across the table to run a finger over the top edge of his shirt cuff—"but doesn't this finder, whoever it is, already have one hundred percent?"

"True enough," he said, clearing his throat. "But there are other considerations. For instance, a person might enjoy the freedom of spending a smaller, yet still substantial sum as opposed to having more but not being able to touch it."

They each doctored their coffee. Ellen drank all her water and asked for a refill. She wished she'd thought to buy some aspirin the day before. The waitress brought their breakfast.

"Too bad you couldn't get the word to this person somehow," Ellen said as she stacked the pancakes one on top of the other. She went light on the butter but poured on the syrup until it dripped off the edge of her plate onto the paper place mat.

"I don't think you're stupid, Ellen. I hope you

aren't greedy." He took a bite of his eggs, chewed perhaps once, then swallowed. "My clients have limited patience and a long reach. They're like elephants, you know? They don't forget. These are not people you disappoint."

"Or what? And then you're fired?"

He put down his fork and reached for her hand. She made every effort to relax as he separated her fingers and stroked the length of each of them.

. . . *Before they killed her,* that cop said, *they broke her fingers.*

Suddenly Mr. Boney Maroney didn't look so goofy anymore. She pulled back her hand and took a bite of her pancakes. They felt heavy in her dehydrated mouth. Her appetite had also dried up. She reached for his water.

All right, fine, you son of a bitch, she thought. *We'll work ourselves a deal.*

She took a long sip, set his glass back down on the table, and held up her hand like a cop at a traffic light. "Like I said, don't look at me. If I had a bunch of money, I'd be on some beach in Buenos Aries or something."

"Aires," he said. "Buenos Aires."

"Exactly."

He looked at his watch. "You still have a chance to come out on top."

"One can only hope," she said with a bravado that fell flat on the table for all to see.

They finished the rest of their meal in silence, each busy with his or her own thoughts. She watched him pay for breakfast. When the cashier gave his change she asked if she could have it.

"I have a few calls to make," she said.

He smiled knowingly, tapped his watch, and said, "Ten percent and everybody goes away happy, that's the deal."

They walked outside. He started in the direction of her apartment, but she stopped short at the phone booth.

"This is as far as I'm going," she said.

"All right. I'll be in touch."

She fumbled in her purse as he walked away. When she did glance up, he was getting into the gray Mustang. She considered writing down the license plate, but didn't know what good that would do her. The important thing right now was to hold her mud. These guys wouldn't eliminate their only link to their money. Of course, she was assuming they were logical—not the kind of people who would batter a fool old woman into the next life. She put her hand against the wall of the phone booth and leaned into it. The front of her head throbbed. She grabbed a hank of her real hair and pulled it hard. Her eyes burned with unshed tears, but this was not the time to let down.

What did he mean by a long reach? Fuck 'em anyway, she wasn't planning on hiding. But if she had a mind to, he wouldn't find her. Nobody was that powerful. Her mama had taught her that much.

She used his change and dialed Munch's number. Halfway through the second ring, Munch picked up the phone.

"You are home," Ellen said, speaking in her slow, distinctive style.

"What's going on?" Munch sounded surprised but

happy. "God, I've been worrying about you. Are you out?"

"Yes indeed. I am a free woman."

"Since when?"

"Yesterday."

"I heard about your mom."

"Yeah, my daddy's going to come out and help me find a funeral home," Ellen said, amazed at how calmly the words came out, like she was talking about someone else—someone she barely knew.

"Your dad?"

"Uh-huh. My real dad."

"I thought he was dead."

"He used to be."

"Since when do you talk to him?"

"The Colonel wrote me a couple months ago. Just out of the blue. Said he wanted to be back in my life."

"The Colonel?" Munch asked.

"I'll tell you all about it when I see you."

"Why didn't you call me when you got out? I would have come and gotten you."

"I know that."

"So what now?" Munch asked. "Where are you staying? Do you want to go to an AA meeting tonight?"

"I don't think that's for me."

"You gonna try staying sober on your own?" The friendliness in Munch's tone was a tad guarded now.

God, Ellen thought, *who said anything about staying sober?* "I'm just taking it a day at a time," she said, feeding Munch back one of her own lines.

"Listen, I'm sorry about your mom, but I can't have you coming around here loaded."

"Who said anything about getting loaded? Why is everything either/or with you?" Ellen was getting tired of eating shit all the time, of everyone in the world being so sure of how she should handle her private affairs. "Now you're sounding like all those shrinks at CIW, always talking about 'changing my attitude.' Shit, it wasn't my attitude that put me in the joint." She paused for dramatic effect. "It was my actions."

"Had a personal breakthrough, did you?"

Ellen didn't miss the tone. "Maybe your way isn't for everybody. You ever think of that?"

"I'm not saying it is," Munch said, her voice sounding resigned. "All I know is since I've been sober, things have always come out for the best."

"Well, I cannot say that that has been my experience."

"You didn't give it much of a chance."

"You told me God wouldn't let me go to jail again," Ellen said, letting her anger boil through her voice.

"What I said was what's supposed to happen will happen." Then Munch's voice went soft. "I was really hoping that that wouldn't include you having to do more time."

"Yeah, well it did."

They both said, "Hmm," in the verbal shorthand that evolves from the closest of human experiences—friendship between comrades-in-arms. In their case, two women who had earned their bones on the street. They waited a moment while all the things that didn't need to be said out loud passed between them.

"How did you hear about Lila Mae?" Ellen asked.

"This cop came to my house and told me."

"That Becker guy?"

"No, his name was Chacón, Rico Chacón. I met him once before."

"You and your cops. I don't know how you can stand to be around them."

"They're not all assholes," Munch said.

"I guess that depends on your perspective."

"It does indeed."

"You got a car I could use for a little while?" Ellen asked, reading the graffiti scratched into the Plexiglas around her.

"Oh yeah, right," Munch said. "The last time you 'borrowed' one of my vehicles, I had to ransom it back from the Mexican *federales.*"

"I thought we were all right about that," Ellen said. Shit, she'd paid for the repairs and then some.

"I'm not mad at you. I've just got a lot at stake now. I own stuff now. Stuff I could lose if someone sued me. Besides, I was just getting ready to go over to the U-Haul place to rent a hitch and trailer and then it's going to be a real pain in the ass to drive around. Where do you need to go?"

"I thought I would run a few errands."

"Can your dad help?"

"He won't be getting in town until tomorrow." A car full of low riders cruised by slowly and hooted. Ellen turned her back on them. "Are you going to be home all day?"

"In and out. I'm up to my elbows in boxes. We're moving this week. That's why I need the trailer. I bought a house."

"Moving?" The word came out in a croak. Ellen's stomach went thoroughly sour. Her ears rang and black fluttery things developed at the edge of her peripheral vision.

"Yeah, too much shit has gone down in this house. I've been broken into twice. First by that maniac last summer, and then by that creepy rapist guy I told you about. Kinda wrecked the vibe around here."

"You gonna move in with your boy Garret?"

"No, my landlord sold the place to some company that's gonna build an apartment building and bought me out of my lease. Gave me enough to make a down payment on my own house."

Ellen loosened the phone cord wrapped tightly around her palm when she realized she'd cut off the circulation to her fingers. "And all this is happening now?" she asked.

"Yeah, you're lucky you caught me in."

"I can't wait to see you," Ellen said. Her focus narrowed to a spot on the phone that read IN CASE OF EMERGENCY. Man, she thought, they could say that twice and put it in the paper. "I'm going to need your help."

"I figured," Munch said.

Back at his desk, Becker went over his notes, coming across the names of Ellen Summers's other visitors while she was in prison. He called the Secret Service's Los Angeles office on Temple and asked to be connected to Agents Carter and Long. The call was transferred to the counterfeiting department.

"Long," a gravelly voice answered.

Becker introduced himself.

"What can I do for you?" Long asked.

"I understand you went to visit a woman named

Ellen Summers in CIW. Can you tell me what your interest was in her?"

"She's part of an ongoing investigation," Long said cautiously.

"Involving counterfeiting?" Becker asked. The guy would have to be a total dickhead not to give him that much.

"What's your interest in Ms. Summers?" Long asked.

"Her mother and stepfather were murdered."

"Let me take your number and get back to you," Long said. "Will you be in on Monday, say before ten?"

"Sure," Becker said, knowing the guy would have to check with his bosses before he wiped his ass. "I appreciate your help." He gave Long his office and beeper number and then hung up. He wasn't overly disappointed. He knew the way the feds operated. They didn't give anything up on the first call. But as Becker often told his wife, his middle name was Persistent.

Chapter 8

Ellen arrived on Munch's doorstep at six that evening. It was already dark and there was the kind of chill in the air that usually foretold a storm. Munch was still feeling guilty for not offering to loan Ellen a car, but she had to think of Asia and their financial security. The last time she checked, there was no such thing as "Ellen Insurance." It would be a losing proposition.

But now, seeing her wayward friend in the flesh, the guilt, even irritation, she'd been trying to talk herself out of all afternoon gave way to joy. She gave Ellen a brief fierce hug that had the dogs barking and brought the kids running. Munch noticed a white pickup truck with utility boxes on either side of the bed parked in front of the house. Some poor working fool must have loaned Ellen his truck. He wouldn't be getting it back while it was still running or had gas in the tank.

Asia and Lindsey now riveted their eyes on the

larger-than-life apparition that was Ellen, with her coiled shoulder-length blond hair piled high and spilling out everywhere; her equally dramatic makeup—eyelids from brow to lash lines embellished with layers of colors ranging from pink to purple. Her long curly lashes were thick with mascara and little rhinestones were imbedded in her nail polish. Her large breasts bulged out the top of her skintight shirt.

"Well," Ellen said, looking at Asia and Lindsey, and speaking in her exacting Deep South drawl, giving each word, every syllable, weight, "I did not realize you had twins."

The little girls squeezed each other's hands and exchanged silent looks of merriment.

"C'mon," Munch said, "dinner's ready." She seated the four of them around the small square table in the dining alcove and brought out the food from the kitchen.

"Meat loaf?" Ellen asked, smirking. "Now I have really seen it all."

"Shut up and eat," Munch said, winking at Asia and Lindsey.

"I am just not accustomed to seeing this domestic side of you," Ellen said, also smiling coyly at the little girls, as if to include them in the joke. Asia grinned openly. Lindsey's smile was fleeting.

"Takes some getting used to," Munch said. "If you're real good, I'll let you wear my apron when you wash the dishes."

"I guess that beats a bug in the eye," Ellen said.

Asia giggled. Lindsey looked down and stirred her food.

Ellen shot Munch a questioning look. Munch could

do little more then shrug in reply. Both of them knew the signs of an unhappy kid.

"Did you know my dad?" Asia asked Ellen. She'd met Ellen only once before when Munch explained that Ellen was an old friend. Apparently, she'd been saving this question.

"Sleaze John?" Ellen said. "Honey, we *all* knew him."

Munch cleared her throat and shot Ellen a warning glance.

"He was a lot of fun, your daddy," Ellen said, ignoring Munch.

"Ellen—" Munch said, her tone a threat and a plea.

"Relax," Ellen said, adjusting her cleavage. "I think I know what to say and what not to say to a kid, for chrissakes. Why do people have such a hard time trusting me?"

"You want a list?"

"What else?" Asia pressed, scooting her chair over toward Ellen, her little face blocking Ellen's reach for her fork.

"Asia," Munch said, "let her eat."

"Your daddy could charm the feathers off a goose." Ellen leaned over to Asia, rolling her eyes skyward. "Hmm. Sleaze John." She shook her head and chuckled. "There was this one time"—her lips curled into a smile, then she stopped and looked at Munch. "Well, maybe *that* story can wait."

Munch reached over to Lindsey's plate and cut up her carrots. "You want some butter on your potatoes?"

Lindsey looked at her plate and said, "Uhh . . ." as if not sure how to answer.

"Asia likes butter."

"Okay," Lindsey finally said in a quiet voice.

Munch felt the little girl's solemn eyes on her as she cut a pat of butter and transferred it to Lindsey's plate. It was as if the kid was suspicious of the attention, cautious about how much to accept. Munch could relate. She also didn't like receiving anything without a clear understanding of what it might cost later.

When Munch was finished mashing the butter into the potatoes, Lindsey took a bite.

"How is it?" Munch asked.

Lindsey's hand, the one holding her fork, stalled on the plate. A quick flash of desperation shadowed her eyes and then in a formal voice she said, "Thank you very much."

Munch sighed to herself. That hadn't been what she was fishing for. She gave Lindsey's arm a little squeeze wishing she could gather the girl in her arms and give her all the hugs she'd missed in her young life. Asia broke the moment by burping.

"Asia," Munch said.

Asia laughed and said, "Excuse me," through her fingers. The apology would have been more convincing without the giggles.

Munch thought about Lila Mae trying so vainly all those years to exercise some kind of control over her daughter.

Good-bye, Lila Mae, she thought, *I love you.*

She looked over at Ellen and wondered how it felt to lose one and discover another parent in such a short span of time. She hoped Ellen's real dad wouldn't turn out to be a jerk. Even though the majority if not all of Ellen's misfortunes were brought on by her own actions, Munch couldn't help feeling some of Ellen's sense of outrage. Ellen did try, but then she'd get some wild hair up her ass and the next thing you knew she was calling from an airport in Chicago, having remembered too late about an appointment with her PO, and looking to Munch for an alibi. Finally Ellen's PO had said "enough" and violated her.

Ellen had spent her last night of freedom on Munch's couch six months earlier. Lila Mae had refused to take time off work to drive Ellen to the courthouse where she would turn herself in to the deputies. Munch had done the duty, partly out of selfishness. It never hurt to remind herself of the price to pay for jumping back into the life—keep that attitude of gratitude alive and strong.

The rest of the meal passed quietly. As they were scratching the last bites of food off their plates, Ellen looked up with a wicked gleam in her eye and addressed Asia. "Who you should ask me about is this little gal here," she said, nodding toward Munch. "I've got a lot of stories about her."

"All right, all right," Munch said, feeling the heat rise in her cheeks. "You girls go get ready for bed. After you both brush your teeth, we'll all play a game." Waiting until both girls left the room, Munch added in a quiet voice intended only for Ellen's ear, "And it damn sure won't be truth or dare."

"I heard that," Ellen said.

Munch chuckled. Ellen was the last person you would ever want to trade dares with. She didn't care about crossing points of no return; chances were she wasn't planning on coming back anyway. Munch had been just like her once—anything to shock or surprise or further her personal legend of craziness. "We sure do have some stories, don't we?"

"Yes, we do," Ellen said. "And no man is going to get the best of us."

"No man standing," Munch said, finishing the second part of their joke.

Ellen gestured with her head to Lindsey's vacated chair. "What's the deal with the kid?"

Munch filled her in on what had happened at the aborted birthday party as she picked up the plates with the remains of the kids' dinner. "I should have realized what a jerk he was when we went out to dinner and he wanted to split the check. But I'm the real idiot because I went on to sleep with him anyway." She lowered her voice to a confidential whisper. "It wasn't even good."

Ellen nodded. "Kind of thing makes you want to douche with bleach. Call me old-fashioned, but when I fuck a guy, I want him to pay for dinner."

"At least." Munch smiled and then grew somber again. "She's not even asking when she can go home again."

"I can't say as I blame her," Ellen said.

Munch made her voice gentle. "How are *you* doing?"

Ellen's face lost its color. Tears filled her eyes. The sight of Ellen's tears spurred Munch's.

"I thought I saw Lila Mae on the way over here," Ellen said. "I yelled out to this woman, and when she turned around she didn't look anything like Lila Mae. Must have thought I was crazy."

"Yeah," Munch said, wiping her eyes on her sleeve, "I know exactly what you mean. The same thing used to happen to me after Sleaze died. It's called denial." Denial, Munch knew, had its function. Sometimes the truth is so horrible, such an abomination, that your mind just has to recoil, to believe—if only for a short while longer—that the world hasn't just taken another sudden turn for the worse. She looked at Ellen, wanting to hug her, but waiting too long to act on the impulse. "What's your dad like? Must be a trip to see him again after all this time."

"I haven't actually seen him yet, not in the flesh anyway. I called him when they told me about Lila Mae."

"How did he take the news?"

"He said he was real sorry. He told me that he and Lila Mae did not exactly part the best of friends, but it was a real shame all the same. He said he would front the money for the funeral."

"That's cool."

"He's like that." Ellen reached into her purse and pulled out a worn letter. She showed Munch a photograph of a man in a military uniform with a butch haircut. "This is him."

Munch looked down at the stern countenance of a military lifer. "He looks, uh, impressive."

"Yeah, I think so too," Ellen said proudly. "You know, I was going to join the National Guard once. They told me to come back *after* I cleared up my court cases." She made a face to express what she thought of the foolish recruiter's suggestion.

"Like you would *need* to then," Munch said, only half-sarcastically.

"Exactly."

"When are you going to see your dad? I'd like to meet him."

"I'm having dinner with him tomorrow night. He's flying in from North Carolina. Listen, when you do meet him . . . I mean, he knows I was in CIW, but . . ."

"Don't worry. I'll just say that we went to school together."

"That is true enough."

Just then Sam and Nicky jumped to their feet in unison and ran to the back door—barking hysterically. In their excitement they even turned on each other, lips curled back into snarls and jaws snapping without connecting.

"All right, all right," Munch yelled above the din, clapping her hands. She followed the dogs and peered out the window. When they continued to bark, she raised her hand as if to swat them. The dogs settled down reluctantly, their heads resting on their front paws and their noses inches from the crack at the bottom of the door.

"What was that all about?" Ellen asked.

"Probably a cat or something," Munch said, kneeling down to stroke each dog's head. She was rewarded with two wet kisses. "The time to worry is when they don't say anything."

"What do you mean?"

"I guess it's something Mace St. John taught them. The other day some salesman came to the door. Before he had a chance to knock, they were waiting on the other side, standing at attention with their hackles up. I guess that silent threat stuff works great if you have a cop with a gun on your side of the door, but I'd just as soon they bark their heads off if they hear someone outside."

Ellen peered out the darkened window. "I know how scary that can be."

Munch nodded, knowing her friend was seeing things from the trespasser's point of view. "Especially when you're already keyed up," she added. She'd only been involved in a couple of burglaries. Even in the midst of her drug addiction years, the experiences had left her feeling shitty. Some types of crimes are more easily justified than others.

"I had a fellow come see me today," Ellen said, following Munch to the kitchen sink. "He said he was a private investigator but seemed more like a lawyer. You know how they come off geeky at first and then you can just tell they have no heart at all?"

Munch filled the sink with hot soapy water. "What did he want?"

"He thinks I have some money—a whole lot of money—that belongs to some client of his."

"Didn't you tell him that if you had money you would have hired a lawyer of your own?" Munch watched Ellen's face for a reaction as she scraped the leftovers into the dogs' bowls.

Ellen was busy modeling in the kitchen window's reflection. "I figured that went without saying."

Munch put the dog dishes on the floor. Sam and Nicky made short work of the scraps. "Did he make you an offer?"

"What makes you say that?"

Munch shrugged. "That's what those kind of people do. They start with a deal and before you know it you're fucked either way."

"Ten percent," Ellen said. "He said if I gave back

the money, I could keep ten percent. Shit, he's probably taking thirty."

Munch plunged her grease-stained hands into the hot soapy water. A couple more days off work and they'd be completely clean. "What else?" With Ellen, there was always the question, What else?

"He said I'd live to spend it."

"Just like that?" Munch asked. She realized she was washing the same clean plate and handed it to Ellen to rinse and dry.

"Close enough."

"Does this have anything to do with your mama and Dwayne getting killed?"

"The thought has crossed my mind."

"Sounds like the kind of people you wouldn't want to mess around with."

Ellen stacked the plates on the counter. Munch reached over and opened the cabinet where they belonged. Ellen caught on immediately and put them away. When she spoke again her tone was indignant. "This is like extortion."

"Not exactly."

"Close enough."

"I don't know if this has anything to do with anything, but a couple months back some guy called my work looking for you."

"What guy?" Ellen asked.

"He said he was from UPS and had a package for you, but not a valid delivery address."

"Sounds bogus," Ellen said. "Probably some kind of bill collector."

"Yeah, that's what I figured. Since when does UPS go to that much trouble?"

"What did you tell him?" Ellen asked.

"I made out like I didn't have anything to do with you anymore." She hadn't been acting. "I figured he'd leave me alone if I came off hostile. I never heard any more about it."

"Honestly, none of these people give a gal a chance to think."

"Who else?" Munch asked.

"I just meant—"

Munch cut her off. "You said people. Who else?"

Ellen held up a handful of flatware. Munch impatiently opened the drawer to the right of the sink. Ellen was stalling now.

"Who else?" Munch repeated.

Ellen sighed. "These two guys from the government came to see me in CIW. They wanted to know where I had gotten my money from. It seems they traced some large bills back to me. I said I didn't know what they were talking about."

"What did they have to go on?"

"Well, I did make a few purchases before my unfortunate incarceration. I told them that cash came from turning tricks. I even took my time admitting it."

Munch put the roasting pan in the sink to soak. Her ears were ringing as Ellen's words and all their implications took hold. "Did they buy it?"

"Before they left, I told them I was going straight."

"Did you say straight to where?" Munch asked, her aggravation growing, knowing that Ellen was missing the point. She hadn't said anything about the liquor she smelled exuding from Ellen's pores, but knowing that her friend hadn't wasted a minute before drinking disappointed her. She was disappointed, but not surprised. Running to the bottle was what they always had done—with or without excuses. Her promise to Lila Mae was quickly growing more complicated. She had to sell the idea of sobriety to Ellen in terms she would relate to.

"Getting loaded makes you stupid," she said, "and getting drunk makes you sloppy. Not to mention it screws up all your emotional reactions, puts them all out of sync and proportion. You might think it's helping you get through a tough time, but that's bullshit. We have a saying in AA: 'You can pay now or you can pay later, but you're going to pay.'"

"Oh, we're back to that now," Ellen said, rolling her eyes.

"It's always going to come back to that," Munch said. Munch had been a hard case back in the day. Every face she showed the world either seethed with hostility or was I-don't-give-a-fuck blank. And yet, every word sincerely directed to her in an effort to help her had been heard by some part of her brain and stored for later reference. "I know you get tired of hearing me say this, but you're not going to last very long if you don't make some big changes."

"Getting sober ain't going to get my mama back."

"And getting drunk will? Ellen. This is me you're talking to. Don't start hanging a bunch of excuses on the shit that goes wrong in this world. It won't get you anywhere. Believe me. If you're hoping to get through this thing all right, you're going to need all your wits. And I'll tell you another thing," Munch continued, "if you keep using and drinking you're better off without all that money. I've seen too many dope fiends killed by windfalls."

"Yeah, well, the way it is looking I am going to get myself killed with or without it." Ellen closed an overhead cabinet with enough force to make the glasses within chatter against themselves.

"No," Munch said with certainty. "That's not going to happen."

"And that's another thing; if it was really those people's money, from what I hear, they wouldn't be so all-fired anxious to get it back."

Munch started to ask what that was supposed to mean when the phone rang. She answered it on the only extension still hooked up.

"Hi," the familiar male voice said. "How are the poochies?"

She looked at Ellen and caught her eye before replying. "The dogs are fine, *Mace*. How are the mountains?"

"Cold." And then in a quieter, more confidential tone he said, "I'm going fucking nuts up here."

She couldn't help but feel an odd little thrill of satisfaction that his time alone with his wife wasn't enough for him. She sometimes pictured a life with Mace in some alternate reality. In this parallel universe, she had done the normal things in life: finished school, never done drugs, hadn't ruined her body for having kids. She and Mace were a couple, a couple who never had arguments and were always there for each other. He understood everything she said, even (and especially) those things she couldn't put into words. When something went badly in her life, she'd consult with this dream Mace and he'd always say, *Yeah, I know what you mean, they were wrong, you were right.*

And then there was Caroline St. John—the woman whom Munch called in real life her reference guide to the straight life. Their relationship had been established long ago. Caroline had been her probation officer, the woman who held the golden key to Munch's continued freedom. Caroline had watched her pee in a cup, seen her drunk and smack-backed, smiled gently through her lies, and been much more tolerant of her than any addict deserved.

Sometimes Munch suspected that everyone else, especially kids who went to high school, kids who hadn't spent their formative years learning how to hustle while staying a step ahead of both the man and the monster, had received some sort of instruction manual. The people who did it right learned what they needed to learn in safe increments, got to practice all this dating shit before they had a little kid watching their every move. The only rules Munch had ever learned about who you had a relationship with were born of observation. *If the guy hit you, you had to split, because once he hit the first time and got away with it, you could be sure he'd do it again.*

Then there were some hidden rules that guided her from someplace deep in her psyche, edicts that she followed without articulation or conscious decision, that she was only just now realizing existed.

Don't ever love them more than they love you.

And, *Don't spend it all.* The *it* being ego in the purest sense, the "I" that distinguished her self from other selves. So far, she hadn't found fault with that decision.

"Hey," she said now to the real Mace St. John, the one who pretended along with her that she and he were nothing more than friends, "I ran across a friend of yours. Rico Chacón."

"Yeah?" Mace said, his tone guarded. "Where did you see him?"

"Tell him 'hi' from me," Ellen said.

Munch tried to cover the speaker part of the phone, but she was too late.

"Who was that?"

Munch hesitated, sorely tempted to tell him anything but the truth. "Ellen."

"What's *she* doing there?"

Munch wanted to tell Mace about Ellen's recent loss but felt uncomfortable blurting it out with Ellen standing there. Instead she lowered the phone and said to Ellen, "Mace says, 'Hi.'"

"What's going on?" Mace asked.

"Ellen is out of prison."

"Yeah, I got that. But why is she at your house?"

"We just had dinner," she said, then walked with the phone around the corner out of Ellen's earshot. "Her mama got killed right before she got out. Rico stopped by to give me the news."

"Is it his case?"

"Apparently."

"Do you need me?"

"No, everything's under control. Ellen's daddy is coming into town tomorrow to help out. I couldn't very well turn her away at a time like this. I know you think she's trouble."

"I don't think. I know."

"Well, I can't abandon her now. Hey, listen," she said, not wanting to hear another protective tirade from him, "what kind of guy is Rico?"

"He's a good cop. He's not a jerk." This was Mace's highest praise about anyone. "How are the dogs?"

"They're great. No need to worry."

"Tell Ellen I'm sorry about her mom."

That was one of the many things she loved about Mace. Under all that gruff exterior he had a big heart. "I'll do that," she said. "Thanks. I'll see you in a week." Munch hung up the phone and turned to Ellen. "We need to talk."

The phone rang again. Munch answered with, "Forget something?"

"I know what you're trying to do, you dirty little bitch," the woman caller whispered. "And you won't get away with it."

"Who is this?"

"You're not going to step into my life and take over. I won't let that happen."

Munch hung up on her.

"Who was that?" Ellen asked.

Munch lowered her voice so as not to be overheard by the girls. "That woman I was telling you about, Lindsey's mom, Noreen. She's a head case. I mean like seriously mental." She told Ellen about the prescription medicine she'd seen at the house.

The phone rang again.

"Let me take this one," Ellen said, grabbing the phone before Munch could. "Hello?" she said sweetly. Disappointment showed clearly on her face when she handed back the phone. "She hung up."

"Payback," Munch said, returning the phone to its cradle. It rang again. This time Munch answered, "What?"

Noreen said, "I'm not going away."

Reason told Munch to just hang up again. Nothing was to be gained by jumping into this woman's head trip. Partly it was Ellen's unspoken influence, partly the accumulated stress of the last few days, but mostly it was because she'd taken all the shit she could stand. "Why don't you do the right thing," she said in a reasonable enough tone, "and commit yourself to Camarillo? Maybe you can fall in love with some nut your own age."

Noreen's voice lowered to an unnaturally low octave. "You're going to regret that."

"Bite me," Munch said and then unplugged the jack. She turned to Ellen. "Sometimes I wish I was a man so I could say, 'Blow me.'"

"Yeah, it really loses something in translation."

She wanted to laugh, but trading insults with Noreen had made her feel juvenile and petty. There was irritation in her voice when she told Ellen, "I'm going to put the kids to bed and then you and me are going to talk. You might as well spend the night."

Chapter 9

Munch had just returned from overseeing the kids' face washing and teeth brushing when the dogs ran past her with an eerie intensity. This time they ran to the front room and just stood there.

Ellen looked up from her magazine. "What is this all about?"

The dogs' eyes locked on the lower panes of the window that faced the street. When the hair stood up along the dogs' spines, Munch's own skin responded with goose bumps. She reached over to stroke Sam's back. Which of them she intended to comfort, she wasn't sure. The dogs' muscles were rigid.

"Someone must be out there."

She went to the back bedroom to check on the kids. The girls had changed into their pajamas and were playing with a game of Cootie that Munch had set up for them. She walked across the room and made sure the windows were locked. "Stay in here, guys."

She made a small detour into the bathroom and retrieved the twelve-inch pipe wrench that she'd used earlier in the day to work on the sink. Holding the tool in one hand, she returned to the front room.

Ellen, meanwhile, had gone back in the kitchen and found a cast-iron skillet. She gripped the handle firmly, the lip of the pan resting on her shoulder as she stared intently at the window.

Something went thump against the side of the house and the dogs went ballistic, barking and snarling and throwing themselves against the sill.

"Get the gun, George!" Ellen yelled. "I'll call the cops!"

The dogs barked a few more times, then went quiet with their heads cocked in concentration. The ten-second silence following their outburst was broken by Asia, calling from her bedroom.

"Mom," she yelled. "What's happening?"

"Nothing," Munch called back. "Ellen was just telling me a story and got carried away." The dogs paced circles around the living room with their tails lowered, making small urgent whimpering noises.

"They sound like they're in pain," Ellen said.

Munch glared at Ellen, then shook her head at her own idiocy for allowing Ellen to be there in the first place as she clipped the dogs' leashes to their choke chains.

"Hey," Ellen said. "This is not about me."

"You sure about that?" She laid the big pipe wrench against her shoulder, turned on the porch light, and peered out the front window. The limo, shrouded in its king-size car cover, was untouched. The street was quiet.

She grabbed a flashlight from the kitchen and said to Ellen, "I'm going to check it out. Wait here."

Clutching the big wrench in her right hand, the leashes and flashlight in her left, she walked outside and around to the side of the house where she'd heard the noise.

Noreen stepped out of the shadows of the neighbor's garage. "Where is he?" she asked, her voice low and dripping with venom.

"I don't know and I don't care," Munch said. Her fingers tingled unpleasantly with adrenaline. The dogs snarled deep in their throats. "What are you doing here?" If this woman thought Munch would hand over a nine-year-old child to a person in her condition, she had another think coming.

"I just want to talk to him."

"He's not here."

"I'm not leaving until he talks to me."

Munch felt a rush of anger surge through her. She wasn't even asking about Lindsey. "Fine then. Stay out here all night."

She returned to the house and switched off the light.

"Was that the witch?" Ellen asked.

"Yeah, she thinks Alex is here. I'm not going to give her the satisfaction of taking her seriously."

"See? I told you this was not about me."

"This time."

"God almighty," Ellen said. "Now you sound just like my moth—" She stopped midsentence and for just a split moment her attitude threatened to crumble.

Munch waited several seconds for her friend to collect herself and took a few deep breaths. Outside she heard a car start and speed off into the night. "Okay," she said. "You're right. I'm sorry. That had nothing to do with you." *For once.* "I'm going to get the kids squared away."

Thirty minutes later, Munch and Ellen were sitting on the living room sofa. Munch had brought out pillows and blankets, and the two of them swaddled themselves on opposite ends of the couch. "I think it's time you told me all about the money."

"I found it."

"Found it where?"

"He wasn't going to take it with him," Ellen said.

Munch knew without hearing another word exactly who Ellen meant. Yes, the guy was dead. And, yes, he needed killing. The guy had been a fucking pervert and a murderer. Six months ago he'd broken into Munch's house at the height of his killing spree. The evidence of his visit had been discovered in Asia's underwear drawer. Then, as the cops closed in, he had kidnapped Ellen and led them all on a hairy chase through the downtown freeway system, ending in a wreck that nearly totaled the Cadillac he was driving and Munch's limo.

That Ellen had somehow managed to profit by the guy's death was no skin off Munch's nose. There was also the point that she and Ellen contributed to the asshole's demise in pretty much self-defense—if you could convince a jury of a self-defense plea when the victim met his death after he was unconscious. Moot point. It wasn't going to get that far.

"How much are we talking here?" she asked, knowing it would have to be a sizable amount. "And who else knows about it?"

Ellen picked up the notepad by the telephone, ripped off the top sheet, and wrote down a number. Silently she handed it to Munch. The number of zeros to the left of the decimal point sped up Munch's heart and made her mouth go dry: $150,000. Enough money to put a 50 percent down payment on a house on the Westside, ample money to buy a house outright in the Valley, even in these boom times. "Holy shit."

"Yeah, and there was more than that even." Ellen ripped the paper into tiny pieces. "It was in a bag in the backseat. You can't tell me he earned it honestly."

Munch knew it was time to ask the question. "What else?"

"Let's just say I am not about to take anybody's word for anything."

"Word about what?"

Ellen walked into the kitchen and dumped the shreds of paper down the garbage disposal. "There have been some questions raised as to the legitimacy of the currency."

"It's never simple with you, is it?" Munch said, not caring whose mother she sounded like. "But I guess that explains the feds' interest."

Ellen pouted. "Well, how was I supposed to know? Besides, Suki will clear up any doubts."

"And who's Suki?"

"She's okay. I did some time with her. You don't have to worry about her. She knows how to keep her mouth shut."

"I used to think the same thing about you," Munch said.

Ellen affected a hurt expression.

Munch looked at her friend a good long minute

before she said, "You know this must be why they killed Lila Mae."

Ellen nodded. "Becker said they thought robbery might have been the motive. One of those home-invasion things. They beat her face so bad we might have to keep the coffin closed. The only way the cops identified her for sure was from fingerprints. The guy at the mortuary said he'd do the best he could with her once the coroner released her to him. I brought him a picture so he could try to make her look like she used to."

The vision of Lila Mae's suffering filled Munch with an itchy distress and then she felt a murderous rage. She wanted to get this guy, this killer, and she wanted to put a pillowcase over his head and beat his head in with a baseball bat. The anger was so powerful, so consuming, that she immediately recognized it for the danger it was. For the first time in a really long time, she saw the road leading back to hell, and it was paved with self-righteousness. She had to clear her throat before she could speak again. "How about Dwayne?"

"Alls I know is that he got his outside."

Munch grunted softly and met Ellen's eyes. At least there was one bit of silver lining to all this. Hating someone and wishing them dead were not always the same thing, but Dwayne had been a serious jerk, one of those stepfathers who didn't believe in sparing the rod. And although Ellen never came right out and said it, Munch suspected there were other things the guy hadn't spared her. Ellen did say that even by her own admission Lila Mae had never been great at picking men.

"Was anything stolen?" Munch asked.

"I don't know. The cops won't let me inside yet. They said they trashed the place."

"They?"

"He, she, they," Ellen said impatiently. "Whoever did it. I don't know. I was in CIW—how could I know anything?"

Munch looked at her friend. She kept her voice low and calm so Ellen would know how serious she was. "Who knew about the money?"

"Hardly anybody."

"Great. Let's start with them." Munch spread the fingers on her left hand and counted. "You've got the feds. Does that count as one?"

Ellen shrugged uncomfortably.

"You got this guy Purcell who came to see you at your apartment yesterday on behalf of a third party. Let's count that as two more, shall we?"

Again, Ellen had the grace not to answer out loud.

"Suki." Munch just shook her head and held up four fingers. "Who else?"

"That's all," Ellen said. "Except for Billy Vega."

"Billy Vega?"

To save confusion in a community of not-exactly brain surgeons, at six foot four and pushing three hundred pounds, a guy like Billy usually went by the moniker "Tiny." But Billy's oldest brother had already claimed that honor.

The boys' father, Dirk "the Doctor" Vega, had been a charter member of the Hell's Angels. He and Sunny Vega's four sons had a long reputation of mischief all through the Westside. The boys inherited their height and red hair from their ex-show-girl mother, Sunny—their distinctive arched bushy eyebrows and not-to-be-messed-with disposition from their father. Tiny, the oldest, standing in at six foot two, had been booted from the Army for punching a sergeant; the next oldest was serving time in San Quentin. Number-three son died in a scooter crash on the Marina Freeway. Drunk and helmetless, he collided with a white Oldsmobile. The Olds won. The night he died, three houses burned down. The police duly noted that each of those houses had white Oldsmobiles parked in their driveways. The arsons remained unsolved, but not for lack of suspects.

By the time Billy, the baby of the family, came of age, additional adjectives were not needed. The Vega surname held weight enough.

"He was my manager at the Spearmint Rhino," Ellen said.

"That strip joint?" Munch said, thinking that the title "manager" was a bit tame for the services the guy more likely performed.

"Gentlemen's club. It's really classy inside. You would be surprised. They don't even serve alcohol there."

"They don't?"

"Not anywhere where the girls go totally nude. That's the law." She said it as if this was the final word on anything. "Why do you think they call them juice bars? Most of our customers do their drinking first."

"All right. Whatever," Munch said. "Have you talked to Billy lately?"

"No."

"Did that PI guy Purcell give you a way to get ahold of him?"

Ellen grabbed her jeans off the floor, reached into

the back pocket, and retrieved a white business card. She handed it to Munch.

Munch chuckled softly as she recognized the address.

"What?" Ellen asked.

"See this 'Suite 306' on the address? It's bullshit; that's the box number. I use the same Mail Boxes Etc. to make the limo business look more professional and to avoid drop-in clients." The phone number was a recently issued prefix. She got up and grabbed her phone book. Universal Security wasn't listed in the White or Yellow Pages.

"You know I can't just give them what they want," Ellen said. "Not after what they did to Lila Mae. When I close my eyes, I can see her screaming."

Munch locked eyes with Ellen, and for a long moment nothing more needed to be said. What kind of monster could hurt another human being like that? In the silence of the room she heard a clock ticking. Nothing more was going to be solved tonight. She stood and said, "It's getting late."

The comforter dragged after her as she headed for her bedroom. She stopped at her doorway, knowing she needed to say something else, and at the same time knowing how empty words could be. Their eyes met again and Munch tried to convey her shared sorrow, her faith, her friendship, even her love in that long silent moment.

"Ellen," she finally said. "It's going to hurt."

"Do you know for how long?"

"No. Sleep well, okay?"

"You too."

Asia's soft wet snores carried into the room. Munch

thought about God and all His quirky ways. How all the seeming worst things that ever happened to her paved the way for the best things she had now. Her sobriety, Asia, even this move. There were those who believed that their whole path was already laid out for them and the only thing they had control over were their opinions. Let go and let God, they always said. He knows best. Don't fight the flow. Munch knew there was a certain amount of truth to all that. She also knew that He helped those who helped themselves and He didn't like whiners. It was also said that He didn't give a person more than he or she could handle. She knew a lot of people who wished that God didn't have such a high opinion of their stamina.

Unbidden to her mind came the horrible thought, *How would I get through the pain if Asia were to die? Would I even want to?*

Chapter 10

On Sunday morning Munch got up first and made coffee. She reconnected the telephone and was feeding the kids their breakfast when it rang. She felt a slight sense of trepidation before answering, "Hello?" in a neutral voice.

"Hi, it's me," Lindsey's dad said.

"Where are you?"

He gave a little martyred sigh. "I'll be fine. What a weekend."

"She called me last night and then she came by."

"She's gone nuts. I don't even know her anymore."

"I saw some of her stuff at your house. What's up with that?"

"She's trying to move back in. Like I say, she's gone nuts."

"Are you home now?" Munch asked, thinking what a total wimp this guy was.

"No, I think the best action for me to take is to avoid her. I stayed at a friend's place in Malibu last night. I went back this morning to change, but I needed to go into the studio."

Alex worked for a production company in the Marina.

"You might have called."

"Yeah, I'm sorry about that. It's been crazy out. I knew Lins was in good hands."

"Greasy but good," Munch said.

The comment went right past him. "Can you get Lindsey to softball practice?" he asked.

"Sure, no problem. We'll improvise on the uniform."

"I really appreciate all your help."

"You want to talk to her?"

"The studio is breathing down my neck."

"I'll get her." Munch put down the receiver and went into the kitchen. "Lindsey? Your daddy is on the phone. He wants to talk to you."

Lindsey put down her spoon and slid off her chair. When she picked up the telephone, the receiver seemed huge in her hand. She listened and replied with monosyllables. Finally, she said, "I love you too," without enthusiasm and returned the phone to Munch.

"You've been great," Alex said.

"It's what I'm known for," Munch said, wondering if being a good sport was ever a terminal condition. They said their good-byes.

She went outside to grab the Sunday paper. There was a strong smell of bleach in the morning air. She lifted the car cover on the limo but it appeared to be all right. The flowers by the mailbox had been trampled and her trash can enclosure gate was ajar. She took a step closer and saw that her single green plastic container was empty. She felt oddly violated by this theft of her refuse.

She walked back to where she had discovered Noreen lying in wait. The muddy ground still showed the imprint of what could be a high-heeled shoe. There was a splattering of whitened spots on the concrete driveway, like the kind you see after a car battery explodes. And on the front lawn she noticed a brown place of dead grass that hadn't been there yesterday. She rubbed the spot and brought her fingers to her nose. The unmistakable odor of bleach again assaulted her senses. Jeez, what had Noreen come there to do? Blind someone?

She wondered if she should report the incident to the cops. Or to be strictly honest, a certain cop with a slightly crooked nose who smelled of musk. Wouldn't she get better service if she tapped into an already established rapport?

No, she decided, Rico Chacón tracked down murderers. His time was more important than to be wasted on some stupid case of vandalism. And even if she was inclined to snitch, it wasn't like she had any solid proof pointing to Noreen. So what could he do? If she was going to call anyone, it should be the child welfare people. Lindsey was the real victim here. Noreen's harassment was minor league compared to the emotional damage being inflicted on the poor kid.

Munch went back inside and washed her hands. Ellen had rinsed the breakfast dishes and left them to dry in the drain board. "Ten minutes," Munch called out to everybody.

Ellen walked into the kitchen wearing only a sleeveless T-shirt and bikini underpants. Munch stared for a moment at the quarter-size scar across her friend's shoulder. She'd asked Ellen once how it happened, and Ellen had just shrugged, saying she couldn't really remember; some vaccination gone wrong or something.

"I'm doing a load of laundry," Munch said. "Got anything you want to add?"

"I guess I will be having my own washer and dryer now," Ellen said.

"You're getting the Maytag?"

The two of them exchanged sad smiles.

Lila Mae had a thing about her washer and dryer. She didn't think anyone but she could operate it correctly. She also believed another person's mishandling would surely lead to the machine's breakdown. Like if you didn't clean the lint screen just right, the thing would short-circuit and walk away.

When Ellen had turned eighteen, Lila Mae and Dwayne had gone to some guidance counselor who said that the best way to deal with their wayward daughter was to set strict boundaries. Their house was not Ellen's house. If she wanted to come over, she was to call first and under no circumstances was she to bring any of her friends. Ellen hadn't thought that would include Munch, since she'd been over lots of times and long before those sanctions had been imposed. Still, she knew not to push the issue. They had come over one afternoon and found the house empty. This was when Ellen and Munch were living in Munch's car—a big old Chevy convertible they affectionately referred to as their "wide bike."

The living arrangement worked out well. The driver's seat was of course Munch's, the passenger seat Ellen's. The glove box served as their bathroom cabinet; they stored their hair stuff, makeup, and toothbrushes there. The trunk was their closet. They were also known to occasionally entertain in their backseat parlor.

The problem was laundry, especially at a time when every bit of spare change went for either gas, dope, or booze, and not necessarily in that order.

So that one day, when Lila Mae was noticeably absent, they decided to get that little housekeeping chore out of the way. The wash cycle went off without a hitch, but Lila Mae's car pulled into the driveway before their jeans had a chance to dry. Ellen told Munch that she would stall her mother while Munch retreated out the side door. The dinging of the dryer betrayed them. Lila Mae ran to her precious laundry room and found the girls hopping on one leg, trying to pull on uncooperative wet jeans.

Ellen's mom hadn't seen the humor in the situation, but Munch and Ellen had almost peed themselves laughing.

Poor Lila Mae, Munch thought, trying to remember if she'd ever seen the woman laugh.

Munch was shaking her head in a mixture of regret and amusement when Ellen entered the kitchen. She handed Munch her jeans, panties, and socks. "Want some help moving?"

Munch was touched. "Yeah, that would be great." Now that had to be the mark of a true friend, she thought, someone who would help you move. "I can't believe how much stuff I've accumulated. I'm tempted to throw most of it out."

"I know what you mean," Ellen said. "That's why I prefer to travel light."

Ellen liked to brag that she never kept more belongings than would fit in the largest bus locker, a service that she employed on a regular basis.

Munch found Ellen a clean set of underwear and a pair of pants that would fit her. "I need to take the kids to the ballpark." She tried to figure out a delicate way to suggest that Ellen also leave.

"What time will you be back home?" Ellen asked.

"As soon as I can. Call me from wherever you are."

"Not to worry," Ellen said. "You haven't seen the last of me."

Chapter 11

Munch dropped the kids off at the ballpark. Sally Bradbury, one of those moms who had the luxury of a working husband who freed her to be a full-time stay-at-home parent, was already there. She was wearing fleece warm-ups and tennis shoes. Walkman earphones hung around her neck.

"How's the moving going?" Sally asked as she unloaded her station wagon. Her blond hair flipped outward where it brushed her shoulders.

"Hectic," Munch said, "and more work than I realized."

"When do you expect to be finished?" Sally pulled out a duffel bag full of gear and handed it to the waiting children.

"I have to go back to work on Tuesday, so I hope I'll have the bulk of it done by then."

"I sure envy your knowledge of cars," Sally said.

Munch smiled, thinking how it was funny how

there were a lot of days she would trade it all for what Sally had.

"If it would help, I'll keep an eye on the kids," Sally said.

"Are you sure?" Munch asked. "I've got Lindsey Ramsey today too."

Sally waved a dismissive hand in front of her face. "Three kids aren't that much different than two. Go."

"Thanks," Munch said. "I'll be back by three."

"If you'd like," Sally continued, "Asia's welcome to come home with Caitlin on Monday and spend the night."

"That would be a huge help."

"When you get caught up, maybe we can have lunch sometime."

"I'd like that," Munch said. "I'd like that a lot." She left the park in a state of happiness, as much for the found time as for Sally's overtures of friendship. Her next stop was the U-Haul place on Lincoln Boulevard where she rented a trailer, hitch, and dolly. She spent the next few hours packing and loading, her mind often on Lila Mae and the good-byes she didn't get to make. As a treat for the kids, and to use up the ingredients in her cupboard and refrigerator, she decided to make cookies.

At ten o'clock, there was a knock at her door. Ellen. She'd brought a friend. The other woman—one who might charitably be described as a creature—stood slightly behind Ellen and peeked out. Munch caught a brief glimpse of nervous eyes and the sort of expression seen on the faces of animals who were always the prey, never the hunter.

"Who's this?" Munch asked.

Ellen glanced back at the wraith and stepped to one side. "This is Suki."

Suddenly exposed, Suki recoiled a bit, then produced a weak smile that never made it to her dull eyes. She wiped at her nose with the sleeve of her thin beige sweater and nodded her greeting. Munch saw it all—the untucked shirt, the pants with the frayed hems, the scuffed clogs, the smooth skin under mostly gray hair. Junkie. She didn't want to step aside and let this woman into her house, yet at the same time was not immune to Suki's obvious discomfort at standing outside in daylight. Munch knew exactly how she felt.

"I guess you better come in."

Ellen strutted. Suki shuffled past, looking at nothing, demonstrating the thousand-yard stare perfected by cons.

"Suki can help us with our situation," Ellen said.

Munch also noted how now *the situation* was jointly owned. "What exactly is Suki's talent?"

"Paper," Ellen said.

Munch sighed. Paper. Forgery, check kiting, credit card fraud, all those were women's crimes. Men leaned toward burglary and robbery. Possession and sales were anyone's game.

"When did you get out?" Munch asked Suki.

Suki looked to Ellen for reassurance.

"She's okay," Ellen said.

Suki hitched her large bag a little higher on her rounded shoulder. "Last month."

"Wonderful." Munch made eye contact with Suki and indicated the sofa. The aroma of her cookies announcing their doneness filled the house.

"Mmmm. Mm," Ellen said. "Something smells good."

In the kitchen, the oven timer buzzed. Munch glared at Ellen and reluctantly left her so-called guests. Ellen followed her into the kitchen and leaned against the sink while Munch pulled the cookie sheet from the oven.

She kept one eye on Suki through the hallway mirror even though there was nothing loose lying around to nick-knack. *Nick-knack*—that polite junkie term for ripping off whatever small item wasn't nailed down and would fit in or under your clothes. Suki was perched on the couch, barely making a dent.

"I don't like this kind of shit in my house," Munch said.

"You are moving, aren't you?" Ellen said, reaching for a cookie.

"Still, I don't like it." Munch scooped spoonfuls of cookie dough onto another sheet, scraping out the last of the brown sugary mixture from a red ceramic bowl.

Ellen took the empty bowl from her and filled it with hot soapy water. Then she wiped her hands dry and reached for another cookie. "These are pretty good."

"They're for the kids," Munch said, piling the still-hot persimmon cookies onto a Pyrex reindeer platter. The other plates were already packed. She had bought the platter at an after-Christmas sale. The reindeer's red nose and tail formed the handles on either end.

When she glanced back at the sofa in the living room, she saw that it was vacant. The bathroom door shut, the lock clicked. Munch waited for what she felt was a decent interval of time and then took up a position just outside the door.

"You okay?" she yelled.

"Just a minute."

Munch heard the toilet flush and water running. She'd give Suki thirty seconds tops, then she was going in. The doorknob turned, and Munch took a step back.

Suki emerged looking composed and said, "I'm ready." She had twisted her hair into a neat bun and the sheen had left her face.

"Ready for what?" Munch asked.

"You got a desk lamp we could use?" Ellen asked Munch.

"There's a bedside lamp in Asia's room."

"I'll get it." Ellen went to Asia's room and returned a long minute later with the fixture.

"You get lost?" Munch asked.

"Relax, will you?" Ellen said. She had taken off the shade and was unscrewing the bulb. Suki reached into her large macramé purse and took out several items. The first was a two-hundred-watt photo floodlight, which she handed to Ellen; the second was a microscope, which she set down on the table in the dining room. Ellen screwed the brighter bulb into the lamp and handed Munch the cord to plug in. As Suki prepared her equipment, Munch was amazed at the woman's personal transformation. Suki was no longer a nondescript middle-aged urchin; she now exuded confidence. Even her clothes seemed a little less shabby.

Ellen pulled an envelope from under her shirt and spread five one-hundred-dollar bills across the coffee table. Suki picked up one after the other and held them up to the bright light.

"These are great," she said. "Different serial numbers, clear portrait. Paper feels good too. Twenty weight." She rubbed a bill across her cheek. "Definitely a cotton, linen blend."

"So they're real?" Ellen said.

Suki placed a bill under her microscope and invited them each to take a look. "You see how the ink is actually laid down. This is no copier work. You're looking at genuine intaglio product."

"What's intaglio?" Munch asked after taking her turn peering through the microscope, curious despite the warning chimes sounding in her head.

"Kind of printing press the BEP uses."

"BEP?"

Suki looked at her like she was dense. "Bureau of Engraving and Printing. Intaglio printing presses cost millions to own and operate. They use engraved steel plates. You've heard of those, right?"

Munch shrugged, making her face say, "Who hasn't?"

"The intaglio method is a form of embossing. The plates are smeared with ink and then wiped clean. Then plate and paper are pressed together at pressures reaching fifteen hundred pounds per square inch. The result is this three-dimensional image on the substrate."

"Substrate?"

"Paper."

"So this is real?" Ellen asked.

"Almost," Suki said. "I've heard rumors about this stuff. Comes out of the Middle East, part of a big conspiracy to undermine the American economy. They say it even makes it through the Federal Reserve." Suki looked directly at Munch and used a tone one adopts when speaking to the hard of learning. "In the course of normal business, all money passes through a Federal Reserve bank every three or four days. That's the last stop for most counterfeit bills."

"Have you ever thought of using your powers for good?" Munch asked. She returned to the microscope and studied the portrait of Benjamin Franklin under magnification. "Oh, I get it. It's like the difference between letters that are typed and stuff that's xeroxed."

"Exactly." Suki smiled like a professor whose student has had a breakthrough.

Munch had to fight the feeling of pride swelling her head.

"You're sure this is fake?" Ellen asked.

"Yeah." Suki slid the microscope across to her. "You see the blue and red fibers in the substrate?"

Ellen looked through the eyepiece. "What about them?"

"Photocopied. Genuine treasury paper has the fibers imbedded in it."

"Shit," Ellen said.

"I could get you thirty cents on the dollar for these," Suki said. "You'd make more if you passed them yourself. And with quality like this, it would hardly be a gamble. Just forget about Disneyland. Vegas is a bad risk, too. Too many eyes in the sky, if you know what I'm saying."

Ellen held one of the bills and looked pensive. "What's wrong with Disneyland?"

"As soon as they pick up a bad bill, security is on the phone to every cashier within three minutes," Suki said.

"How about the track?" Ellen asked.

"Ellen, don't even think it," Munch said as she unplugged the lamp. She turned to Suki. "Who have you told about this?"

"Not a living soul," Suki said.

Munch met her eyes, but Suki's expression was deadpan. "Would you please go outside and wait in the truck?" Munch asked her.

Suki packed up her equipment and left. Munch watched her sidle out the door. Ellen had a proud smirk on her face. "Didn't I tell you? Lady friend's got some depth."

"Yeah, I'm impressed."

"She wasn't always a junkie."

"I figured." Munch scooped up the bills, counting them as she did so. "Where's the rest of this?"

"I have most of it stashed."

"Most of it?"

"Okay, I'll go through the whole story and this is the God's honest truth."

Munch smiled in spite of herself; this should be interesting.

"I took the money. It was in the backseat of the car. That murdering psycho showed it to me, promised to give me some. And you *know* that was a lie. He planned to kill me all along, just like he did all those others. I hope there's a special corner in hell for the likes of him."

Munch nodded. Ellen didn't have to convince her that last summer's serial murderer, aka "the Band-Aid Killer," needed killing. "So you took the money," Munch prompted.

"Well, yes. Yes, I did," Ellen said, attempting to

look virtuous. "What you don't know is that I left the bag and a whole lot of that money right there at the scene. I only took what I could stuff in my clothes and although I got a little crazy with it in the beginning, I've been real careful with the rest."

Munch couldn't speak for a moment. There was so much wrong, on so many levels, she didn't know where to begin. "You think it makes you less guilty to take only part of what's available to steal? Did you rehearse that in your head for the jury?"

Then Munch's stomach twisted as the full personal impact of Ellen's words sank in. She balled her fist at the memory of the fold of hundred-dollar bills Ellen had pressed into her hand last summer, money Munch had taken with no questions asked. The pieces were all falling together. The terrorist factions who had bought the plutonium last summer used funny money. "Who else did you pass money to besides me? You know, the one with 'unwitting accomplice' stamped on her forehead."

"Hardly anyone. I'm not stupid."

"How about any big purchases?"

"Well, I bought my mama a car, but my name was never on any paperwork. And believe me, I was shocked as anybody when the feds came to see me in CIW and said they were investigating a counterfeiting ring, a matter of national security they said. I never had nothing to do with no counterfeiters, and I sure wouldn't do anything to hurt my country."

"Who else?" Munch asked again.

"Just different people. People in, like, you know, need."

"Peddle it elsewhere, would you? I want names."

"A few bills fell Billy Vega's way. I better give him a heads-up."

"Yeah, you wouldn't want to get on his bad side."

"Billy's okay. He always liked you."

"Yeah, I worked on his mom's car a few times. I always thought that was pretty advanced of him to trust me to work on it. You'd think it would go against his macho instincts. When's the last time you saw him?"

Ellen looked back nervously toward Asia's bedroom. "I've been trying to get hold of him since I got out, but he left the club. I called there yesterday, but the fool on the phone wouldn't tell me anything or let me talk to anybody else. The girls were all busy, he said. They were having a two-for-one special. Though why they would do that on a Saturday does not show me much good business sense."

Munch held up a hand to stop her. "Sounds like you might just have to go there in person."

"I can't." Ellen studied her nails. "I had a small disagreement with the current management."

"No sense in leaving any bridges unburned, huh?"

"Maybe if we could send someone else. One of the other girls probably knows where he is." Ellen made a point of not looking directly at her.

Munch realized that somewhere the music had stopped playing, and she, the one with all the bright ideas, was the one left standing without a chair.

"All right. I guess I could swing by there today and see what I can find out. What are you going to do?"

"I got the truck so I could help you move," Ellen said. "How about I take a load of stuff over to your new house?"

"Don't take Suki over there."

"No, I'll drop her off first," Ellen said, heading for Asia's room and going straight for her toy chest.

"Wait on the big stuff," Munch said. "I've got a dolly over at the new house."

"No problem," Ellen said, straining as she lifted a large box. "No problem at all. I can take some of those boxes by the door, too, if you want."

Munch helped Ellen lift the solid oak toy chest into the back of the truck. Suki stayed slouched down in the passenger seat while they filled in the remaining space with boxes. Munch topped off the load with her Texaco uniforms. She wrote Ellen directions to the new house. As she handed over the map and a key, she felt a familiar warning tingle. *Fuck it,* she thought. *This is what friends are for, to help each other in times of need.* She hadn't realized what a huge ordeal moving was going to be.

Ruby, Munch's sponsor, was always telling her to stop being the Lone Ranger and to let other people lend a hand. Munch argued that she valued her self-sufficiency. Ruby said even the best traits could be taken too far.

So really, she was just acting on her sponsor's advice. Not to mention that some good honest labor wouldn't hurt Ellen. Besides, after tonight, Ellen would have her daddy and plenty else to keep her busy.

Chapter 12

It was almost noon when Munch pulled into the parking lot of the Spearmint Rhino in the City of Industry. She had unhooked the U-Haul trailer and left it in the garage of the new house. The club was a two-story white building, located slightly north of the 10 freeway underpass right where it split into the 110 and 60. There was a ragged man on the off-ramp with a homemade sign that read I'M HUNGRY AND I'M UGLY.

A black awning shaded the entrance. Old-fashioned, carriage-house, black wrought-iron sconces flanked the front door. The door, which was shut, was one of those pretty wooden types with the faux leaded glass at eye level. She'd looked at front doors for the new house just last week at Builders Emporium and knew this one was the most expensive model.

Munch parked near the sidewalk marquee that advertised a free lunch buffet on weekdays. Security cameras bolted to corners of the building were trained on the parking lot.

Munch stepped through the door. The foyer was carpeted. Discreet uplights in the corners provided soft light. Women in photo portraits smiled seductively from the walls. Munch scanned the faces and stopped when she recognized the third girl from the left. Darlene, also affectionately known as Ba-Boom-Ba.

Munch herself had come up with the nickname when they had first met. Darlene had short hair then, a booming voice, and she walked like a truck driver. She was one of those Midwestern, corn-fed types, strong and stout, a Baby Huey in drag. She used to hustle drinks by challenging guys to arm-wrestle and then winning. All those unfeminine traits had been forgiven by the cadre of bikers they hung with because Darlene had two assets that didn't escape notice, one on the right and one on the left. Munch had watched Darlene cross the barroom floor on some wasted afternoon early on in their acquaintance. Seeing those two double-D breasts swaying unfettered, Munch had greeted her with, "Ba-Boom-Ba." The name had stuck. And now here she was, nine, ten years later, baring it all in some sleazy strip club with pretensions. Munch never danced for money. It wasn't a moral issue; she had never felt she had the body for it.

The curtains leading into the club parted, and a short, balding man in a tuxedo emerged.

"Can I help you?" he asked.

Munch pointed to Darlene's picture. "Is she working today?"

"Is she a friend?"

"Long time. She still go by Ba-Boom-Ba?"

The guy grinned. "The one and only. Who shall I say is calling?"

"Munch."

The guy left her standing there. Munch's second strongest memory of Ba-Boom-Ba was waiting at the hospital for Ba-Boom-Ba to get stitches the time she stabbed that girl at the bar. Ba-Boom-Ba had felt real bad about it and had cried and cried all the way to Marina Mercy. Her white T-shirt had been covered with the girl's blood. Ba-Boom-Ba didn't even remember pulling the knife, or what they were arguing about, only that once she started pounding that blade into the girl's back she couldn't seem to stop herself. Fortunately, she hadn't hit any vital organs, and the vic was a trouper. She, the stabbee, didn't give up any description of her assailant to the cops. Hell, she was drinking at the same bar as all of them, flirting with their men. What was she doing there if she wasn't another scooter tramp?

Their story, rehearsed on the drive to the emergency room, was that Ba-Boom-Ba had been the victim of the same knife-wielding assailant. Technically this was true. Ba-Boom-Ba's grip on the bloody knife handle had slipped, slid down the blade, and she had sliced the inside of her fingers. They were passing the cuts off as defensive wounds, and by the time they got to the hospital, they had pretty much convinced themselves they were telling the truth.

Munch had hung out in the waiting room while the doctors worked on both of them. Ba-Boom-Ba's victim's father was there too. A middle-aged white guy in a suit, understandably distressed. He looked at Munch a few times, but she just made her face go blank as if whatever he was mad about had nothing to do with her. She had been pretty good at stonewalling back then. Thank God she got out of the life when she did. Another year in and she wouldn't have had any feelings left. Hard to believe that Ellen and Ba-Boom-Ba could still be at it and walking around.

The doorman/bouncer in the tux returned. "I'm Sheldon, by the way." He offered Munch a moist hand to shake.

"Nice to meet you." She wondered if he expected a tip.

"C'mon," he said.

She followed him inside the club. The place was filled with guys in suits, seated at little round tables. Some of them had women with them, others were by themselves. There was a model's runway that extended halfway into the room. When Munch walked past the elevated ramp, her head was even with the performer's ankles. A movie camera mounted on a tripod was set up on the edge of the stage. The emcee announced that *Playboy* was filming today for its show on cable.

Well, Munch thought, *aren't I lucky to come on such a special occasion.*

A woman walked out, wearing only high heels and a glittery G-string. Her breasts were bare, but the nipples were covered with flesh-colored makeup. No one in the audience seemed particularly moved. The woman's expression was blank, like a model's. The camera rolled. Frank Sinatra sang "Fly Me to the Moon."

Sheldon led Munch across the floor and through another door that led to a dressing room of sorts. Women were everywhere, adjusting the tiny patches of fabric covering their crotches, and rubbing baby oil on their legs. Ba-Boom-Ba was standing in front of a makeup mirror, dressed in a tattered kimono, and teasing her light brown hair into spikes. She turned when she saw Munch.

"Hey, cunt," she bellowed affectionately. "How the hell are you?"

Munch made her face into a half-smile, grateful no one she knew now was witnessing this greeting, and feeling a tiny bit traitorous for thinking that.

"Sheldon said you were out there. I couldn't believe it."

"Yep," Munch said, "I can't believe I'm here either."

Ba-Boom-Ba charged the distance between them and gave Munch a bone-crunching hug. "You looking for work?"

"Actually, I'm trying to track down Billy Vega."

Ba-Boom-Ba's manner instantly changed. A scowl replaced her smile. "That fool? What do you want with him?"

"I've got a message for him."

"Send it Western Union."

"I take it the honeymoon is over between you two?"

"Been dead and stinking for a long time," Ba-Boom-Ba said. "He got himself into some heavy shit. You best stay way clear of him." She leaned in close and lowered her voice. "You heard about how they found that girl last week in Downey? She was Billy's old lady. Some dude raped her and left her in a Dumpster naked."

Munch conjured a mental image of how horrible it would be to find herself naked and just thrown away.

Ba-Boom-Ba brought her face in close again. "The

only way they found her is because of the smell. It was so hot in the Dumpster, she was decomposing."

Oh, Munch thought, dead was worse. You don't come back from dead.

"Yeah, some sick shit going down. The freak broke all her fingers." Ba-Boom-Ba shuddered for emphasis, her massive breasts parted her robe. Since Munch had seen her last, she'd gotten a butterfly tattoo above one of her nipples.

"You know where I can find Billy now?"

"He's bouncing at that club out by the airport on Century. Losing that girl really fucked his head up, I heard."

"Century Entertainment?"

"Yeah, that's the place."

Munch nodded and looked down all the spray cans and bottles of beauty aids on Ba-Boom-Ba's dressing table. "How about you? You doing okay?"

"I'm getting by. You're not handing out Bibles, are you? I heard you got religion."

"It's not like that."

Two hot, sweaty naked women pushed past them on their way to the back of the room. They looked young, like nineteen or twenty. That had to be demoralizing, like going to Westwood on a date and being surrounded by college coeds. Munch looked back at her friend and saw the hardness in her eyes. The music changed to the country-western song "Take This Job and Shove It." Ba-Boom-Ba started mouthing the words. She looked like she'd happily shove a saddle up anyone's ass.

Munch grabbed her arm and pulled her to a quieter corner. "You remember Ellen?"

"What about her?"

"Her mama got murdered, and her stepdaddy."

"She's in the joint, right?"

"No, she got out a couple days ago. The murders happened when she was inside."

"Life is hard all over." As if to emphasize her point, another pair of perky young things bounced past, all giggles and energy. Munch thought that that kind of attitude probably really helped them up onstage.

"So you didn't hear anything about it?"

"No, but it's been raining shit all month."

"Yeah?"

"The boss split, nobody's getting paid. There's some rumbles in the jungle, if you know what I'm saying."

"Management changes a lot, does it?"

"It does when money gets lost, and loans don't get repaid."

Sheldon returned with an unopened jar of maraschino cherries, which he handed to Ba-Boom-Ba. "Would you mind?" he asked.

Ba-Boom-Ba popped the lid easily and handed it back to him.

"Loans from who?" Munch asked, after Sheldon had walked away again.

"I shouldn't say."

Munch knew from the look in Ba-Boom-Ba's eyes that she was proud to be on the inside, and would be just as pleased to prove it.

"The Boys?" Munch asked, using the euphemism for the local mob.

Ba-Boom-Ba made her face go solemn, as if to say a wise woman wouldn't say something like that out loud, but she didn't dispute Munch's conclusion either.

Munch thanked her.

"Hey, let me get your number," Ba-Boom-Ba said.

Munch tore out the address from one of her bank deposit slips. The phone number would be the same at the new house. They talked about going to a movie together or something. Even as Munch wrote Ba-Boom-Ba's name and number in her phone book, she was certain they'd never get together. As Munch exited the club, she stopped to admire the row of scooters parked outside. The first was fully dressed with fat-bob tanks, a solo seat, and saddle packs. The other three were chopped and extended, with lots of extra chrome and custom paint jobs. What caught her eye was the panhead on the end with the straight pipes and Springer front end. It was painted a color she had never before seen on a Harley: pink. Somebody's dreams were coming true.

Becker had been sitting in the parking lot of the Spearmint Rhino checking his notes when the blue GTO pulled up. He was mildly interested to note that the driver was a lone woman. She was small and cute, with her face scrubbed clean and hair pulled back in a ponytail. When she turned to lock her car, she looked familiar. He ran her plate. Miranda Mancini.

Bingo.

He waited while she talked to the doorman. The guy took her inside.

Becker called in his location, then paid the cover charge and followed. The place was dark and loud. Some bimbo was dancing onstage. He took a seat in the back row and spotted the Mancini woman being led backstage. A six-foot-tall black-haired Amazon in a sheer nightgown winked at him. *Geez,* he thought, *my wife is not going to believe this place.*

An Asian girl in a bikini stopped at his table. "Can I get you a drink?" she asked, all smiles.

He reached for his wallet. "Bring me a Coke."

His drink arrived several minutes later followed by one of the working girls. The girl put a hand on his shoulder and leaned over so that most of her tits showed. "Looking for some company, honey?"

"Still shopping," he said. "Thanks."

She pouted for only a second and then moved on to the next man. He feigned interest in the floor show while keeping an eye out for Mancini. The door she had gone through opened and he saw her enveloped in the arms of a broad with Carol Doda tits.

"Six dollars," the waitress said and waited.

He pulled out a ten. "Give me a receipt, will you?"

The waitress returned with his change and a wet register receipt. He gave her a dollar tip.

Several minutes passed and then Mancini bade Big Tits good-bye. Becker watched Mancini leave, then waved the Amazon over.

"What's your pleasure, honey?" she asked.

He pointed at the stage door. "The one in the robe," he said. "Tell her I'd like a private meeting."

"Sure thing," she said. "What's your name, honey?"

"Art."

"Hi, Art. Private dances are fifty dollars. We do accept American Express, Visa, and MasterCard."

He unfolded his badge holder and gave her a quick peek. "I just want to ask her a few questions. Won't take long."

She sighed, rolled her eyes skyward. "All right. But try to make it quick, will you? We're filming today, and she's on deck in ten minutes."

She grabbed his hand and led him through the dressing room door.

"Boom-Ba," she called, "you got company. I told the *officer* to make it quick."

The Amazon disappeared, leaving him toe-to-toe, in a manner of speaking, with the woman she had called "Boom-Ba."

Becker gave her a business card as way of introduction.

"This about Corinne again?" she asked.

"Corinne," he repeated, waiting for her to give him more.

"The murdered girl."

"She worked here?"

"Used to," she said. "Till she got herself killed." The woman laughed hard at her own punch line.

He pulled out his notebook. "What's your name?"

"Darlene Tarrel. Two *r*'s."

"How long have you worked here?"

"Two years, this time, but it's only temporary. I'm saving my money to go to chef school."

"Good for you." He scratched the side of his face and gave her his sheepish look. "So what's the dumbest question you ever get asked?"

"Oh, I get the same ones night after night. I just smile and act like I haven't heard it all before."

Becker nodded sympathetically.

"Not a night goes by, some joker doesn't want to know, 'Who shaves you?'"

Becker almost got a crick in his neck not looking down.

"For your information, I shave myself."

Out on the floor, men's voices roared with lusty appreciation. Darlene Tarrel looked annoyed.

He showed her the strip club flyer found at Lila Mae's house with Ellen's picture on it. "How about this woman?"

She looked. "What about her?"

"You know her?"

"I might. A lot of girls pass through here."

"Look closer." He handed her a copy of the handbill with Ellen's photograph on it. "You sure you don't remember her? Her name is Ellen Summers."

Darlene removed a pair of glasses from the pocket of her robe and studied the flyer. "Uh-huh, oh yeah. I know her. She worked here six months ago. I don't know where she is now."

"That woman you were talking to earlier. The little one with the ponytail."

"Yeah?"

"What did she want?"

"Just an old friend, looking for some guy we used to know."

"She have a name?"

"Yeah, I guess so. I just know her as Munch."

"What guy?"

"Some asshole named Billy Vega. I don't know what she wanted with him. I told her to steer clear. As a matter of fact, he's the one got that other girl—" She stopped.

"What?"

She bit her lower lip for a moment. "He was Corinne's man. You know what I'm saying? He was supposed to be looking out for her."

"Was Ellen one of Billy Vega's girls?"

The dancer laughed then, a deep rumbling chuckle. "Billy is lucky to have one girl at a time, the red-haired freak."

"Were Corinne and Ellen friends?"

"They might have danced some sets together. What they did outside this place, I don't know."

He took back the flyer. "Thanks for your help, Darlene. You call me if you think of anything else. And good luck."

"Thanks, Officer." Darlene opened her robe. "How do I look?"

"Uh, great. Very photogenic. Break a leg."

"Hey," she said with a wink, "you never know who might be out there."

On his way out, Becker noticed a small television on the dressing room table. It was tuned to a cooking channel. Julia Child was pulling a quiche from a sparkling stainless-steel oven.

Darlene went to the ladies' room to use the pay phone. She retrieved the number from a piece of paper folded in thirds and stuck in the back of her lipstick case and dialed the seven digits.

"Someone just came in asking for her."

She put a finger on her free ear so she could hear better.

"A cop." She read off the name on Becker's business card. "He didn't say. I told him she worked here six months ago. He put her name together with Billy's.

I said I didn't know anything about that. I got something else for you, too. Some broad I used to know was here, asking questions about Billy, seemed to know a few things about Ellen, too." She listened a minute, laughed, and then sang, "If you've got the money, honey, I've got the time."

Chapter 13

Ellen found Munch's new address easily enough. Munch had already been there. The U-Haul trailer, still loaded with boxes and furniture, was inside the small attached garage. It was a cute house. One of those Spanish stucco jobs with arched windows and a red-tile roof. The inside smelled of fresh paint with a faint undertone of insecticide.

She'd unload the trailer, but her first priority was Asia's toy chest. She got the dolly from inside the garage and wheeled the large wooden box into the room Munch had told her was Asia's.

The walls were pink. Bright white bookshelves waited to be filled with novels about flying nuns, magical broom closets, and phantom tollbooths. She placed the toy chest in the corner away from the window, opened it, and removed the toys. Then she used a long thin screwdriver to pry up the sheet of cedar lining the bottom. The hundred-dollar bills were bundled in stacks of fifty. Hard to believe now that it was only six months ago that the money had come into her life. It felt like years, what with all the waiting for things to cool down and her being in jail and all.

She had wound up with thirty bundles. Not too shabby for a day's work, until the money turned out to be counterfeit. Quality counterfeit to be sure and not completely worthless, but still a disappointment. The money had been safe enough stashed under a floorboard in Asia's closet. But Munch's decision to move coupled with the impending demolition of the house had required an alternate plan.

She picked up two bundles, stuck them down her pants, and then replaced everything else as it had been. The weird part was, she hardly cared about the money anymore, even if it were real, it was just paper—not worth a human life.

She spent the next hour hanging up Asia's little dresses in her closet. She also put books away on the bookshelves, assembled the kid's dresser, made her bed, and dragged the chest to its place at the bed's foot. Then she went out to the garage and brought in all that stuff. Most of it was marked KITCHEN or BATHROOM. She put the boxes in the appropriate rooms for Munch to unpack.

She patted the money wedged in her underpants and locked the door behind her on her way out. She had a plan.

Munch was hungry. She was also low on gas. She had a fortune cookie left over from a few nights ago. She unwrapped the cellophane, broke open the cookie, and devoured it.

She stopped at a Hancock filling station with its ten

choices of Blendomatic gasoline. From the menu she selected number four, which was a high-octane blend of leaded ethanol. She always went with the greatest octane to minimize the pinging in her high-compression engine. Lead protected her valves although she'd heard that there was legislation under way to remove all the lead from gasoline by 1988. The ethanol was something she'd been meaning to try. It was supposed to burn cleaner, be easier on the environment. While waiting for her tank to fill she unrolled the small white banner that held her fortune.

"Tomorrow," it read, "do something unusual."

She threw back her head and laughed. She was still smiling to herself when she pulled up to the ball field. Sally Bradbury was over by the dugout speaking to one of the coaches. Sally waved and nodded to where Asia was waiting for Munch on the bench by the side gate. Munch parked and went inside to sign her out. Asia had a consent slip for an away game the following week. Lindsey wasn't with her, but there was a crowd of kids around the park's bulletin board.

"Hey, honey. Where's Lindsey?"

"Her mom came and got her."

"Who let that happen?"

Asia looked at her without comprehension. And why should she understand what was wrong with that picture? Nothing in her short life had prepared her for the concept that a parent could be the worst company for a kid.

"I need to make a phone call," Munch said. They walked over to the pay phones, and Munch called Alex at the studio. "I'm at the park. Noreen got here first and picked up Lindsey."

"I know," he said. "She's here now."

"Well, that's a relief." Munch looked over to see that the crowd by the bulletin board had grown to include the coaches as well as arriving parents. Some of them glanced at her and then looked away just as quickly. "You've got to get that woman some help before she does some permanent damage."

"Tell me about it," he said. "You don't think this hasn't been hard on me? My whole life has been disrupted."

"I was thinking more of Lindsey. Somebody has to."

She hung up and walked over to the bulletin board to see what had everyone's attention. It was a long printout. At the top of the page was her own name followed by a string of aliases. Next to the familiar police codes of 647B PC, 11550 H&S, and 11350 H&S someone had written in ink the civilian translations: prostitution, under the influence of heroin, and possession of heroin. After each charge the jurisdiction, disposition, and subsequent incarcerations were also listed. She tore the document down and wadded it into a ball. Seeing the expressions of the older kids, she knew her action had come too late. Her face stung with a million small pinpricks, as if an electrical shock had passed between her ears.

She grabbed Asia's hand and led her to the car. There was little she could do about her shaking hands, but she could keep her pace measured and her expression neutral. She felt the eyes of the playground on her and knew that she was probably mistaken. Most of that stuff wouldn't mean much to these kids, maybe some of the sixth-graders, but not the little ones. The adults, of course, were a different story. Her main focus now was not to transmit her feelings to Asia, not until she could figure how to deal with this public revelation of her history.

It wasn't that she didn't admit most of her past openly, but she liked to work up to the worst parts.

Asia hurried along beside her. "What's wrong?"

"Nothing," Munch said, slowing her pace.

They reached the car. Munch opened the passenger door and waited for Asia to climb in.

"Then why the mean face?" Asia asked as her mother made sure her seat belt was fastened.

Munch tweaked Asia's nose. "I was just thinking about something."

She came around to the driver's side and got in. The car's engine roared to life and she felt the same little self-satisfied thrill that its powerful V-8 engine always gave her. She goosed the throttle a few times, turned on the air-conditioning, and directed the flow of cold air toward her face.

What did she have at stake here? Her reputation? With whom? Anybody she cared about, anybody she was close with already knew.

She always had the talk when she went out with a guy and it began to look like things could turn sexual. Not that that happened all that much, relatively speaking. In the past seven years she could count the men she had had relations with on one hand. That was some kind of record. She was proud of it.

The personal revelations would start with the guy asking what she did about birth control. She could easily tell him, "Don't worry, it's taken care of," and let him assume she was on the pill or had an IUD. But what if they fell in love and he thought they'd have babies together someday? No, it was better to begin with the truth.

"I can't have kids," she'd say. "I have scarring in my fallopian tubes."

If the guy asked how it happened she could just as easily say it was a result of endometriosis—a condition any woman could get and that was almost true in her case. But to be fair, she would lay out the whole scenario. She'd tell him about when she was younger she had a venereal disease that went unchecked. Gonorrhea. The disease had spread to her reproductive organs and ruined them. It was also true that in women gonorrhea can be asymptomatic. And for her it was. No symptoms whatsoever. Not if you didn't count all the men who were complaining.

Back then she didn't really care who she infected, finding special irony that time when the Satan's Pride Motorcycle Club members passed her around on their meeting night without her consent. Served the bastards right.

Anyhow, she would lay her past open before she embarked on any relationship that had a hope of a future. She would include the part about how she'd obviously changed a great deal. That she was a different person back then—crazy from drugs. Getting off drugs had restored her to sanity. Etcetera, etcetera, etcetera. Then if the guy was still around and willing after all that—

Munch jolted upright as the realization of what must have happened struck her. Alex. That little fink. He must have told Noreen.

She looked down at Asia, who was practicing snapping her fingers. How much was Munch's policy of truth going to affect her? Asia must have felt the attention because she stopped snapping and said, "I love you."

Munch turned down the radio. "I love you, too, honey. We do all right together, don't we?"

"Yep, so far, so good," Asia said, and went back to entertaining herself, now singing a song from last summer's school production of *Pinocchio.*

Munch had to laugh. Had to be *Pinocchio*, didn't it? The little wooden boy whose nose grew with each lie he told. A moral lesson set in the realm of make-believe. Maybe that's where it belonged. How well did absolute honesty go over as policy? She had had some fantasy when she first got sober that her new world was going to be a place where lies were never necessary. She had soon learned different. Even people with straight jobs and straight lives didn't always tell the truth. Still, she clung to the belief that when you shared your life with a person, total honesty was important.

Six years ago the guy had been a cop named John "Jigsaw" Blackstone. They'd worked together to solve the murder of Asia's daddy. In the course of their adventure they'd saved each other's butts. Besides the respect that had ensued, there had also been a measure of attraction. They got together for lunch a few times, and were working their way up to dinner.

Then one day the love lives of cops had come up. Blackstone said he knew guys, other cops, who got involved with strippers and hookers—even marrying them on occasion.

"Oh, yeah?" she said, thinking this might be the perfect opportunity to come clean with her past.

"Yeah," he said, "the guys think they're helping the girls, reforming them or something. But the truth is nobody forgets about where these women came from. Everybody laughs at the guys behind their backs."

Munch had changed the subject then. After that, she stopped calling him. When he tried to make plans, she was always busy. Eventually they lost contact. Mace St. John told her once that Blackstone had transferred out of Homicide and was working sex crimes. She said she hoped he was happy.

A minivan full of kids passed them. Asia waved to her friends.

Fuck it, Munch thought. It's not like she was planning to run for some political office. Still, this was embarrassing. Goddamn embarrassing.

"Man," she said out loud, slamming her palm on the steering wheel.

Asia looked at her wide-eyed. "Are you okay?"

"Yeah, just ducky." She smiled to take the bitterness out of her tone then glanced at her watch. She had time to make another run between houses and to check her machine for messages before her afternoon limo run. She also needed to feed the dogs.

She stopped at the new house first, saw all that Ellen had done, hitched up the trailer, and went over to the old house. Ellen was waiting for her. She still had the truck. Munch pulled into her driveway. Asia had fallen asleep in the passenger seat and was snoring loudly. Munch left her there.

"Thanks for unloading all that stuff."

"How did it go?" Ellen asked.

Munch pulled her rap sheet from her pocket and handed it to Ellen. She explained where she had found it and who she believed was responsible.

"What are you going to do about this bitch pulling your covers?" Ellen asked, following Munch up the walkway to the front door.

"The woman's sick."

They were almost to the door. Munch could hear Nicky's tail thumping the wall. It was kinda nice how they were always so happy to see you again.

"So what does that mean?" Ellen asked. "Are you going to carry your message to her now?"

"She's got problems I can't begin to touch. I'm worried about Lindsey."

"I still think you should kick the mom's ass," Ellen said. "Just on general principles."

"Don't think I don't want to, but that never solves anything." Munch turned the key in the lock and opened her door. The dogs greeted her with little whimpers of pleasure. Maybe after they were settled she'd finally take Asia to the pound like she'd been promising and pick out a dog. Or perhaps Mace St. John would come up with a pet for them. He had a propensity for taking in strays.

"How did the other thing go?" Ellen asked, following Munch inside.

"You didn't tell me Ba-Boom-Ba worked there."

"You saw her?"

"Yeah. She said Billy Vega left the Spearmint Rhino, and if I was smart, I'd stop looking for him."

"Did she say why he left?"

"He got into something too heavy, and one of his girls got killed."

"Which one?"

"I didn't ask. It happened over in Downey. Sounded pretty brutal. All her fingers were broken."

Ellen sank to the floor as if all her muscles had suddenly failed her. The dogs sniffed her face.

Munch crouched on the floor next to Ellen and pushed the dogs gently aside. "Let me guess. There's something you haven't told me."

Chapter 14

"They broke my mama's fingers too," Ellen said, her voice hushed with shock, maybe fear.

"Bastards." Munch shook her head and remained silent for a moment. She rubbed her hand over Ellen's back. "Tell me everything. This time start from the beginning."

"You remember I said I had some trouble at the club—with the management?"

"Um, hmm."

"One day Animal took me aside and said he noticed me living beyond my means."

"Animal? You didn't say your beef was with Animal. I remember that motherfucker. You could always pick his old lady out of the crowd; she'd be the one with the cast on."

"I wasn't fucking him, I was just working there." Ellen wiped her eyes with her sleeve and took a deep breath. "Anyway, he said he had a deal going and was looking for new backers. He told me I could double my investment. The next day I came in to work with two thousand dollars and he brought in a sample of the goods."

"Dope," Munch guessed.

"Mexican Brown. We went over to some other guy's pad to shoot up. I went first. We were sitting at this guy's kitchen table. I stood up and walked over to the refrigerator. The next thing I know my head was bouncing off the linoleum."

"You OD'd?"

"Enough to put me out. I woke up in bed, naked, some guy I didn't know on top of me. Animal was gone. So was my bundle of bills."

"So, raped, robbed, and left for dead. Sounds like a typical day in the life. What did you do next?"

"I took the guy's car keys after he, uh, fell asleep and drove his Lincoln through the office of the club. Unfortunately, Animal wasn't there at the time. Couple people saw me, so I split. Don't worry, they didn't call the cops or anything."

"Back up a moment. If you had all that money, why were you dancing?"

"I had to show some means of support, and I didn't want to draw attention to myself."

Munch didn't pursue that string of logic. Instead she said, "You're lucky he didn't kill you." Then everything fell into place. "He didn't kill you because he knew there was a lot more where that came from. You bragged, didn't you?"

Ellen nodded miserably. "That, and when Billy showed up on his new scooter . . ."

"You bought Billy Vega a motorcycle?"

"It was more like a loan."

"You see? This is what I mean about getting loaded. It makes you stupid." Munch didn't need to say that her big mouth had probably gotten Lila Mae and Dwayne killed. Ellen would have to live with that for the rest of her life. "What's the tie-in with the finger-breaking?"

"Okay, I didn't know about the mob connection until after I started working there . . ."

"Who do you think owns places like that? Bank of America?"

"Well, sure, I mean I knew they were laundering, that's sort of to be expected. But then the books started coming up short, and Animal figured it was one of the girls. He lined us all up in the office one day and said he'd break the fingers of anyone who ripped him off. Even Ba-Boom-Ba looked scared and you know what a hard ass she is."

"So broken fingers are like his trademark? Why didn't you think of this before?"

"I thought he was just being, you know, figurative."

Munch rolled her lip with her finger, thinking. "Why don't we just get the message to him that the money is counterfeit? Take the heat off."

"You think he would believe that?"

"Probably not." Munch wondered if there wasn't some way they could make the truth work for them. It would be sweet to see Animal and company pay for the murders without getting Ellen thrown back into the joint or worse.

"Billy told me once that he had my back if I ever needed it," Ellen said. "I'd say it was time I called him on that."

After a moment, they both stood. Ellen shook out her arms and rolled her head a few times. The expression on her face was resolute. Munch could hear her friend's thoughts as clearly as if they had been spoken out loud. The same thoughts Munch would be having in her place. That these guys didn't know who they were fucking with. Munch also knew that that kind of thinking was bullshit, fueled by haywire emotions and an exaggerated sense of yourself. She'd been there too. Recently.

"I'm sorry about your mom, you know that," she said, hearing how inadequate the words sounded. "But, Ellen, c'mon, you're no match for these guys. Mace St. John is getting back in town next week. I'll tell him the situation and he'll—"

"What? You think he gives a shit about me? I see the way he looks at me."

Munch considered. Ellen did have a point. Mace St. John thought she was beyond redemption and had made his feeling abundantly clear. She thought again of her promise to Lila Mae. "You're right. Your best hope is to deal with the feds."

"The ones that came to see me in the joint?"

"Offer them a deal. In exchange for immunity, you'll give them the location of the money and let them take it from there. No questions asked."

"I'm supposed to just hand it all over and walk away? I think I have more coming to me than that."

"You want blood, I know, but you're going to have to settle for poetic justice." Munch opened the front shades so she could keep an eye on Asia. "Maybe you can ask to go into protective custody or something until this whole thing shakes out." Munch wondered if this was a bad time to ask for her house key back.

"No way am I going into any kind of custody."

Munch looked at her friend and wanted to whack her upside the head. Ellen was hardly in a position to be refusing options. But until Ellen saw that herself, there was no point arguing. "When did Billy and Ba-Boom-Ba break up?"

"Oh, they've been off and on forever; you know how that goes."

"Yeah, I shouldn't be surprised."

"Does she know where he is now?"

"She had an idea," Munch said. "But I don't want you to go off and see him by yourself. You're not alone in this thing."

"I appreciate that. And I'm going to help you deal with your situation too. Noreen Ramsey has messed with the wrong women."

Munch made a dismissive gesture with her hand. "I'm not worried about what she's done to me as much as what she's doing to her kid. I know it can't go on much longer. The rate she's going, she'll self-destruct."

"You really think so?"

"How long can she keep it up? She has a big job. Surely she can't spend all this time running around and doing her crazy shit without it screwing that up."

"What does she do?"

"Sells real estate. You see her name all over town. Alex says she pulls down big bucks in commissions. Actually, I feel sorry for her. She makes all the money in the world and she's miserable."

"Oh, that reminds me," Ellen said. "Garret called, said he was all through with some tool he borrowed.

He said to stop by his house, that he'd be home all day. He had a real nice voice. You want me to go over there for you?"

Munch considered the offer briefly. No, she couldn't do that to Garret. Besides, she owed him a visit, a final ending. "I'll swing by later."

"You sure now?"

"Yeah, positive." She checked her watch. "Listen, Ellen. I hate to rush off again, but I need to load the car and make another run to the new house. You want to come with me?"

"No, you go on. I'll be fine. You want your key back?"

"Yeah, good thing you said something."

Ellen handed Munch the house key.

"Promise me you won't do anything until at least tomorrow," Munch said, slipping the key onto the ring that already held her car and toolbox keys. "Whatever you think you need to do can wait another day. It wouldn't hurt for you to chill out a little. Go to a movie or something. Give all this a chance to soak in."

"I won't do anything stupid."

Munch closed her eyes and rubbed them. She really didn't have time for any of this. She walked across the floor to what was left of her home limo office, now reduced to a two-line telephone and an appointment book set atop a folding card table. She had arranged with the phone company to have the service switched to the new house on Monday.

"I couldn't come with you now, anyways," Ellen said. "I've got to go see the fella who owns this truck before he reports it stolen or some damn silly thing."

Munch was still smiling when she played the messages on her tape. Rico called. Twice. In the second message he told her that he'd be at the Inglewood Youth Center all day in case she was in the neighborhood and wanted to stop by with the kids. He left the number and directions. The Youth Center was only about a mile from the airport. Not even out of the way really. She wasn't kidding herself; it would also be a good excuse to show up in her limo outfit of tailored black slacks, high heels, and wearing makeup and jewelry.

Time to feed the dogs. They came running when they heard the can opener. She split the can of Nature's Recipe between the two compartments of the dog dish, then added kibble and water. The dogs attacked their dinner with their usual enthusiasm.

Ellen joined her, reaching down to heft a cardboard box full of pots and pans. "You want these to go?"

"Yeah, might as well," Munch said. She'd cooked her last meal in this house. The plan for tonight's dinner was McDonald's. Drive-through mom strikes again. She had enough of those little Happy Meals toys to open her own franchise. Asia received Flintstone vitamins every morning to compensate for any nutritional needs lacking in Chicken McNuggets and french fries. Munch tried not to notice how she was seeking and finding an easy solution in a pill. She hoped she wasn't setting a precedent. The kid's genes were already stacked against her with both birth parents being drug addicts.

She picked up a box of plates and followed Ellen out.

"Listen," she said as they stacked the boxes in the back of the trailer. "I've been thinking. It's probably not safe for you back at that place in the projects. Why don't you stay with me again tonight? I'll meet you over at the new house. Come there after you're through with your dad."

"You are a true friend."

Were those tears in her eyes?

"I'm going to be back and forth a lot," Munch said. "And I have a limo run to the airport at five o'clock."

"You do keep busy, don't you?"

"Yeah, another day, another fifty cents. Give me a time when you think you'll be around and I'll be sure to be there."

"Oh, now, don't you go rushing your business on my account," Ellen said. "I have my own key."

Munch looked down at her key ring and saw that the new key dangling there was indeed a copy. Why was she not surprised?

Chapter 15

Ellen didn't tell Munch the entire truth. She did need to get the truck back to its owner (or at least extend her lease) and she was having dinner with her dad, but the nature of her other errand would only upset Munch.

The truck belonged to a longtime trick named Roofer Russ. She'd called the old guy the day before and discovered he was home convalescing with a broken leg. He was more than happy to loan her his truck in exchange for a little home nursing. Now it was time to make another deposit in Russ's goodwill bank before he got all excited and did something they would both regret.

Twenty minutes later, Ellen was at Russ's little wood-shingled house in Venice. She knocked on his door.

"Who is it?" he yelled.

"It's me," she replied, using the door key that she had found on the truck key ring. He was stretched out on his living room couch and in a grouchy mood.

"What happened to a couple of hours?" he asked.

"I am sorry, honey. I know I should have called. I've been helping a friend move and you know how exhausting that is." She sat down next to him and patted his cast. "Did you miss me?"

"Me and Mr. Pokey both," he said, finally putting a grin on his old sourpuss face.

Ellen stopped herself from rolling her eyes. She hated it when guys named their dicks, hated it even more when she had to play along. She reached into her pocket and pulled out a wad of hundreds. Russ stared.

"You rob a bank or something?"

"Believe me," she said, "I earned all of this." She peeled off two bills and stuffed them in his shirt pocket. "Can I use the truck a few more days? My friend has a lot of stuff to move."

Russ shrugged. "Why not? It ain't doing me no good."

She bent over and planted a kiss on his forehead, smelling his old-man smells of scalp oil and denture breath. She promised herself that this was the last time she was touching this old coot. "Thanks a million, darling," she said, smiling sweetly. "I'll see you in a couple days. You got everything you need here?"

"My sister has been doing for me, but a man gets lonely." He rubbed his crotch. She pulled back before he could grab her.

"I have got to go. We will have us a little party when I come back. How does that sound?"

"I'll be here."

Don't hold your breath, she thought as she walked

out his door. Fifteen minutes later she pulled up to the address Patrice had given her when they saw each other at the parole office. The house was an old Victorian-style monstrosity near the canals. The once-white paint was peeling and the front yard was full of dated furniture with sun-bleached upholstery. Several seat cushions had blackened holes from small fires probably started by cigarettes and put out by God-knows-what. The station wagon parked at the curb had two flat tires and a thick layer of dust. She locked the truck and let herself in the front gate. There was a red-painted line on the front walk. Stuck in the dirt beside the edge of the line was a sign that read BEWARE OF DOG.

Just then a large black Doberman came charging out from the side yard. She screamed and jumped back, making it all the way to the gate before the dog reached the red-painted line and snapped back. The chain holding him drew taut.

"Nigger!" a man's voice called from in the house. "Shut up!"

"Hello?" Ellen called.

A bare-chested, long-haired, tattooed blond guy came to the door. He eyed Ellen suspiciously. Well, what did she expect? The guy didn't exactly trade in Avon products.

"Are you Lenny?" she asked.

"Who wants to know?"

"Patrice sent me."

"All right," he said. "Come on in."

"Uhh," she said, pointing at the dog who was still eyeing her like all he saw was cat meat.

"Nigger," the guy yelled, "sit."

The dog sat. Ellen smiled weakly at the dog as she

passed him, thinking she'd have an attitude too with a name like that. She'd always hated that word, only using it herself on the rarest occasion.

"What you looking for?" Lenny asked when they entered his front room. A television blared in one corner. Old TV dinner trays littered the coffee table. A trail of oil spots led to a black stain in the center of the floor, no doubt left by a Harley.

"A gun. Didn't Patrice tell you?"

"You think they only come in one size? You want a revolver, automatic, what? How about a thirty-two magnum, two-shot? I've got a sweet little derringer." He held out his palm, showing her the small gun concealed there. "You stick it right in your panty hose."

"Two shots seems a little . . . limiting. What else do you have?"

"Revolver or automatic?"

"What's the difference?"

"None to me. You want a wheel gun, I can give you a good deal on a Ruger. I'll even throw in a speed loader."

"No, I think I'm looking for an automatic. Something easy."

"I've got just the thing," Lenny said. He left the room and returned a moment later with a black felt drawstring pouch. He opened it and removed a gun with a gray cross-hatched plastic grip. The words PIETRO BERETTA GARDONE V.T.—MADE IN ITALY were stamped on the brushed chrome barrel.

"Can I hold it?" she asked.

He racked the chamber and removed the bullet there, then popped out the magazine and handed the weapon over.

She held it first at her side, then tried a few quick-draw maneuvers.

"Seems a mite small," she said.

"You want something fits your hand. Won't do you any good if it gets away from you." He looked at her pointedly.

"No, I suppose not."

"Don't worry, it'll get the job done," he said. He showed her how it loaded and fired. "Two hundred, twenty-five. I'll throw in a box of rounds."

She turned her back on him and separated three one-hundred dollar bills from her fold of bills. "How much for the derringer too?"

"That'll cover it." He wiped both guns down carefully before slipping the one back into its pouch and handing over the other still wrapped in the cloth. She put the automatic in her purse and slipped the smaller weapon down the front of her pants. He reached behind the sofa cushion and retrieved a box of .22 shells.

"Here you go."

She put the bullets in her purse. "Pleasure doing business with you."

"Forget you ever met me," he answered.

"Ditto." She was all set to turn around and leave when she saw the small coke mirror on his table. "Hey, Lenny, you got a taste?"

"It's going to cost you."

"No problem," Ellen answered. A small part of her brain told her that that sounded just like something Munch would say.

Chapter 16

Munch changed into the clothes she considered her limo uniform. She didn't wear a hat, but she did have a ruffled shirt and a wide red elastic belt that she hoped gave the illusion of a feminine tuxedo. She slipped on a pair of black cotton gloves to complete her transformation. The run was a simple pickup in Brentwood with a drop-off at LAX. This meant Munch wouldn't have to leave the car other than to load luggage from the house. She hoped her customer had packed lightly. Her back ached already from multiple trips of moving boxes and furniture. Fortunately, she was just about done. By Monday night she figured to be completely moved. Now that Asia was spending the night at the Bradburys', Munch would have time to unpack enough of their stuff so that their life could resume some measure of order. This routine included her returning to work on Tuesday morning at the gas station so she could make some money.

She brought along Asia's *Highlights* magazine and

elicited a promise from the eight-year-old to stay quiet in exchange for the privilege of coming along.

The trip to the airport went off without a hitch. The client was a regular, some big-shot family lawyer. Family lawyer was what his business card said; what it really meant was that he specialized in divorce cases. She also serviced his cars, so she liked to keep him happy.

"We've got one more stop to make," Munch told Asia, after leaving the airport. "Remember that Rico guy who came to the house the other night?"

"The one with the candy."

"That's the one."

"I liked him."

"Me too," Munch said.

The Inglewood Youth Center was a new facility. Built on an acre of donated land and surrounded by a ten-foot chain-link fence to keep out vandals, it boasted an Olympic-size swimming pool, a large indoor basketball court, and a playground with a swing set and jungle gym. Local artists had painted the wall mural behind the outdoor boxing ring, creating a colorful mélange of homeboys who had risen to some degree of fame. Graffiti was noticeably absent.

Munch and Asia wove through the crowd of young children busily burning up the time between when school let out and their parents got off work. The majority were black, a few Hispanic, and the rest various mixes of the two.

Munch saw Rico first, working in the cage by the swimming pool, his head bowed over paperwork. Steam lifted from the surface of the pool like morning fog. The smell of chlorine stung her eyes and reminded her briefly of the previous night's vandalism. The lifeguard blew his whistle, and Rico looked up. When he did, he saw her. His eyes lit up appreciatively, and she was more glad than she let herself show. He opened the side door, and invited her and Asia inside.

"Thought we'd come check you out," Munch said. "The place, I mean."

He smiled like he knew exactly what she meant. She was glad for the distraction of the crowd of little girls clamoring at the window.

One who looked Asia's age spoke first. Her hair was sectioned off into dozens of different cornrows, each one fastened with a yellow or pink plastic barrette. "Officer Rico," she said. "we want to go swimming. I left my quarter at home, but I'll bring it tomorrow."

Rico regarded her suspiciously.

"Cost a quarter to use the pool," he explained to Munch.

"Please," the little girl added, hopping on one foot. She smiled and dimples appeared on either side of her mouth.

"Me too," a second little girl in a pink sweatshirt added. This one had brown hair curling down to her waist and the heart-shaped face of an angel. She batted her thick lashes. "I'll pay you back tomorrow," she said. "I promise."

Rico still hadn't smiled. He picked up a clipboard. "I'm going to write down all your names."

The girls bounced up and down like little cheerleaders after their team had scored.

Rico wasn't finished. "Tomorrow, if you don't pay me back, you'll never go in the pool again."

The little girl with the long hair and big brown eyes turned to the other kids. "All right," she said, emerging as their interpreter and spokesperson. "You understand? If we don't pay him back, we can't ever go in the pool again."

One by one, the kids nodded their heads. Understanding the consequences, they each gave Rico their names. Munch thought they were even more precious when they weren't trying to be cute.

"As I read off your name," he said, "you go inside. All right, Sharell, Mercedes, Claretta, Antonia."

They watched the kids strip off their sweatshirts and pants and leap into the steaming pool. She turned to Rico. "I could never do it," she said, using her statement as an excuse to rest her gloved hand on his arm. "I'd give them all my money. How can you resist those faces?"

"These kids need to learn that if they want something, they have to pay for it."

His words brought even more of a reaction to her body than his touch had—a warmth in her stomach that quickly spread downward. In her teens and twenties, she had been drawn to men who offered excitement, good times, even danger. These days, the responses from her groin seemed directly correlated to her perception of how good a daddy the guy would make. She realized her eyes had strayed to his crotch and looked away quickly, hoping he hadn't noticed. This Rico had definite potential.

"Can I go play?" Asia asked.

"Sure," Munch said. "Just stay where I can see you."

Asia headed for the jungle gym. *Great,* Munch thought, *now I can watch her break her head open.*

"Be careful," she called out, knowing the look on Asia's face without seeing it.

"You have any kids?" she asked Rico.

"Oh yeah." He chuckled and was quiet for a moment as he looked up and to his left. *Does he need a moment to count?* Mace St. John had once told her that people looked to their left when they were accessing the memory half of their brain. They looked to the right when they needed to construct images or use their imagination, such as when they made up a lie. "A girl," he said.

"Are you married?"

"Not for a long time," he said. "Came close to doing it again a couple of times." His expression was wistful. She felt an unreasonable surge of jealousy. But when were those kinds of emotions ever reasonable? Even now she noted her relief that he already had a kid, as if it took the pressure off her to produce his heirs. Man, was she getting ahead of herself.

He pulled out his wallet and showed her a picture of a beautiful, exotic-looking teenager with what looked like a mix of Asian- and African-American features.

"How old?"

"Fourteen."

"How old were you when she was born?"

"Too young," he said, smiling wistfully. "Her mom was my high school girlfriend. My dad said I didn't have to deal with it, that I could go back to Mexico." He pronounced it *Meh-he-ko*. "We still have family there. But I couldn't do that. I had to be responsible."

"How long did you stay married?"

"Eight years."

"Do you see her much?"

He wiggled the picture. "When I go visit Angelica."

"That's who I meant." Munch felt a weird stab of jealousy again, then caught herself. What was she thinking? She wasn't about to get involved with this guy, this cop. Even if the electricity between them was burning holes in her concentration. He was obviously a total horn dog, probably sniffed every tail that wagged past him.

"Oh," he said, looking abashed. "Yeah, I see my daughter as much as I can. She's the main reason why I transferred up to L.A." He grinned. "That and the chief wanted me on his team for the Police Olympics this year. I won the gold in my division last bout."

"So you're a ringer?"

"Nope, just good at what I do. What time have you got?"

Munch glanced at her watch. "Quarter to."

Rico grabbed her wrist and held it so he could read her watch.

"You don't trust me?"

He smiled. "It's not that."

She felt a small twinge of disappointment when he let her go.

"I need to get ready for my workout." He reached under the counter and pulled out rolls of white bandages. "Want to help?"

"What do you want me to do?" she asked, looking into his eyes as she spoke, her smile conveying her willingness.

He smiled back, not missing the signal. "Wrap my hands, for starters."

He sat in a straight-back chair. She stood over him and wound the bandage around his hand, following his instructions and alternately routing it under and over his thumb. They were fully in the mating dance now, touching as often as possible: knees, toes, forearms. She could smell his hair, traces of cologne, coffee on his breath.

"Have you heard from Ellen?" he asked.

"Yeah, she's been helping me move."

He handed her a pair of bag gloves. They weren't as padded as boxing gloves, but still required lacing. She helped him put them on, sliding the loop over his thumb.

"How's she doing?"

"Oh, you know. She's trying to stay busy and get her life together. She's about as okay as can be expected. Any luck finding the guys who did this?"

"Guys?"

"Whoever," she said, trying to sound casual. Mace also told her that he solved the majority of his cases because somebody talked, usually the bad guy.

"Want to get the door?" Rico asked.

"Oh, sure." She opened the door and they both walked out. He headed for a heavy bag suspended from a sturdy wood A-frame.

Behind them, two boys wrestled on the ground. The sounds of little girls shrieking filled the air. Asia stood by one of the picnic tables with a semicircle of kids around her. One of the little boys in the group picked up a rock the size of his head and held it face high.

"Look what I can do," he said to Asia.

She looked him up and down, made a small moue of

her mouth, and dismissed him with, "It's not *that* big."

Rico's eyebrows lifted. Munch didn't know whether to blush or be proud. Mama's little ball buster.

"What's Ellen doing now?" he asked, giving the heavy bag a few warm-up punches.

"She's having dinner with her dad tonight."

"Her dad?" He let off a flurry of punches, putting his whole body into it, grunting as he connected. The chain holding the bag creaked in its eye bolt.

"Her real dad."

Sweat spread to Rico's armpits. He paused to wipe a trickle running down his brow. "I was under the impression he was deceased."

"Yeah, me too."

Rico delivered a few low punches she was sure were capable of doing grave bodily injury. She took a step back, a little awed by his power. "I guess we were both wrong."

Rico stopped and steadied the bag. "You got a name for this guy?"

"No, I've never even met him. She just called him 'the Colonel.' He's flying in from North Carolina today." Munch saw Asia hanging by her knees on the parallel bar, and wondered how she'd managed to get herself there. It was a good thing that the little girl was wearing overalls instead of a dress.

Rico let the bag swing gently to a standstill and took one step so that he was standing close to her. "We really want to close this case. All we care about is the homicide. Anything, anything at all that you can think of." He waited, as if he were giving her time to say something else. As if he knew she knew more than she was admitting.

Munch hesitated for a minute and then said, "Ellen told me that they broke Mrs. Summers's fingers."

"That's right."

She chewed her lip and looked at the wall. The most surprising thing about police investigation that Mace St. John had taught her was that the case didn't end like in the movies when the detective pointed a finger at the bad guy and said, *Aha, it was you.* Cops measured the successful end of a case with the conviction and sentencing of the bad guy. And that meant building their solution on irrefutable evidence. "Maybe there's other cases like that. You know, where someone's fingers got broken."

The look he gave her was speculative. "Maybe we should check on that."

"Had to be some kind of animal," she said, wincing inwardly at her own choice of words. She was trying to be subtle.

"They usually are."

He hadn't moved away. She was filled with the smell of him and didn't find it unpleasant.

"Mom," Asia yelled, "I'm hungry!"

"Well, I guess we'd better get going," she said.

"Thanks for stopping by," he said.

"Yeah, it's been . . ." She realized she didn't know how to complete her sentence.

"Yeah, it sure has," he said, a twinkle plainly visible in his eye.

Munch called for Asia. The nice thing about high heels, she thought as the two of them walked to the limo without looking back, was that they made it easy to twitch your butt a little. She was pretty sure she hadn't heard the last from Rico Chacón.

"Can I sit in the back?" Asia asked when they got to the limo.

Munch opened the back door with a flourish, then buckled her daughter in.

"How about some music?" Munch asked as they pulled away. She pushed in the cassette tape already in the player and turned up the volume. Pat Benatar's soprano voice declared, "I need a lover who won't drive me crazy."

Amen to that, Munch thought, acutely aware of the crumpled printout in her pocket and already worried about Rico's reactions when she told him about her past.

Rico came in from his workout and made a call. "Ellen Summers's father is living and coming into town from North Carolina." He listened for a minute before replying, "I thought so too."

Munch drove to Garret's new house—the one he had envisioned her and him renting together. It was a three-bedroom brown stucco one-story job, circa 1960, six blocks away from the old house. She tried the doorbell. There was no response, so she walked down the long driveway that ran the length of the house. The driveway widened into an RV-size concrete slab and ended at the two-car garage that Garret had wanted so badly.

She reached the end of the driveway and stopped. For a weird second she felt as if she were having an out-of-body experience. Before her was an El Camino with the hood up. Under that hood and working on the engine was a woman in dark blue uniform pants and a lighter blue button-down shirt. Just like Munch's uniform at the Texaco station. The woman had long, dirty-blond hair, which she wore tied back but unbraided. She looked up, and Munch realized she knew her. The woman from the pet store. Garret went there often while they were together to get aquarium supplies or to check out new fish.

"Hi," Munch said. "Jenny, isn't it?"

Jenny straightened and gave Munch a long, slow, even slightly disapproving up-and-down and then flipped her long hair over her shoulder with a practiced toss.

"Yes."

"Have any trouble getting those fingernails clean?" Munch asked, making her face into a mask of congeniality.

"No," Jenny said, with a sniff, "I never have."

Well, fuck you too, Munch thought. "Is, uh, Garret around?"

At that moment Garret emerged from the house. The expression on his face, seeing the two of them together, was a mixture of supremacy and undeserved confidence. Munch knew him well enough to know how fragile his facade was.

"Jenny is a real mechanical prodigy," he said.

Munch wondered what or who else he was teaching her to be. "You got my torque wrench?"

"Sure, I'll get it."

A loud squawk came from inside the house.

"What's that?"

Again Garret had that same self-satisfied look on his face. "Come in. I'll introduce you."

She followed him through a sliding door into a

room furnished with a desk, couch, and low coffee table. There were magazines on the coffee table. It looked like the waiting room at a car dealership. The carpet was tracked with grease in a pathway that she assumed led to a bathroom. A large open perch took up one corner of the room. Seated on that perch was a huge blue and gold parrot. Bird crap and discarded sunflower seed hulls plastered the carpet beneath it. The animal let out another loud screech that made her ears pop.

"What's his name?"

"Papagayo. It's Spanish for 'parrot.' "

"Nice," Munch said as she reached out her arm to the bird.

"Watch it," Garret said, holding up a bandaged wrist. "He bites."

Munch withdrew her arm and looked around the rest of the room. "Looks like you've got things just like you want them," she said.

He smiled. The bird squawked and made a lunge for them. They each took a step away. "And to think," Munch said, "all this could have been mine."

He gave her a look of pity. It was all she could do to look as if she were sorry. "I'd better go," she said. "I left Asia asleep in the car."

Chapter 17

Ellen stopped to make another call.

"Jeff Doogan Realty."

"Yes," Ellen said, adjusting her tone to sound moneyed and businesslike. "I'm interested in one of your properties. The listing agent is Noreen Ramsey."

"She's not in right now, would you like her voice mail?"

"When is she expected?"

"Not until tomorrow morning. She usually stops in at nine."

"I'll try again then," Ellen said. She got back in Russ's truck and headed for Santa Monica and her meeting with her father.

She wished she knew the Colonel better. Her last real memory of him was from when she was a little girl and had chicken pox. She was at the kitchen table of the old house. The walls were yellow, the refrigerator avocado green. In front of her was a bowl of Sugar Pops. She could almost taste their sweet crunchiness. See them floating on the white milk. The spoon in her hand seemed huge, unwieldy. The chicken pox covered her body. Lila Mae had rubbed thick pink calamine lotion on her legs and torso to control the itching, but she was still feeling miserable. One eye was swollen almost completely shut due to the large pustule on her lid.

"Hey," her dad said, "you've got a Sugar Pop on your eye."

She had laughed and laughed, silly Daddy.

"Oh," he said, smiling, "I mean chicken pox."

In later years, she realized he'd said what he said to amuse her, to act the fool and take her mind off the disease.

Superimposed over that memory was something that happened years later. She was fourteen or fifteen, and Lila Mae was telling her that her eye makeup made her look like a whore. Ellen couldn't very well explain that that was the point, but still. Would it have been so difficult for Lila Mae to just once express a little approval? Make a little joke?

Much of their early mother-daughter conflicts stemmed from the root fact that Lila Mae had taken or driven Ellen's daddy away. In Ellen's mind, that was when her world had grown dark. That's when her childhood became a blur of new schools and small apartments with no furniture. She was the kid with no friends, no siblings, no father, always the outsider, constantly having to reinvent herself. But always there was the risk of being the kid they whispered about if they noticed her at all.

Ellen was still a long way from forgiving her mom when Lila Mae had made her life more isolated by hooking up with Dwayne Summers and changing both their names. Ellen made it clear early on that if she couldn't have her real daddy, she didn't want her mom to be with another man. Lila Mae said she was being selfish, but as far as Ellen could see, that was just the pot calling the kettle black.

"What if my daddy wants to visit?" Ellen used to ask. "How will he find us?"

"Never you mind about him" was all Lila Mae would say. "As far as we're concerned, he's a dead man."

She used to write him letters, especially during the worst years with Dwayne. They were all bad years, but reached new lows starting when she was thirteen. That's when the arguments turned to face slaps and belt whippings. That's when she'd write her letters to her real dad, using her newly acquired vocabulary. She called her mother a gutter whore and a cunt bitch. Told her dad how much she missed him and all those breakfasts they used to have together. She addressed the letters to Elliot Dane, care of various General Deliveries in the larger Southern towns, Louisville, Kentucky; Thomasville, North Carolina; Memphis; Macon. She even tried Dallas, Texas, once.

It was a lot like praying, sending out those messages with their vague addresses, like lying alone in your room at night and speaking to God in heaven—hoping you'll get a line through. That He'll see what's happening on earth and send down a lightning bolt to smite your enemies.

But none of her letters was ever answered. Eventually Ellen accepted that her father must really be dead. And now she was going to see him again in person, finally.

When he'd written to her in prison, she'd had many questions. Where have you been? for one. He promised he would answer everything at dinner. They arranged to meet at Bob Burns in Santa Monica, a dark restaurant with a piano bar and a menu that favored red meat.

Ellen checked her nose for any residual white traces. She would have to load up on goldenseal in the next couple days. The herb did nothing for the head unless you counted peace of mind. But any self-respecting dope fiend knew that it flushed residual traces of drugs from your system and ensured that urine tests came back clean.

The Colonel was waiting for her. He had taken one of the red leather booths near the back.

She recognized him from the photograph he'd sent her. A photograph she had spent hours studying, looking for clues in his blue eyes and square jaw. Lila Mae had burned all his old photos, so Ellen had to refresh her childhood memories. His smile looked tight, as if the muscles of his face didn't go there often. He had short hair. A military cut. Yes, she had his mouth and nose. He had signed his letter *Colonel Elliot Dane*. She hadn't even known he had stayed in the service. Maybe that explained her attraction for men in uniform. It was one of those genetic things.

Colonel Elliot Dane, she would repeat to herself, relishing the sound of the title. Her own daddy, a leader of men, a hero. Something to be proud of. An anchor.

"Ellen," he called to her, half-rising from his seat.

She smiled awkwardly, feeling suddenly shy. He had a drink in front of him, some amber fluid in a highball glass. The waiter followed her over to the table and asked what she'd have.

"One of those would be just dandy," she said, pointing to her father's drink.

They shook hands. Another awkward gesture. His hand was clammy with sweat but firm. She slid into the booth from the other side.

"Glad you could make it," he said.

"Have you been waiting long?" she asked, not missing the irony of her first question.

"No, I got in early. I'm nervous, I guess."

"Me too," she said, giggling. She didn't tell him how she almost didn't come, that she'd been gripped with a fear she couldn't explain. And there was the guilt too that had to be pushed away. It wasn't as if Ellen was switching camps. Lila Mae was gone; the Colonel was here. Life was full of reversals and a person had to learn to swing with them. Ellen had long practice in making the best of a situation.

"I guess we have some catching up to do," he said. "We've got over twenty years to cover."

"Twenty-three," Ellen said. "I was six."

He gave her an almost hostile look. "Can you hear my side of the story before you go accusing me of not caring?"

The waiter brought her drink and she sipped it greedily. It was scotch on the rocks—not her first choice of poison, but she had to knock down what the cocaine was doing to her nervous system.

"When your mama and me went our separate ways, it wasn't easy. My job had its own demands, and I'm not trying to say this as any kind of excuse. I was young still and I had to make it while I could. Time kept passing. I got transferred, you all kept moving. She married again, changed her name. When I tried to call, the number had changed. I had no way to find you."

"When's my birthday?" she asked. The question just slipped from her mouth unfiltered, and she regretted it instantly. Of course he would know her birthday, the day his baby girl came into the world.

"Is this a test?" he asked. "Can't we just start fresh? Let's just put all the bad stuff behind us. I know you've had some tough breaks. If I could go back and change my priorities, I would. But all that is yesterday's news. I'm here now. First thing we're going to do is get you back on the right track."

Ellen drained the last bit of scotch from her glass, wondering when would be a decent enough interval of time to order another. He solved the dilemma by flagging down the waiter and ordering a second round.

"Would you like to see a menu, sir?"

"No rush," the Colonel said. "We're going to just take our time."

Ellen returned his smile, relieved that he didn't seem in any big hurry to take off again.

"Did you ever think about me?" she asked.

He reached across the table and took her hand. "All the time, baby."

Baby. He used to call her *baby.* That much she remembered.

"So what have you been up to?" he asked.

"I've been helping my friend Munch move."

"Munch." He pulled a notebook from his pocket and flipped through the pages. "That's the one you told me about on the phone. The mechanic?"

She nodded.

He made a notation and put the book back in his

pocket. "I'm retiring from the Army this year. I figure I'll have all the time in the world to mend my fences."

The waiter arrived with the fresh drinks.

"To us," the Colonel said, lifting his glass in a salute. "To new lives, with new friends."

She drank half the glass in one long gulp, already beginning to feel loved. She couldn't wait to tell Munch what a great guy he was.

Munch heard the truck pulling up to the curb and Ellen calling out "Good night." She parted her bedroom curtains in time to see a white Ford Crown Victoria with a Hertz rental sticker on the bumper driving off down the street and Ellen waving at it. Munch heard the key clumsily scraping into the dead-bolt lock on the front door. The dogs were already standing on alert when she got up to greet her friend.

"How did it go?" she asked.

"Great."

Munch smelled the liquor immediately. The frustration she felt was on many levels. The odds that any alcoholic could get or stay sober were dismal, even when the person was trying. She couldn't make Ellen choose her way of life. The best she could do was set an example and hope Ellen noticed.

"He followed you home?" Munch asked.

"That's the kind of man he is," Ellen said. "If I had known you were up, I would have had him come in and meet you. I told him all about you."

"You did, huh?"

"Well, you know. All about you being a mechanic and raising a kid you adopted. Just the good stuff."

Munch knew this was not the time to address the

drinking issue. Not with Ellen half-lit and obviously feeling the best she had in the last few days. Munch didn't have the heart to bring her down, not that this would be the optimum moment to confront her. She'd wait until Ellen was hung over and preferably feeling guilty over some disaster that arose as a direct result of her drinking.

"Tomorrow, after I drop off Asia at school, I'll take you to see Billy Vega."

"I got a bone to pick with that sucker," Ellen said, laughing. "You know he didn't come see me once while I was inside?"

"That must have been heartbreaking given your close emotional bond," Munch said.

"He owes me something."

"Ellen, how many trips do you have to make to the same well before you get it in your head that it's empty?"

"Alls I'm saying is he could have made an effort, the selfish son of a bitch."

"Go to bed," Munch said. "We'll talk tomorrow."

"I love you, man. You're the best. I mean that."

"I put out some blankets on the couch. Get some sleep. We're getting up early tomorrow."

"I love getting up early," Ellen said. Her voice was filled with real enthusiasm, as if she couldn't wait to see what the next day would hold.

Chapter 18

Munch and Ellen spent the early hours of Monday morning loading miscellaneous boxes of garden tools and small appliances. When they attempted to lift some of the heavier items, Ellen had to pause repeatedly and find her equilibrium. The skin under her eyes looked almost bruised, and her lips appeared sunburned.

"You want to stop and drink some water?" Munch asked.

"I'll be fine," Ellen answered, but her skin was the color of ash.

Just then they heard a loud rumble and stopped to watch the approach of a Chevy Monte Carlo with a caved-in front end. The rusted exhaust system hung close to the ground, emitting a spray of sparks as the car bounced closer. The driver waved and Munch realized it was Ba-Boom-Ba.

Hail, hail, she thought. Now all they needed was a

few Hell's Angels, a keg, and a crack pipe, and the morning would be perfect.

Ba-Boom-Ba crossed to their side of the street, bringing the dilapidated Chevy to a stop facing the wrong way. "How the hell are you?" she roared.

"Ba-*Boom*-Ba," Ellen said.

"I brought breakfast." Ba-Boom-Ba lifted a bag off the driver's seat and showed them her gift. It was a six-pack of Budweiser and a bag of Fritos. The breakfast of champions.

Ellen wet her lips and directed a pleading glance at Munch.

"Make a choice," Munch said. "I won't stop you. You want to go party? Take your shit and go."

"Hey, hey, hey," Ba-Boom-Ba said. "Don't be like that. We don't have to drink. I just came over to see how y'all were doing." She got out of the car. "What are you, moving?"

"That's right," Munch said.

"Is there more shit in the house?"

"My couch and coffee table."

Ba-Boom-Ba shed her black leather motorcycle jacket and threw it in the backseat of the Chevy. She was dressed in too-tight jeans that cut into her fleshy waist, a white T-shirt, and boots. "Looks like I got here just in time."

"A half hour ago would have been better," Ellen said.

Munch looked at Ellen suspiciously as she addressed Ba-Boom-Ba. "You were just in the neighborhood?"

"No, I wanted to tell Ellen how sorry I was about her mom."

"Thanks," Ellen said.

"What happened?"

"Some asshole beat her to death," Ellen said.

"So what do you want with Billy?" Ba-Boom-Ba asked. "You think he had something to do with it?"

"Her fingers were broken," Ellen said. "The asshole broke all her fingers."

Ba-Boom-Ba's right hand flew to her mouth, her left landed on her hip. Her eyes were big as she said, "No."

Something in her reaction seemed to lack sincerity, but Munch didn't have time to analyze exactly what. Asia stood in the doorway of the house, her lunch pail dangling from her hand.

"Who's this?" Ba-Boom-Ba asked.

"My kid. Asia, this is, uh, Darlene."

Asia strode forward and stuck out her hand. "How do you do?"

"Very well," Ba-Boom-Ba answered. "How old are you?"

"Eight."

"You going to school?"

"Yes."

Munch checked her watch. "Ten more minutes."

"Let's go get the rest of your sh—, uh, stuff," Ba-Boom-Ba said. A minute later she emerged from the house with the couch, sans its cushions, balanced on her head.

Ellen nudged Munch. "Comes in handy, don't she?"

"Yeah, she sure does."

Ellen gathered the cushions. Munch followed her out with the coffee table. Asia was sent back inside to grab her overnight bag, leaving the three women alone on the sidewalk.

"I meant what I said before," Ba-Boom-Ba said. "You don't want anything to do with Billy Vega."

"You're right about that," Munch said, clamping a warning hand on Ellen's arm before she blabbed their plans. "Thanks for your help."

"You want me to follow you to your new place?"

"I'm not going there till later, but thanks anyway."

"Well, then," Ba-Boom-Ba said, suddenly looking uncomfortable, even pathetic. "I guess I'll be going."

Asia came back outside in time to wave good-bye to Ba-Boom-Ba and got into her mother's car.

"That was nice of her to drop by," Ellen said.

Munch watched the Chevy turn the corner. "What do you think about what she said about Billy?"

"What do you think she's going to say? They broke up, remember?"

Munch took Asia to school. Lindsey was already on the playground. When Munch waved hello, the child gave her a look of reproach.

Great, Munch thought, *now she's turned the kid against me.*

Asia had a backpack full of overnight clothes. Munch kissed her good-bye. "Want me to call you later?"

"No, I'll be all right."

"Okay, see you tomorrow," Munch said, but Asia had already run ahead into the playground. "Love you," she called after her. Asia raised her hand in a backward good-bye.

Munch drove to the new house. She wrestled the

couch out of the trailer and in through the front door. It fit perfectly in the new living room, as if it had been custom-made. She saw this as a good omen. Two hours later she had the pictures leaning against the walls where she thought they would look best. She would let Asia be in on the final decision. Munch's other priority was to get the limo stuff squared away on the odd chance she would get a call for business. The last thing she did was go out to the garage. Tenpenny nails studded the raw two-by-fours on the garage walls, and she used them to hang the gardening tools.

Ellen was sitting cross-legged on the living room floor reading the *National Enquirer* when Munch returned to the old house. The truck was parked in a different space.

"Where have you been?" Munch asked.

"I went out for breakfast."

"You seem awfully pleased with yourself."

"Just happy to be free, white, and twenty-one," Ellen said. "You ready to go?" She had chosen the blond, curly wig for the occasion and big rhinestone-studded dark glasses. As always, Munch felt undazzling next to her friend in a simple T-shirt, pair of blue jeans, and brown leather bomber jacket.

"Yeah, let's get this over with."

Rather than hassling with unhitching the trailer, they took Roofer Russ's truck to the club in Inglewood that went by the name of Century Entertainment. Ellen drove.

"Let's not make a big party out of this," Munch said. "If he's here, we're just going to tell him what's going on and find out what he knows. If not, we'll find out when he'll be around and then we split."

"Fine by me."

They timed their arrival at Century Entertainment to be around eleven-thirty, figuring the chances of most of the staff being there were greater during the lunch rush hour. Munch wondered how Rico was proceeding with *his* investigation.

The club where Billy worked was close to the San Diego Freeway, highly visible to the traffic going to LAX. LIVE GIRLS, the billboard overhead proclaimed. ALL NUDE.

They had to circle the block several times before entering the entertainment complex off Century Boulevard. When it had been Century Bowl, there were accesses to the grounds from the side streets. But now all those other entryways were barricaded, and the long driveway running alongside the main building was laden with steep speed bumps. Everybody's approach to and departure from Century Entertainment was carefully controlled.

They parked the truck in one of the spaces in the back. Ellen and Munch joined a group of businessmen jostling toward the entrance of the club. One of the guys whipped out a credit card. Ellen attached herself to the arm of one of his companions.

"You here to party, sugar?" she cooed in his ear. The guy grinned like an idiot. The doorman pulled open the door, and she sashayed in with her new friends.

Munch followed, telling the doorman, "I'm with them."

She detached herself from the group as soon as she

could and started looking for Billy Vega. With his size, booming voice, and flaming red hair, Billy was not the kind of guy one missed easily in a room, even a dark strip club.

"Buy you a drink?" Ellen's new friend asked, staring at her breasts.

Ellen started to answer, but Munch grabbed her arm. "Your makeup needs freshening."

Ellen pinched the guy's arm and said, "Let me go make myself pretty."

The guy grinned like a drunk puppy.

When they were out of earshot, which was only a few steps, Munch directed Ellen toward the video arcade. "Just look. If you spot him, come and get me."

They wove their way through the tables and scantily clad hostesses. The stage was smaller and rounder than the one at the Spearmint Rhino, but it was still elevated. Century Entertainment was also darker and louder. Munch knew it was one of those places you wouldn't want to see in bright light. Half of the tables were filled, especially those closest to the stage. The attention of most of the men was focused on the show in progress.

Munch spotted Billy coming out of an office marked PRIVATE. He was fatter than she remembered. He filled the doorway. A long-sleeved shirt concealed most of his tattoos, his beard reached to his collar, and his once fiery red hair was punctuated by wings of white above his ears.

Billy scanned the noonday crowd. Munch wondered how well he could see out of his dark glasses. Then he turned her way and froze. She lifted her head a short half nod to acknowledge his stare, but didn't smile. With a guy like Billy you had to be careful which signals you sent.

Ellen had noticed him too, and started to make her way across the rows of tables. Billy raised his arms in greeting to Ellen, as if to say look what the cat drug in.

Ellen went straight into his arms and hugged him. Billy squeezed her back, lifting her off her feet.

Munch pulled her hands out of her pockets, smiled slightly, and said, "Billy."

Billy looked at her without recognition until Ellen said, "You know Munch."

He lifted his sunglasses. The light was slow to reach his eyes, but then he finally said, "Didn't you used to be about six inches taller and fifty pounds heavier?"

Munch laughed. "It was all attitude."

"Wait here a minute," Billy said. "I've got a little bit of business to finish and then I'm all yours."

Billy was almost to his office door when a tall, skinny guy in a suit emerged.

"Son of a bitch," Ellen said, pointing at the guy in the suit. "That's that Fred Purcell guy. The PI I told you about."

Munch looked. She had the sensation for a second that they had stepped backstage before the play was over, and were seeing the players without their masks, the props without stage lighting.

The look of surprise on Purcell's face when he saw Ellen confirmed her suspicion. The standoff lasted only a few seconds and then Purcell smiled. One of those okay-so-you-busted-me smiles. Then he shrugged as if to say, *It doesn't matter.*

"Why that lying dog," Ellen said. "Client, my ass." She reached down into her waistband.

The next expression on Billy's face was pure evil, and Munch had no trouble interpreting it. He and Purcell were in this together. There was no mysterious client with a long memory, just someone who was supposed to be a friend, but had decided to go for the easy-looking cash score. They were out to rip off Ellen, and there wasn't a fucking thing she could do about it.

Something made Munch look back at Ellen. She saw the gun in Ellen's hand, saw Ellen taking aim.

"No!" Munch yelled, pushing Ellen's hand down. "Not like this. Not here."

Tears coursed down Ellen's face. "You see that motherfucker. You see the way he's looking at me."

Munch grabbed Ellen's arm and hustled her toward the door. "Yeah, I saw. Let's get out of here."

Only a few patrons noticed when Ellen brandished the gun, and even then they seemed torn between which show to watch, except for one guy sitting at the table directly in line between Ellen and her target. Munch even heard the guy's brief girlish scream as he overturned his table and then crouched behind it. His act of self-preservation blocked Billy Vega's forward motion toward them.

Munch pulled Ellen after her, heading back the way they came in. The doorman, a big no-neck guy with a shaved head, was checking the ID of two kids. His sumo-wrestler build filled the doorway.

Munch tried to slip around him. The guy put out a hand to stop her.

"We're leaving now," Munch said. "We don't want any trouble."

"Not this way you ain't," the guy said.

Ellen grabbed for her gun again. Munch threw a desperate look around. There had to be another alternative. Billy Vega was still occupied with the customer on the floor, trying to pry the overturned table from the guy's grip. The bartender had lifted the telephone, but Purcell gestured for him to hang up.

"You gotta exit through the bookstore," No-Neck said.

"Bookstore?" Then Munch realized the doorman hadn't been trying to prevent them from leaving. She pushed Ellen in the direction of the attached shop and through its one-way door. Ellen staggered ahead of her, bumping into the aisles of merchandise as she fumbled for the street exit. They burst through the door and into the bright sunlight.

"What the fuck was that about?" Munch yelled, pushing Ellen to the truck. "You want to go back to jail for a parole violation?"

"They're not going to get away with this," Ellen said.

"Put that thing away and give me the keys," Munch said when they got back to the truck. Ellen's hands shook badly as she handed them over.

They clambered into the cab. Munch glanced toward the club, waiting for Billy Vega to emerge. He didn't. Ellen rolled down her window. "That's the skinny motherfucker's car," she said, pointing with the gun at a gray Mustang. She fired off three rounds, puncturing the driver's door and flattening a tire.

"Would you quit?" Munch screamed, using both hands and feet to maneuver the pickup out of the parking lot. The truck bounced hard over the speed bumps. Munch felt the differential scrape over the last one, but the oil pan was spared.

Ellen was still screaming, "Fuck you!" when Munch turned onto Century and headed for the freeway.

"I think he got the message," Munch said.

Rico had spent the morning burning up the phone lines. He told Becker that Ellen Summers's real father wasn't deceased after all. It took several calls, working from Dwayne Summers's background information, to discover the county and then the town in which Dwayne and Lila Mae had filed their marriage license: Macon, Georgia. The clerk in Macon wasn't about to give up any additional information until Rico requested it in writing on LAPD stationery, which he then faxed. Finally he was able to get the name of Lila Mae's ex: Elliot Dane.

DMV checks showed no California driver's license. Voter's registration also came up blank.

"Elliot Dane," Rico said, trying to remember why the name seemed familiar. He went back over Ellen's CIW records. It wasn't until he got to the mail records that he found what he was looking for. Elliot Dane had written Ellen Summers while she was in custody. His return address was in Fort Bragg, North Carolina. A call to the registrar of voters supplied Elliot Dane's Social Security number and date of birth. Rico also noted that the call Ellen made after being notified of her mother's and stepfather's deaths was to a Fort Bragg area code. Just to be on the safe side, he called the airlines to check if any flights from local airports to North Carolina flew in the time frame between the murders and when the man he presumed was Elliot Dane had received the call. There were none. But even if there were, there was no guarantee that Elliot Dane would be listed on the manifest. If Rico were planning to fly somewhere to commit a murder, and then fly back home to establish an alibi, he would pay cash for his ticket and travel under an assumed name. Lack of evidence was rarely proof of anything.

Becker waited until ten o'clock before giving up on his return call from Agent Long. He decided to try the guy again after lunch. The Summers's autopsies were scheduled for this afternoon. He and Rico would be in attendance, learning as much as they could. For now there was field work to follow up on.

He had contacted the Downey sheriff's station and spoken to the investigators there. They were still actively working the case of Corinne Adams and eager to trade information. All her fingers had been broken ante-mortem, and the autopsy showed that she had recently had sex, although there had been no signs that it was forced. The investigators had immediately gone to her boyfriend, Billy Vega. Vega had an unshakable alibi for the time of the murder, and he had agreed to submit to a lie detector test. The investigator faxed over a transcript of the polygraph interview. A technician named Claudia Juárez had conducted the interrogation. Becker read with Rico looking over his shoulder.

> JUÁREZ: Do you have any knowledge of how the murder of Corinne Adams was committed?

Vega: No.
Juárez: Did you have Corinne Adams killed?
Vega: No.
Juárez: The last time you saw her alive was the day she was killed?
Vega: Yes.
Juárez: And this was at the club called the Spearmint Rhino?
Vega: That's right.
Juárez: Do you know who she left the club with the evening she was killed?
Vega: No.
Juárez: Do you have any idea who she went to meet that night?
Vega: Nope.
Juárez: Have you discussed her murder with anyone?
Vega: Nope.

Liar, Becker thought as he read. The last question was a control question. Kind of like, Are you getting enough sex at home? Subjects who answered "no" and "yes" to those two questions respectively were being less than candid. You know someone who gets killed, you talk about it. It was human nature.

Juárez: Prior to Corinne Adams's murder, did you have any idea her life was in danger?
Vega: None at all.
Juárez: Did you have any reason to want her dead?

VEGA: I didn't kill her.
JUÁREZ: Just yes or no, Mr. Vega.
VEGA: No.
JUÁREZ: Do you know who killed her?
VEGA: Nope.
JUÁREZ: Thank you for your help, Mr. Vega. The interview is concluded.

According to the examiner's findings, Billy Vega was less than truthful when he declared that he didn't know who had killed Corinne Adams.

Becker searched the station's archives and found two things that pleased him very much. The first was a current photograph of Billy Vega, and more precious than that, Vega's last arrest report with the ever helpful 5.10 form on the back.

"You use these in San Diego?" Becker asked Rico.

"No."

Becker flipped over the cover sheet of Vega's arrest report and revealed a second form filled out in longhand. "Pure gold. The detectives take the information during booking. We tell the suspects it's totally voluntary. The beauty of the five-ten is that you don't have to Mirandize the suspect because this is all just background information. You tell the guy that it's for the judge. If the mope cooperates, he has a better chance of bailing out, maybe even getting an OR." The first half of the form pertained to relatives: mother, father, siblings, spouses, kids. "You always want to get the mother's birthday. Hardest gang-bangers I know always have a soft spot for their mom. I can't tell you how many guys we've picked up on warrants at their mom's house on her birthday. Kids' birthdays too."

The other categories on the form were employment, hobbies, education, even where the subjects got their hair cut. This last was not applicable in the case of Billy Vega, who probably had never seen the inside of a barbershop.

"Information," Becker said, waving the form, "is our biggest tool."

When Billy Vega worked at the Spearmint Rhino, he listed his boss as one Lawrence Whitley. Becker knew the name. Lawrence Whitley had been the sergeant-at-arms of the now defunct Satan's Pride Motorcycle Club, and last Becker heard, he was prospecting for the Hell's Angels. His street name was Animal.

"You drive," he told Rico, throwing him the car keys.

The two men settled into their seats. "I got one for you," Becker said. "This guy goes to the doctor, finds out he's got AIDS. The worst part of it is that now he's got to go to his parents and tell them he's Haitian."

Rico cracked a smile.

They were heading up Airport Boulevard when news of a shooting came over their radio. The location given was their destination: Century Entertainment.

"Small world," Rico said.

"The club's right by the freeway," Becker said. "The suspect is probably long gone."

"Let's go see what there is to see," Rico said.

Becker radioed in their intentions, and within minutes the two detectives were in the parking lot of Century Entertainment. A skinny white guy in a cheap suit was standing by a gray Ford Mustang, surveying the damage.

"Howdy, partner," Becker said. "This your ride?"

"Who are you?" the skinny guy asked.

Becker badged him. "Can I see some ID?"

"Why do you need my ID?"

"For our report." Becker glanced at the sex-shop window. There was a sale on Luscious Lucy's Love Oil. "Is this your vehicle?"

"I don't want any problems," the skinny guy said.

By "problems," Becker assumed the guy meant police involvement. "Looks like that's not your choice." Becker turned to Rico. "Start taking names of witnesses. Ask them how many shots were fired. See if anyone saw the shooter." He turned back to the skinny guy. "And I'm still waiting to see some ID."

The skinny guy finally produced a driver's license.

"What are you doing here, Mr. Purcell?" Becker asked.

"Monthly service call. I make sure all the surveillance cameras are working, and I rotate out the older videotapes."

Purcell handed him a business card.

"Universal Security," Becker read out loud. "What are you, some kind of a private investigator?"

"Actually we specialize in preventive security."

"Did you get a videotape of the incident?"

Purcell looked cornered for an instant, and Becker wondered what that was about. "No, the cameras weren't running. I was right in the middle of changing tapes."

Becker posed his pen over his notebook. "You want to tell me why someone would want to shoot up your car?"

Purcell scratched the back of his head. "I have no

idea, Officer. I guess I was just at the wrong place at the wrong time."

A big guy in a tight black T-shirt exited the club. Becker recognized him immediately as Billy Vega. As a rookie, he'd busted the guy's dad. This was not unusual. In poorer neighborhoods where teenage parenthood abounded, he'd followed criminal careers spanning three generations. Still, seeing this younger, bigger version of Dirk Vega made him feel his years.

Vega walked right up to Purcell. "Everything all right, bro?"

"The fucking bimbo shot up my car."

"What bimbo?" Rico asked.

Becker jumped a little, not having realized his partner's proximity.

"How should I know?" Purcell said. "Just some crazy broad. Stormed into the club and pulled a gun. Next thing we know she's popping caps in the parking lot."

"But you never saw her before?"

"I don't think so," Purcell said.

"Who looks at faces?" Vega chimed in.

"Billy Vega," Becker said, turning his attention to the big man. "Just the guy I came to see." He noticed Purcell's expression go noticeably blank. Fucking idiots. Like that didn't tell him something. "Funny, isn't it?" he asked, addressing both men. "I come here to ask a couple questions, and I run smack into a crime in progress. And you two don't have any idea who the shooter is. Am I getting it right?"

Purcell and Vega remained mute and motionless.

"No," Becker said. "Of course not. Probably some fluke."

"Stranger things have happened, Officer," Billy said, widening his stance and crossing his hands over his crotch, which showed his San Quentin breeding.

"Yeah, I understand you've been having a run of bad luck with your women." Becker noticed the tip of a baggie hanging out of Vega's pocket. He reached over and tugged it free. "What have we got here?"

Vega sighed when confronted with what looked like a gram of hash. Becker took his handcuffs out of the pouch clipped to his belt. "You know the drill, Billy." He had to use two sets of handcuffs due to the girth of Billy's arms and back. Becker didn't care about the dope, but it would serve his purposes. Not only did he now have a hammer on this guy, he'd also have a lot better luck with his interrogation once he got Billy away from his comfort zone.

Billy slumped in the backseat of the detective's sedan, being very careful to avoid looking at Purcell. An Inglewood squad car rolled into the lot. "Wait here," Becker told Purcell and walked over to meet with the uniforms.

Rico was speaking to witnesses on the sidewalk. Becker waved him over.

"What's up?" one of the Inglewood cops asked. "Any casualties?"

"Just the car," Becker said, and gave them a quick rundown on what was happening.

Rico pointed to an elderly woman by the bus stop. The woman was dressed in dark clothes and clutched her purse to her chest with both hands. "She says the shooter was probably one of the dancers."

"How's that?"

"Large, possibly silicone, breasts, tight clothes, and the blond hair was a wig."

Becker smiled in amusement, looking over Rico's shoulder at the elderly woman. "She got all that?"

"They were in a white pickup with a utility bed. The witness didn't get the make or a plate."

"They?"

"The driver was also a woman. Took off like she was driving the Indy 500."

"How many shots?" Becker asked.

"Three. Everyone I talked to agreed."

"According to the mope in the suit," Becker said, pointing out Purcell, "the shooter came into the club, pulled her gun, came back outside, and then shot up his car."

The four cops walked over to the Mustang and counted bullet holes.

"You're going to want to get this fixed as soon as possible, sir," Becker called over to Purcell. "Patrolmen tend to want to speak to drivers of cars riddled with gunfire."

"Thanks for your concern," Purcell said.

Becker answered with a little half salute, and then the two detectives walked back to their car.

"You thinking what I'm thinking?"

"That the shooter was the Summers broad?"

Rico nodded. "I think something she saw pissed her off."

They left the scene to the local law and headed back to the station to book Vega. Their next order of business would be the drive downtown to the Office of the Coroner to observe the Summerses' autopsy.

* * *

Munch jumped on the freeway, then took the first exit. She felt too exposed on the open road. She knew all the side streets in the area from limo runs during rush hour. She kept to them now, avoiding dead ends and gang turf.

"Where are you going?" Ellen asked as she took off her wig and turned her jacket inside out. Munch hadn't noticed before that it was reversible.

"Long-term parking. We'll request a space inside."

"Then what?"

"We'll take the tram to the airport and then catch the shuttle into Santa Monica. And you're losing the gun."

Ellen pulled the gun from her waistband. Munch threw her a rag. "Wipe it down. You've got some explaining to do."

"I'll just give Russ the parking stub. It's not like we wrecked the truck or anything. And he does have a pretty good alibi. I'll tell him to wait a couple days in case anyone got the plates and then he—"

"Not to him. To me. What are you doing with a gun? When did that become part of the plan?"

Munch pulled up to a storm drain and pointed. "Here." She waited while Ellen pitched the gun.

"What *is* the plan?" Ellen asked.

"Now you ask." Munch checked the rearview mirror, then pulled out into the empty street.

"Fucking Billy," Ellen muttered.

"Yeah, well at least you know where you stand, who your friends aren't."

"So what's next?"

"You're going to make some calls."

"Who first?"

"Your dad. Tell him you want to stay with him for a while."

"What about the rest of them?"

"It's simple," Munch said. "You know how they say, 'Watch what you pray for'?"

"Not really."

"We're going to give everyone what they want. They want that money so fucking bad? We're going to make them choke on it."

Chapter 19

Munch drove Russ's pickup to a long-term parking structure six blocks from the airport. From there they took the free tram ride to the airport, getting off at the upper level. They took the escalator to the lower level and then boarded a Santa Monica–bound Super Shuttle. She hated supporting the service, but knew cabdrivers sometimes had long memories.

"What do you have against the Super Shuttle?" Ellen asked. "Competition?"

"It's more than that," Munch explained, settling down into the backseat of the bus. "The mayor owns a large interest in the company, and now all of a sudden limo businesses have to have a separate insurance policy to conduct charters at the airport. Every time I pick up a client at LAX I have to stop at a booth on Sepulveda and buy a trip ticket for another buck-fifty. If I don't have a sticker on my windshield and a trip ticket on my dash, the cops pull me over. Who profits by all this? Tell me all that isn't a conflict of interest."

"Just criminal," Ellen said.

Munch lowered her voice. "Which brings us back to the matter of you packing."

"Let's just say I had a feeling," Ellen said, looking out the window as if she now also had a feeling about the other cars on the road.

"It was dumb," Munch said. "You're not going to outgun these assholes. The only way to get over is to be smarter than them. I shouldn't have to tell you that. Tomorrow you're going to get all that funny money and hand it over to these guys. Then we're going to tell the feds where to find them. Until then, you just lay low and stay out of trouble. That means don't get loaded. *Capeesh?*"

It took an hour of bus transfers to get back to Munch's old house. Munch uncovered the limo and loaded it with the last of her clothes. She had Ellen follow her in the GTO over to the new house.

After securing the limo, feeding the dogs, and checking her messages, Munch took Ellen to her apartment to collect her stuff.

"Someone's been here," Ellen said, pulling on a black hairpiece styled into a shag cut.

"How do you know?" Munch asked, standing in the bedroom doorway of Ellen's apartment.

"I put some hairs on the dresser drawers. They're gone."

"Someone looking for the money?"

"I expect so. Like I would be so stupid." Ellen stuffed her remaining wigs into a red shopping bag.

Munch grabbed an armful of clothes out of the closet. "I'll put these in the car."

Ellen followed her out with a suitcase and the shopping bag full of hairpieces. Munch noted that Ellen had toned down her makeup and buttoned her blouse to reveal no cleavage.

They stopped at a pay phone and Ellen called the Colonel.

When she got back in the car, Munch asked, "What did he say?"

"He will be expecting us."

Ellen's dad was staying in a WWII vintage barracks on the grounds of the Veteran's Administration in Westwood. They pulled up to the address. The white Crown Victoria Munch had seen the night before was parked in the driveway. A man was pacing on the front gravel, smoking a cigarette. He glared in their direction as the car rolled to a stop. He took a last irritated pull on his smoke before crushing it out underfoot.

"Is that him?" Munch asked.

"Yeah, come in and meet him."

The Colonel bent down and picked up his cigarette butt. He deposited it in the red coffee can by the front door before turning to greet his daughter and Munch. He stood erect and offered Munch his hand in a firm shake. "Nice to meet you," he said. "Come in."

"We've got some stuff to unload," Munch said, wondering what it was about the guy that made her so nervous. Maybe it was the intensity of his eyes. They were gray-blue, sharklike. His mouth was set in a grim line and the furrows in his brow were deep. He obviously didn't appreciate that Munch was the best friend Ellen had, probably figured she was another loser from Ellen's past. She'd be thinking the same thing if she were in his spit-polished wing tips.

When he looked at his daughter, his expression softened.

"Hi, Daddy," she said, struggling with her suitcase.

"Let me help with that," he said. She set her luggage down, and the two faced each other for an awkward moment. Munch noted the indecision in both their faces. Elliot Dane made the first move, reaching out to his daughter and enveloping her in a hug that was both tender and stiff. After a moment he broke the embrace with a self-conscious clearing of his throat.

"Well then," he said, hefting the large suitcase easily and making a crisp about-face for the house. Munch wondered how she was supposed to address the guy. Elliot? Mr. Dane? As usual, Ellen's nickname for her dad was right on, and in Munch's mind the guy remained *the Colonel*.

The inside of the military motel was pathologically neat. All the living room furniture was in straight and perpendicular formation. The nap of the carpet at strict attention. No knickknacks on the coffee table. The only pictures on the wall were of old guys in uniforms with lots of medals on their chests.

The Colonel walked into his small open kitchen, took three glasses from the cupboard, and set them on the counter dividing the rooms. "What'll you have?" he said, opening a jar of olives.

"Just water," Munch said.

The Colonel plopped three olives into the first glass. "Ellen?"

Ellen licked her lips and shot a quick sideways glance at Munch. "Uh, got any apple juice?"

The Colonel poured gin and vermouth over his olives. "Check the refrigerator." He poured Munch a glass of water and indicated the couch. Ellen came around into the kitchen and opened the refrigerator.

Munch took her drink with her own glance sideways at the open fridge. There was a quart bottle of vodka in the door, along with opened bottles of wine, and some barbecue sauce. The main shelves of the refrigerator held a carton of orange juice and the kind of Styrofoam containers restaurants package leftovers in.

"I'll just have some orange juice," Ellen said. She took her glass and poured her drink out of Munch's line of sight.

Munch didn't have to stretch her mind much to hear the bottle of vodka being stealthily removed from its cradle. Great role model this guy was turning out to be. She knew his type. Dead set against drugs and completely blind to the fact that alcohol was every bit as destructive. She wondered if Ellen would be willing to give a recovery house another shot after all this was over. Her best bet was an all-women facility for obvious reasons. If Ellen didn't want to go, then Munch had some serious decisions about her own loyalties to make.

The Colonel was standing at parade rest in the living room. Munch joined him there.

"Have a seat," he said.

"Thanks."

Ellen came into the room and perched on one of the chairs.

"Ellen tells me you're buying a house," he said.

Munch was surprised that Ellen had even remembered she'd said that. It was such a big deal to her, but Ellen seemed to not have heard her when she told her. "That's right," Munch said.

"And you have an adopted daughter but no husband?" He pulled a notebook from his pocket.

Again Munch felt on guard, sensing no friendliness in the guy's interest. And what was the deal with the book?

"Your daughter's name is . . . ?" he frowned, flipping back a few pages.

"Asia," Ellen said.

The Colonel clicked open a ballpoint pen and wrote.

Munch wondered if this was a military thing. Either way, she didn't like it. "Are you planning to stay in town?"

The Colonel strode over to where Ellen sat sipping her "orange juice" and clamped a hand on her shoulder. "I'm not leaving until things are settled." Ellen looked up at him with an expression of adoration. "They're going to let us bury your mama soon," he told her.

"What about Dwayne?" Munch asked.

"The fool who got himself shot?" The Colonel's expression turned amused. "I expect he's got his own people somewhere."

Munch thought about Dwayne. She didn't harbor warm feelings toward the guy either. He hadn't been Ellen's real dad, but he had been the one who was there. He deserved more than a quick cremation or internment in a potter's grave. She looked over to see Ellen's reaction and found her friend studying the floor.

Munch stood, crossed the room into the kitchen,

rinsed out her glass and left it to dry by the side of the sink. "Call me later," she told Ellen. "Nice to meet you, sir."

"You have to go?" His question was more of a formality than any entreaty to stay.

"Yeah, I'm trying to have my new house in some sort of order before I go back to work tomorrow."

"Thanks for everything," Ellen said.

Munch pointed a finger at her. It was at the tip of her tongue to say, "Be good." She didn't. It was already too late for that.

Chapter 20

At eight o'clock that evening, Munch pulled up to the house. The old house, as she now had come to think of it. This would be her last trip. She let herself in through the front door, feeling the dwelling's emptiness. As much as she had happily anticipated this move and the prospect of owning her own place, it was still sad to be saying good-bye to her home of five years. There were so many memories tied up in these four walls. Christmases and Easters. Asia losing her first tooth. The tooth fairy almost getting busted.

She lifted the telephone receiver, and hearing no dial tone, she unplugged the instrument and put it in a box. Then she did a last circuit of checking closets and cabinets, turning off the lights in all the rooms. Her footfalls echoed off the empty walls and the shadows played tricks on her eyes. Something went crack outside. A branch breaking by the front window. She went to investigate and noticed the porch light was out even though the switch was still on. Leaves brushed the window. She backed away. Startled.

She debated with herself if she should turn on the living room light. With the curtains removed, the house would be like a lighted stage making her even more vulnerable to the unknown, perhaps hostile, audience outside. Maybe she was just being paranoid, but given the events of the last few days she had certainly earned that right.

The front door pushed in against its jamb ever so slightly. The back of her neck prickled with itchy terror as the doorknob turned, slowly. Anyone with honorable intentions would have knocked. She had locked the door, hadn't she? She looked around her at the empty house with no telephone. She wished she had the dogs, but was glad Asia was safe at the Bradburys'.

Her options were limited. Screaming would only make her neighbors raise the volume of their televisions. She could wait and hope whoever was out there went away. She could try going out the back and sneaking around to her car. Going to a connecting yard was out of the question. Tall oleander hedges separated her from her next-door neighbors, and she really didn't feature sprinting across the open backyard to her adjoining rear neighbor if there was some evildoer out there. Her fourth option was to stand and fight. She searched the boxes by the door for a weapon, coming up with a rolling pin. Great. Lucy Ricardo fends off home invasion.

Headlights from a passing car lit the room. The doorknob jerked back a half turn. She waited, straining to hear.

Out of her peripheral vision she thought she saw a movement by the side window, but she couldn't be certain. Was it the shadow of a figure running or an innocent phantom created by trees and distant headlights? Her heart hammered, but she waited. She heard noises in the back and realized she couldn't remember if she had bothered to secure the windows back there.

Maybe this would be a good time to make a break for the car. What if there was more than one of them? She quietly twisted the doorknob with her left hand; her right still held the rolling pin. She threw the door open and sprinted across the porch, the front yard, and then onto the street. She *had* remembered to lock her car, she realized too late. Crouching on the asphalt, she switched her bludgeon to her left hand and reached into her pocket for her keys.

"What's up?" a man's voice asked from behind her.

She spun around, screaming and swinging as she did so. He was ready for her and caught her hand before she could inflict any damage.

"Hey," Rico said. "It's me."

"Was that you at the door?" She gasped, trying to catch her breath. "God, you scared the shit out of me."

"What are you talking about? I just got here."

"Somebody was trying to break in. I saw them try the door."

"I didn't see anybody," he said, putting a protective hand on her arm and pulling her behind him as he scanned the area.

"Maybe they're gone. I think I heard something in the back."

Rico saw the keys in her hand. "I'll check it out. Get in your car and lock the doors."

He waited until she was inside her car and then said, "Wait here."

He went back to his car, leaned across his front seat, and retrieved something from his glove box. In the light of the street lamp, she saw he now held a gun and a flashlight. She watched him crouch-walk to the house, staying to the shadows. He kept the gun and flashlight aimed in front of him, but hadn't switched the light on. Indecision gripped her. It felt wrong to send him off into unknown danger while she sat passively by, clutching her stupid rolling pin. The least she could do was go to the neighbors and call in some backup.

A minute passed. Her eyes strained to make sense of the hulking shadows into which Rico had vanished. This was taking way too long. She popped out the dome bulb before opening her door, not wanting to distract him or draw attention to herself, and got out.

Just then, Rico came back around from the side of the house and walked in the open front door. She saw the beam of his flashlight bouncing off the empty walls. After a seeming eternity, he finally emerged.

"Whoever it was is gone," he said.

"Why would anyone want to break into an empty house?"

"Kids, maybe, looking for a place to party."

Munch threw the rolling pin onto the floor of her backseat, crossed her arms across her chest, and rubbed her shoulders as if the cold had brought on her quaking. Rico holstered his gun and walked over to her, stretching out his arms as if to embrace her.

She turned from him and walked out to the street. Adrenaline prohibited her from standing still. She was also unused to a man being there for her in time of crisis instead of being the crisis.

"Thanks," she said.

"I told you to wait in the car."

"I couldn't. What if you needed me?"

He cocked an amused eyebrow at her.

"What were you doing here anyway?" she said, wanting to sound annoyed and invulnerable. The tears of relief streaming down her face defeated her bravado.

"I was in the neighborhood," he said, wiping away one tear with a surprisingly gentle hand.

She felt flustered by his attention. He seemed to be taking up all the space around her. She didn't know whether to push him away or pull him close, so she changed the subject. "Getting close to the killers yet?"

"Everything takes time. We only performed the autopsy this afternoon. Dwayne Summers died of a bullet wound. That gives us strong evidence if we find the weapon."

Her thoughts went immediately to the day's events. Ellen shooting up that little jerk's car. Three rounds and each hitting its target. Made her kinda proud despite herself. "You've known for a while he was shot, haven't you?"

"Not for certain. We had to wait until the coroner took some X rays—"

"And the bullet lead showed up white," she finished.

He raised an eyebrow in surprise.

"The things I know, eh?" She said it as a joke, but her laugh sounded false. He was close enough that she could see the stubble on his chin. "So then."

He didn't say anything.

"Just happened by?" Her voice sounded foreign to her. Breathy and soft.

"I came to see you." He said "you" like she was the operative word in the sentence.

"You did?"

"I tried to call, but I couldn't get through."

"What did you need?"

"This is going to sound weird. I can't stop thinking about you."

"I'm glad you're here," she said, feeling her expression go solemn the way it did when serious lust was involved.

He grunted softly and closed the distance between them. The kiss seemed natural. It began as a question, a tentative toe in the water, but soon turned into something much more serious. Their tongues met and she allowed herself to get lost in the sensation. She wanted all of him then. They were still standing in the street, below the street lamp.

"Want to come in?" she asked.

"You're sure?" he asked, his lips just barely touching hers.

She could only nod an answer. They turned and walked to the house, his hand resting on the small of her back. She wrapped her fingers around his wrist and led the way.

The door was still open. He closed it after them and locked it. She took him to the back bedroom, where they were guaranteed privacy. They kissed again and then clothes began falling away. She felt suddenly shy and closed her eyes against his nakedness. She only wanted to feel. His skin rippled under her touch, smooth and warm. Sensations of pleasure purled down her body as he did delicious things with his mouth to the front of her. She interlaced her fingers in his hair, urging him on.

She was only vaguely aware of the feel of the carpet on her back. All her cognitive powers were focused on his fingers, his mouth. She also explored his body, hungry to know every inch of him. The sparse curly mass of hair on his chest. The lean hardness of him. She murmured endearments and then stopped forming intelligible words.

"Oh God," she said as he finally joined her. They coupled furiously for incredible minutes that left them both sweating and delirious. Her body took over, moving with an intensity that surprised her.

Later they lay sated. Her head rested on his shoulder. His arm encircled her. She felt incredibly light-spirited, unlocked somehow, and started to tell him things she'd never told anyone. How she loved the ocean. What her mother had been like. He listened quietly. She kept a hand on his chest throughout her recital, loving the feel of it rising with each breath, the steady, even beat of his heart. It didn't occur to her he had fallen asleep until he snored.

She laughed and poked his shoulder. "Hey."

He startled awake. "What?"

"I've gotta go."

He pulled her on top of him and into another long kiss.

"Well . . . ," she purred, "maybe not right this minute."

Afterward, they both fell into an exhausted sleep until the cold woke her up. She sat up and found their tangle of clothes.

"What time is it?" he asked as she pulled on her shirt and underpants.

"I don't know." She handed him his clothes.

He grabbed her hand and kissed it. "You're beautiful."

She grinned and ran a finger up his thigh. "You're not too shabby yourself."

"Where's your kid?"

"Now you ask." She laughed. "She's spending the night with a friend." She watched him stand and pull on his pants. He smiled down at her and offered his hand. She allowed him to help her to her feet and then pulled on her own pants.

He slipped into his shirt and buttoned it.

Munch stretched, enjoying the feel of all her muscles.

They kissed again. Her hands had seemed to develop a need of their own to be touching him. She buried her face in his shirt and inhaled the scent of him. Still holding her in one arm he reached into his pants pocket, pulled out his watch, and checked the time.

"It's one o'clock."

"I guess that answers that."

"Where's Ellen?" he asked.

"With her dad. I met him finally."

"The Colonel?"

"Talk about a lifer. *I* almost saluted him."

"Where's he staying?" Rico asked.

"Are you working now?"

"We are going to want to talk to him."

Munch nuzzled his chest as she considered what to say. What the hell, she could give Rico that much. "He's got a place in that tract of military housing inside the VA. Ellen's going to stay with him for a couple days."

"Good," he said.

"Why good?"

"You've got enough going on." He looked around the empty room. "Looks like you got all your stuff moved."

"Yeah, tonight was the last of it."

"Spent all day moving, did you?"

She rubbed a hand over her face and spoke through her fingers as if to dilute her less than 100 percent honesty. "I feel like I've been moving for a month." She brought her hand back down. "This week has been so intense. In fact, it seemed pretty natural that you would show up just as I needed you."

"Timing is everything."

"Right," she said. "They always say God doesn't give you more than you can handle. Even lately, when all kinds of shit has been coming down, I still get enough perks to keep me going."

"Like you and me?"

"Definitely. Sex is one of nature's better inventions." She said sex instead of lovemaking. More of her "good sport" attitude raising its people-pleasing head. She knew how guys were more comfortable with some words over others. "Love" ranking high on the uncomfortable list. If either of them was going to start using the "L" word, he was going to have to go first.

"I don't know where you're at with God," she said, "and I don't want you to think I'm some kind of religious freak, but I think there's a divine order. Everything happens for a reason."

"So not everything is cause and effect?" He kissed her neck below her ear and goose bumps erupted down her body all the way to her feet.

"Oh, yeah."

"You still talking about God?"

"Was I saying something?" She wrapped her hands in his shirt and pulled him to her.

"What else has been happening?" he asked, pushing her back so he could see her face.

"You mean besides Ellen's mom getting killed and my moving? One of Asia's friends has a psycho bitch for a mother. She was here the other night and made a big scene."

"You think it was her tonight?"

"With that woman, anything is possible. She needs some serious intervention. I'm trying to get the father to do something, but he's being a wimp. She came by here the other night, thinking I had her husband here. He wasn't, but her kid was. She didn't even ask about her kid."

"Why would she be looking for her husband here?"

"Ex-husband, and she's just nuts, obsessed-like."

"Sounds like a real piece of work."

"I keep waiting for her to wind down, but she seems to be just warming up."

"What else has she done?"

Munch thought of the printout at the ball field. This was definitely not the moment to bring it up or maybe it was. She wished there was time to duck away and call the small select group of women she turned to for advice. Women like her sponsor, Ruby, or Caroline St. John. She didn't always follow their counsel, but it helped to take a vote sometimes of people outside the committee that raged in her head. She realized Rico was still waiting for an answer. "The next morning after she came over to the house I found a dead spot on the lawn like someone had thrown some chemical there."

"She sounds dangerous. Did you report her?"

"No. And she took my trash out of the can."

"That sounds like something a cop or a private investigator would do."

"Well, she's got the money to hire one." Munch slipped her hand under his shirt and ran her fingers along his chest, stopping to play with the nub of his nipple. He didn't stop her.

"You got a name for this bitch?"

"Noreen Ramsey. She's a Realtor. If you run across her, bust her for me, will you?"

He smiled. "I just might do that."

She reached up to kiss him. Their mouths opened to each other, and once again she let herself get lost in the postorgasmic warmth of him. It was some seconds before either spoke again.

Rico looked down at her and ran a hand through her hair. "You want to come home with me?" he asked.

"I can't. I have to go back to work tomorrow." She paused and stifled a giggle. Her happiness was threatening to bubble out of her. "I mean today. I need to get home and change and walk the dogs. Why don't you come over to my place?"

He looked genuinely sorry. "Same problem. I'm pulling an early shift tomorrow. How would it look if I came in wearing the same clothes?"

She smiled slyly at him. "Like you got lucky."

"Very lucky," he said.

She knew then she was in some seriously uncharted waters.

Chapter 21

Munch drove to the new house. She turned up the radio and sang along with Grace Slick, who was belting out the ballad "Somebody to Love." When she pulled into the garage of her new house it was almost two in the morning, but she didn't feel like sleeping, far from it. Nothing to break the spell. She wanted to luxuriate in the amazing sensations her tryst with Rico had aroused. She felt agile and unfettered. All this and sober too. Such a deal.

She was still singing when she entered the house. The dogs greeted her with wagging tails. Sam jumped up and Munch caught her paws and danced with her. Nicky barked.

"Shhh," Munch said, ruffling Nicky's ears. "Don't wake the neighbors."

She turned on lights and took a critical look at the work she had remaining. It would take another week before everything was unpacked and put away. Asia's room was her first priority. Although she was also seized by an almost irresistible urge to bake cookies and bring them to Rico at work. Instead, she grabbed a hammer and nails from the kitchen drawer and went into her daughter's new room.

When Asia came home after school, she would be greeted by all her familiar artwork. Again, Munch would let Asia decide where she wanted to hang her Disney animation cells, pictures of horses and dogs, and the prized signed poster of Menudo with the group's teen heartthrob ensemble. Asia's current crush was on the group's cute little blond singer Ricky Martin. She'd drawn a heart around his face. In Munch's day the cutest boy on the earth had been Mark McCain, son of Lucas McCain aka "The Rifleman."

She hammered a nail into a spot in the wall centered above Asia's dresser. She then lifted the matching mirror and hung it in place. Her reflection showed her two large red hickies on either side of her neck.

"Oh, man," she said out loud, feeling proud and embarrassed at the same time. A shiver of remembered pleasure stabbed her between the legs. *God, what that guy could do with his mouth.* She paused to smile at herself and run her fingertips over the love-bruised flesh when she noticed that the lid of Asia's toy chest behind her was ajar. This was not the way she remembered seeing it earlier.

She was instantly on alert. She turned and studied the large wooden chest. She immediately thought of Noreen. Had there been some piece of paper in her trash with the new address on it? How far would Noreen go in her campaign against her? Would she dare to go for Asia? Because if she did, she was going to find herself in a world of hurt.

Slowly Munch lifted the lid, wary of booby traps, thinking about that lawyer who went after Synanon and found a rattlesnake sans the rattle in his mailbox. She listened carefully for movement but heard nothing stir. She lifted the lid the rest of the way until it was all the way open and resting against the foot of Asia's bed. The toys were in their usual disarray. The lid of a Chutes and Ladders board game had come off and the game pieces had fallen to the bottom of the box. One was wedged beneath the edge of the cedar panel lining. When she removed the piece, the panel remained tilted. Suddenly, she had no doubt what she would find under the aromatic piece of wood. She unloaded all the toys, setting them in a heap on the floor, and then pried up the plank of cedar. Stacks of hundred-dollar bills wrapped in rubber bands lined the bottom of the chest.

Fucking Ellen.

She sighed in exasperation, her hands on her hips.

"Sloppy," she said out loud. She went into her bedroom and grabbed her driving gloves and a pillowcase. Stuffing the bills into the makeshift bag, she thought of the old mechanic's adage of not taking the time to do the job right the first time meant you'd be taking the time to do it again. It was no accident that she had the lowest rate of comebacks in the shop. It was a matter of work ethic, something Ellen obviously lacked. Still shaking her head in disgust, she took the pillowcase full of money into the backyard and looked around. The dogs padded after her.

"Not here," she told them. Sam cocked her head in question. Nicky squatted and marked the spot.

"C'mon." The dogs followed her around the house to the garage. She lifted the big door and waited for them to come in before closing it again. After distributing the packs of bills evenly throughout the pillowcase so that she was left with a floppy but flat rectangle, she used duct tape to seal the end. She went into her household set of tools, selected a ratchet, five-inch extension, a deep 9/16 socket, and slid underneath the car. The dogs stood sentry at her feet.

It took only a couple minutes to loosen the nuts holding the gas tank straps. She ran them down the studs until the tank dropped a couple of inches then she crammed the bag of money in the opening and tightened the nuts until the tank was snug. Only after she was finished did it occur to her that she should have counted the money first, just to make sure that was all of it.

Man, she thought, sliding out from under her car, fucking Ellen was just full of surprises, wasn't she?

On Tuesday morning, Rico walked in the office. "What's up?"

"Did you get anything new out of the Mancini woman?" Becker asked. He noted how the younger man's hand went to the back of his neck before answering.

"Ellen Summers has gone to stay with her father."

"Where?"

"Munch said he had a place in the VA. He's military. Possibly a colonel."

"Munch?"

"The Mancini woman's nickname."

"Anything else?" Becker stared at Rico until the younger man looked away.

"I want to put a unit on the Mancini house at night," Rico said, without looking up from the paperwork on his desk, "step up the patrol. Some crazy woman has been stalking her."

"This related to the homicide?"

"No, I'd just like to help her out. I've got the name and workplace of the woman doing the harassing. I'm going to stop by her office at lunch and see if I can put the fear of God into her."

"Where does she work?"

"Jeff Doogan Realty. The office is in Palms."

"I'll go with you," Becker said. "We've got the Vega interrogation this morning. Let's put in an appearance at roll call and you can bring up your girlfriend's problems."

"I never said—"

"You didn't have to." *Jeez, I have eyes, don't I?* "Where does this leave you and Kathy?"

"Kathy has nothing to do with this," Rico said; his hand returned to the back of his neck.

Becker chuckled, grateful to not be burdened with a young man's libido. Especially not these days with that AIDS virus going around. God, what kind of world was it turning into where the penalty for sex was death?

"Did you find out anything about the shooting at Century Entertainment?"

"No," Rico said, as they walked down the hall, "that didn't come up."

They joined the throng of officers mustering for

the morning meeting that kicked off the day's patrol.

"Detective Chacón has some words," the watch sergeant said.

Rico strode to the front of the room and wrote Munch's new address on the bulletin board. He gave a brief account of Noreen Ramsey's increasing harassment and asked that the patrol officers keep an eye out.

"Who is this Mancini woman to you?" the watch sergeant asked.

"She's a source," Rico said.

Becker rolled his eyes. So that's what they were calling them these days.

If Rico was aware of the elbow nudging among the cops seated in their rows of half-tray desks, he kept his reactions to himself.

Back at his desk, Rico put in a call to the U.S. Army Criminal Investigation Command operating out of Camp Pendleton and asked to speak to Tony DeSiderio, an investigator and longtime friend. In fact, DeSiderio had wanted to be a cop but at five foot seven and three quarter inches had not qualified. The cutoff height at the time was five foot eight. Rico had driven DeSiderio to the recruitment office himself. They went in the morning and DeSiderio had lain down in the backseat for the whole ride in an effort to defeat gravity. Nothing they tried made up for that critical quarter inch. Tony joined the Army instead. Ironically, the height requirement had been lowered six months after he'd committed to Uncle Sam. DeSiderio had made the best of it, rising to the rank of warrant officer, and keeping up friendly liaisons as well as commiserations with Rico.

"CID, DeSiderio," the man answered.

Rico identified himself.

"Hey, you old rattlesnake. How's the LAPD treating you?"

"Can't complain," Rico said.

"What you need, buddy?"

"I'm looking for background information on a man named Elliot Dane."

"Rank?"

"Colonel. Maybe. We're not sure."

"Is he in active duty?"

"I don't know that for sure either," Rico said. "If he is, he's probably on emergency leave."

"You know this guy's duty station?"

"Fort Bragg, North Carolina, I believe."

"What else do you have?"

"Social Security and date of birth." Rico read off the information.

"That's a start. I can run him through WWL," he said, referring to the Army's World Wide Locator database. "That should give us his rank, last known duty station, and tell us whether he's active or not. What are you looking for?"

"His ex-wife and her husband were murdered Wednesday night or early Thursday morning." He described the murder scene with all its brutality. "According to preliminary information, Dane was in North Carolina shortly after the homicides occurred, but that doesn't necessarily rule out his involvement. We believe he's staying somewhere in the Westwood VA."

"There's some BOQs there," DeSiderio said, using the acronym for the Bachelor Officer Quarters, which was lodging available at cheap rates to the commissioned ranks, usually on a base.

"Can you check the records there?"

"Sure. I'll also check with Finance and Accounting. See if Dane owned any insurance policies on his ex. I'll also get you copies of military flight manifests listing passengers going to and from the L.A. area and Fort Bragg during the critical time frame."

"You're way ahead of me, Tony. Thanks."

"It'll take a few days, but I can get you a leave and earnings statement, see if he's been discharged."

"I'll check back with you in a couple of days," Rico said. DeSiderio agreed to get right on it.

When Munch got to work, Lou had a pile of work orders on the counter for her. Three of them were for carburetor overhauls farmed out from other shops. She also had two smog checks to do and an intake manifold gasket on a Buick station wagon. She parked her GTO on the side of the lube bay but had to wait until she had the carburetors disassembled and soaking in carb cleaner before she could sneak around and retrieve the pillowcase. She slid the bag of money under her jacket, then opened her trunk and pulled out her spare.

"What you doing?" Lou asked, coming out from the rest room with his hands still on his zipper.

"I want to pop in a new valve stem," she said. "I've got a leak."

"Go ahead," he told her.

She shot him an irritated look. They'd worked together for eight years. He'd only been her boss for the last two. Both of them knew she made him more money than any other two mechanics in the shop, but he still felt this periodic need to piss on fire hydrants. She was well aware he signed the checks.

She reached in her pocket and pulled out a dollar. "Here," she said, handing it to him.

"What's this for?"

"The valve stem."

He handed her back the bill. "Don't be a smart-ass."

"Yes'm, boss."

"What's that on your neck?" he asked.

Her free hand went right to the hickey.

"That side too?" he asked. "What? Are you dating a vampire?"

She pushed past him to the tire machine and swung her spare over the center spline. She knew better than to discuss her love life at work.

"You getting coffee?" she asked.

"Yeah, you want a cup?"

"Sure."

"You never say no, do you?"

She threw a tire patch at him. He laughed and kept going.

"Oh, and Munch?" he said on his way down the driveway to the bakery next door. "Glad to see you're getting right back in the saddle again."

She pulled out the valve stem and a whoosh of rubber-smelling stale air pushed her bangs back. She waited until he was out of sight before she broke the bead of the tire. None of the other back-room crew had arrived yet, and the only customers were a few early commuters getting gas. After making sure no one was looking her way, she slipped the bag of money out from under her coat and worked it between the now-deflated Michelin and the steel lip of rim until the contraband was nestled safely inside the tire. She then popped in a new valve stem and reinflated the tire. The whole operation took five minutes.

Shit, she thought, *if this sober mechanic thing doesn't pan out, I've got a bright future as a smuggler.*

Chapter 22

Becker set the interrogation room carefully. He'd learned through years of experience what worked best. The room had two chairs, no table. Between Becker and his subject he liked only air, nothing to obstruct his view of telltale body language. He placed the chairs so the room's thermostat was at a point equidistant from where he and Billy Vega would sit.

"We're ready," he told the custody deputy. The officer went out to the anteroom to collect Billy Vega.

Becker put his coat on, as he always did when conducting interviews. This was his own version of dressing for success. He wore muted colors, a somber tie, shirtsleeves down, holster and badge concealed. Any suspect ensconced in this room already knew that he was the man; nothing was gained by overemphasizing the obvious.

"I'll do the strong, silent thing," Rico said.

"Yeah, you seem to have that pretty much down."

Rico rubbed the knuckles of his closed fist.

"Observe and learn," Becker said.

"Yes, Obi-Wan."

The deputy returned with Billy Vega. Becker indicated the chair reserved for him. It was the one facing away from the door. Vega could count the dots on the acoustical wall covering if he wanted, but he would be denied the emotional cushion of seeing a way out.

Becker looked down on his prisoner. "I'll give it to you straight. I'm a homicide cop. I don't give a shit what you choose to snort, smoke, or rub on your belly. All I care about is clearing murder cases. You get me?"

Vega turned bloodshot eyes on Becker. He was paying attention.

Before sitting down Becker asked, "Are you cold?"

Vega shrugged. "I'm fine."

Becker made a show of adjusting the thermostat when in reality he was turning on the concealed microphone. He checked his watch. It was ten after eight. The tapes were good for sixty minutes, and he didn't want to make the mistake of not taking the necessary break needed for the officer outside to put in a fresh cassette. He also wanted to give the impression that he was actively pursuing a hot case. Another subliminal method he used to keep the pressure on.

Billy Vega shifted in his seat, turning sideways and crossing his legs. Becker expected no less. A mope like Vega was perpetually guilty. He would always hunch his body against authority figures.

"How many times have you been advised of your rights, Mr. Vega? Can I call you Billy?"

"Call me anything you want, cop."

"You know I have to do this," Becker said. He

pulled a card from his pocket and read the Miranda rights. He never recited from memory, at times like these or in court.

"Fine," Vega said when Becker finished.

Becker handed him a clipboard with a waiver on it. Vega signed after a cursory inspection. As agreed on before, Becker and Rico left the room, giving Vega plenty of time to worry.

The two detectives had the officer operating the tape recorder check to see all was working properly and then went to get a cup of coffee. While Rico doctored his brew, Becker put a large empty cardboard box on his desk and began filling it with paperwork.

"What's all this?" Rico asked.

Becker checked the binding of the thick brown tome in his hand before putting it inside the box. "Monthly crime reports." He picked up another loose-leaf binder full of interagency memos and placed it on top of the first book. Then he added the Summerses' crime scene photographs, autopsy reports, fingerprint cards, and the Spearmint Rhino handbill now unfolded and encased in a plastic evidence envelope.

"Hand me some of those and a marker."

Rico passed him the large manila envelopes Becker pointed to and a Sharpie Marker.

"No," Becker said. "Give me the red one."

He stuffed the envelopes with various office supplies: a letter opener, a notepad, scraps of printout paper from his wastepaper basket. On each envelope he wrote VEGA in large red letters.

Rico watched all this with interest. Becker checked his watch. Five minutes had passed. "Think he's stewed long enough?"

Rico nodded.

Becker finished the box off with all the paperwork he'd been able to gather on Billy Vega. Rico was still nodding when he followed his partner back into the interrogation room.

Becker entered the room like a doctor at a busy medical clinic. He put the box on the floor and rechecked the "thermostat." Then he sat. Vega gazed with poorly disguised interest at the box. Becker pulled out the 5.10 form and a clipboard. The envelopes with Vega's name in red were clearly visible. Vega licked his lips and blinked. Stress, Becker knew, tended to dry the eyeballs. Vega's feet came down to the floor. His feet vainly trying to point toward the exit he couldn't see.

"Let me tell you what we have," Becker said. "Three homicides." He pulled out the crime scene photos of the victims.

Vega kept his face still while he looked at the picture of the dead naked dancer. "Corinne Adams. An employee of the Spearmint Rhino." Becker consulted the 5.10. "You were employed at the Spearmint Rhino as manager beginning March of last year until the week Corinne Adams was killed."

Vega nodded.

"Is that a yes?" Becker asked. He needed a verbal response for the tape.

"Yeah, that's right," Vega said.

Rico made notes on the legal pad clamped to his clipboard.

"In the statement you made last week to detectives," Becker continued, "you said that on the evening Corinne Adams was raped and murdered you had gone to visit your father."

"Yeah," Vega said. "When that shit went down, I was nowhere near."

"So what you're saying is that when this crime was committed, you were far away." Becker never used profanity when he conducted his taped interrogations. It was a big turnoff to juries; they liked their knights of law enforcement pure. He reached down into the cardboard box, removed a sealed envelope marked EVIDENCE: ADAMS HOMICIDE and set it on his lap. On top of the envelope he placed fingerprint cards, the flyer from the club with Ellen Summers's photograph on it, and photographs from both crime scenes. He picked up three close-ups of the dead woman's broken fingers.

"And then following Corinne Adams's murder, you left Spearmint Rhino. Can you tell me why you made this move?"

"I quit."

"And why did you quit?"

"I got a better offer."

"Better than you got from Lawrence Whitley?"

Vega looked bewildered.

"Lawrence Whitley. The man you knew as Animal."

"Oh, yeah," Vega said, back on track now. "Animal, right." Vega's hand rubbed his inner thigh, moved to his crotch. Becker noted this retrogression with interest. It was almost an infantile response. He'd seen this before. Some crooks went as far as to assume fetal positions when his questions got too close to the bone.

He made a note to himself to follow up on the connection between the two men. "So then you got your new job at Century Entertainment."

"That's right."

"DMV records indicate that you registered a brand-new Harley-Davidson last July. I have copies of dealer receipts in the amount of eight thousand dollars. Can you tell me where that money came from?"

"I thought you said you were only interested in murder," Vega said.

"Are you saying that how you got that money had nothing to do with murder?"

"That's *all* I'm saying."

"All right, fair enough," Becker said. "Tell me how you spent last Wednesday evening." Becker lifted one of the sealed manila envelopes with Vega's name on it and shook it. Unknown to Vega, the object inside was the letter opener off Becker's desk. Then he showed Vega three pictures of Lila Mae Summers. The first was from her driver's license photograph, the second as they found her at the crime scene, and the third taken at the morgue.

"Who's that?" Vega asked.

"Who's that?" Becker answered, his tone disappointed. "This is Lila Mae Summers. Mother of Ellen Summers." He picked up the flyer. "Another coemployee of yours at the Spearmint Rhino. I'm investigating a double homicide that took place last week. Lila Mae Summers was killed in a very similar manner to Corinne Adams."

Vega visibly relaxed. The toe that had begun tapping when Becker pulled the fingerprint card from his box became still. Becker realized that somewhere he had strayed.

"Where were you last Wednesday evening, Billy?"

"I was at the club," Billy said.

"On the floor?"

"I didn't watch every set, but I was there."

Becker stared at Billy for a minute, waiting for the big man to offer more, maybe trip himself, but Billy seemed content with what he'd said and that worried Becker. Interrogation 101: The elegance of honesty needed no adornment. He checked his watch and said, "All right, we're going to take a short break. Billy, you want a cup of coffee?"

"Yeah."

Becker and Rico returned to their office.

"I think we need to find this Lawrence Whitley guy," Becker said.

"What do you want to do with Vega?" Rico asked.

"Ehh," Becker said, wobbling his hand. "I don't know. Let's keep a leash on him." When the two detectives returned to the interrogation room twenty minutes later, they found the big man wide awake. This was another indicator that they were on the wrong track. Innocent suspects tended to stay conscious through the process, but the guilty ones practically always napped.

"Thanks for your cooperation," Becker said. "You can leave, but we might need to talk to you again later. I'm going to wait to file charges on the dope. Who knows? It might even get lost somewhere in the shuffle."

Vega stood, rubbing his wrists where the handcuffs had pinched him. "Why would I want the bitch dead? I loved her."

"Yeah, I know, Billy. You're all heart."

After Vega left the station, Becker sat down at his desk and began wording a request for a search warrant on Billy's home and work. Something was going to break loose soon. He sensed Rico's presence in the doorway. Without looking up he asked, "What?"

"You know," Rico said, "when I talked to Munch on Sunday she said I should look for someone who liked to break fingers. 'Some kind of animal' were her exact words."

Becker didn't miss the reluctance in the man's voice. He stopped writing and looked his young partner in the face. "You think she was leading you?"

"Looks that way. The question is: Who's leading her?"

Chapter 23

Ellen left the house without waking her dad. She didn't suppose he'd mind her borrowing his car. She was doing him the bigger favor by letting him sleep in. Judging by the coffee can full of cigarette butts outside the front door, he'd been up most of the night. The sight of all those extinguished cigarettes made her shudder as she passed them. There had to be a whole pack's worth.

Becker used his connections to track down the DA's file on Lawrence "Animal" Whitley. He studied the mug shot. Whitley was bald with bulging eyes and a walrus mustache. He'd been busted for drunk driving once, and assault twice. Three different women had felt the need to take out restraining orders against him.

Becker put the report down and rubbed his eyes. When he looked up again, his lieutenant was standing in front of his desk.

"Got something you might want in on."

"What's that?"

"We've got another homicide. Sounds like the case you're working on."

"Broken fingers?"

"No, not the fingers this time. Just the twisted neck." The lieutenant handed him a piece of paper with an address on it.

"When did this go down?" Becker asked.

"Best guesstimate is last night."

"All right. We'll check it out."

It took twenty minutes in midmorning traffic for Becker and Rico to reach the scene. This time the victim had been found in a much worse section of town. A notorious stretch of barrio full of illegals and junkies just north of the Culver City border. The victim had been killed in a burned-out motel on Sawtelle that no one had gotten around to demolishing. Now a legion of squatters claimed it and used it as a shooting gallery. The detectives arrived at the round-robin of hovels at ten minutes to twelve. The defunct units without benefit of water, electricity, or gas shared the same barren courtyard. On the brick wall next to the derelict cluster of shacks someone had written a hasty epitaph in black spray paint to the deceased.

WE LOVE YOU, SUKI

Becker shook his head at the hypocrisy that inevitably rose from murder. Some unknown, unloved, ignored individual gets snuffed and suddenly every Tom, Dick, and Mary shows up proclaiming the deceased as a good friend, hoping to share the tragedy's limelight. By this time tomorrow there would be some sort of shrine erected, an overturned shopping cart, perhaps, full of flowers and Teddy Bears. People were assholes.

He and Rico badged their way past the yellow tape. They kicked through the detritus of poverty and addiction: fast-food wrappers, wine bottles, plastic grocery bags decaying in the dirt along with other half-buried bits of rags and rubble. Old shopping carts held collections of glittering objects found on midnight scavenger hunts by tweaking speed freaks. Becker asked around and was pointed toward the detective assigned as primary. His name was Dave Shore, and he was a young blond guy with neat rows of hair implants.

"Shore," Becker said, when he was in hailing distance. "Want some help?"

"Yeah, thanks. We're taking statements from the locals. Amazingly," Shore made his eyes round in mock disbelief, "nobody saw nothing."

"Where's the DB?" Rico asked.

Shore pointed to a unit in the corner.

The victim was a frail older woman. Gray hair. Delicate bone structure. Most of her lay prone on a bare mattress awash in blood. Like Lila Mae Summers, her neck was corkscrewed. Only in this case the victim was face up, chest down. Her forehead was caved in. A length of two-by-four was on the floor beside her. Bits of blood and hair still clung to the wood. It didn't appear that she had put up any kind of a fight. There were no signs of defensive wounds. She looked to weigh under one hundred pounds and was obviously destitute. Rape didn't seem to be the issue as she was fully clothed. An assumption, he knew, but probably a legitimate one.

"Are you thinking what I'm thinking?" Becker asked.

"Why the overkill?" Rico said.

"What does it tell you?"

Rico paused a moment to consider. "Anger, frustration, a lack of control."

Newsome, the detective who worked with Shore, had slipped on a pair of latex gloves and was gently rummaging through a large macramé purse. One of the criminalists brought him a cardboard box lined with white butcher paper. Newsome dumped the contents of the bag into the box. In addition to hair clips, a brush, and a half pint of peppermint schnapps, he found several credit cards with different names on them.

Becker called in the numbers and discovered they were listed on the hot sheet.

Newsome also came across papers with the same names signed over and over. Not surprisingly, the names matched those on the stolen cards.

"Practice makes perfect," Rico said.

Finally Newsome found documents from the parole board and prison system that bore the first name of Suki. Last name: Monash.

"Huh," said Becker. "Suki Monash was only thirty-seven years old."

"I would have guessed closer to sixty," Rico said.

"She'd only been out of prison for a month."

"Poor kid."

When they got back to the office, they would run her name, see what came up as far as connections to the other victims. Becker was pretty sure all roads would lead back to Ellen Summers and the goddamn money. It was almost always about the money.

"Let's go see what we can learn from the locals," Becker told Rico.

The inhabitants of the apocalyptic courtyard scattered at the approach of the police. Only those made legal by methadone or too crazy to matter dared to stay behind. They stood in their blanketed doorways, hollow eyes sad as they watched the coroner lower his cart from his wagon.

Rico approached an emaciated man. "Did you know Suki?"

"She was beautiful," he said. "That chick never hurt a soul. This is wrong, man. Really wrong."

The guy would not have looked out of place at Auschwitz. "There had to be noise, maybe not screaming but something else. Grunting or thumping, something out of place in the night."

"The night around here is filled with all sorts of noise," the wasting man said. "Hard to tell suffering from pleasure."

Rico went on to the next witness, a wild-eyed, Manson-looking wino. The wino had plenty of theories to offer. Rico made a few notes as the guy spoke about avenging angels and the wrath of God. When Rico and Becker walked away to confer, the guy was ranting on and gesturing as if he still had an audience.

"There's a guy who will never be lonely," Rico said.

Becker cracked a smile but hid it quickly behind his hand. This would be just the time some news camera would be trained his way and catch a picture of him grinning at the scene of a vicious murder.

They returned to where Newsome and Shore were standing and shared what little bit of information they'd been able to gather. Becker also brought his fellow cops up to speed on his investigation of the Summerses' murder. Shore took notes. Becker promised him copies of his investigation reports.

"Nothing more to do here," Becker said, feeling his stomach growl. He turned to Rico. "Let's have your little chat with Noreen Ramsey and then grab some lunch."

Becker and Rico found the offices of Jeff Doogan Realty with no problem. Noreen Ramsey was seated at a back desk, surrounded by five-foot pony walls. A woman with black hair cut in a shag passed them on her way out as they entered. Before she turned her face quickly away, Becker noted the rhinestone-studded glasses and something familiar about her mouth. His partner, he saw, had glanced only at the woman's breasts.

I'm getting old, Becker thought sadly. He turned his attention on Noreen Ramsey. The word that best described the woman was "intense." Starting with her makeup. Lipstick, lip-liner, and eyebrows were all drawn in severe dark lines. Her suit was austere and hung on her as if she had gone down a size or two since purchasing it. Her eyes were hard, daring you to piss her off. A real spider woman. She smiled to greet them, and he felt an involuntary shiver run up his spine. There was a weird hunger in that smile.

"How'd you like to wake up next to that?" he murmured to Rico in a show of male solidarity, which he immediately realized he had exaggerated. If there was one thing the job had taught him, it was that everyone was full of shit to some degree. He was no exception other than perhaps to be more aware of it than most.

"I hear you," Rico replied.

They reached the back of the room. "Noreen Ramsey?" Rico asked.

"Yes."

Rico pulled out his badge. "I'm Detective Chacón, and this is my partner, Detective Becker. Do you mind answering a few questions?"

Noreen shot a furtive glance at her bottom desk drawer. "What about?"

"Can you tell me your whereabouts last evening?" Rico asked.

"I had dinner at home. I watched television. I went to bed."

"Can anyone verify this?" Rico said.

"Are you asking if I slept alone?" she asked. Her eyes bored into them with deep anger.

"Did you?" Rico asked.

"Yes. I slept alone. I ate alone. I watched stupid television alone."

"And are you still residing at the Oakwood Garden Apartments on Mindanao?"

"Yes. I also own a home in the Palisades. What is this about?"

"We've had numerous harassment complaints about you," Rico said. "You're sure that at no time last evening you went out?"

"Yes," she said. "I've already told you that."

"Maybe you made a quick run to the store?"

"No."

"What show did you watch on television?"

"Mostly I just flicked through the channels."

Becker knew Rico was pinning her to her story. The follow-up, if Rico wanted to take it that far, would be to check with the neighbors. See if anyone saw Noreen leaving or returning. Then they would have her caught in a lie that would give them leverage in future interviews. Supplying a police officer with false information was against the law.

"Now I have a question," she said with cold composure. "Is she fucking both of you?"

"Who would that be, ma'am?" Becker said.

"Don't be coy. That little whore. I hope you both wore condoms. No telling where she's been."

"All we're here to discuss today is you, Mrs. Ramsey," Rico said. "I suggest you find another way to channel your anger. Get some help from a professional."

"A psychiatrist? Is that what you're saying?" Noreen's eyes flew all the way open, and her dark red lips curled away from nicotine-yellowed teeth. "I don't need some asshole cops dispensing medical advice. I've answered your questions. Now get the hell out of my office before I report you to your superiors."

The muscles in Rico's jaw jumped. Becker pulled a business card from his wallet and flipped it on her desk. "Make sure you spell the name right," he said. Back out on the sidewalk he turned to Rico. "Guess you hit a nerve with the shrink suggestion."

Rico spit into the street. "Yeah, probably always makes her mad."

When Becker got back to the office, a pink while-you-were-out note was taped to his phone. Agent Long from the Secret Service had finally returned his call. Becker called the number Long had left. It turned out to be a direct line.

"What you got for me?" Becker asked after dispensing with brief insincere pleasantries.

"I looked up the file on Ellen Summers," Long said. "Before her incarceration several counterfeit bills were traced back to her. My partner and I questioned her at CIW. She claimed to have no knowledge that the bills were queer, said she got them from a trick whose name was John Smith."

"That's original." Becker turned to a clean page on his legal pad and wrote as he talked. "While I've got you on the phone, let me run a few other names by you: Billy Vega, Corinne Adams, Suki Monash, Lawrence Whitley."

"I'll check my files and get back to you."

"Point of interest," Becker said, before the guy's ass slammed all the way shut. "I think I should mention that Suki Monash was found dead this morning. Corinne Adams was murdered a week before Lila Mae and Dwayne Summers. We're thinking Suki's death is related to the other homicides."

"Suki Monash, did you say? Yeah, I knew her. She used to work for the federal reserve mint in Denver. Got busted for narcotics and lost her bonding."

"Is that how you met her?"

"No. She hooked up with a crew carving plates. We busted them about six years ago. She turned state's evidence and bargained down to a possession beef. Last I heard, she was working all the angles as a jailhouse snitch. Unhealthy business, that."

"Something caught up to her," Becker said. He thanked Agent Long and promised to keep in touch before hanging up. Shore and Newsome hadn't returned to the office. Becker scribbled a hasty note that he had some additional information about their homicide victim and left it on Shore's desk.

He returned to his desk to find Rico studying the autopsy reports on Lila Mae and Dwayne Summers.

"Did you see this?" he asked, holding up a photograph of Lila Mae's back. The picture showed rows of old burn scars, twenty-two of them according to the medical examiner's notes. Their size and shape suggested cigarette burns. Their location told Becker that they weren't self-inflicted.

Munch saw the mailman walk into Lou's office. Fifteen minutes later Lou paged her on the intercom. When she went to see what he wanted, he had an opened envelope on his desk. Next to the envelope, which was addressed to him, was an unfolded sheet of paper.

"What?" she asked.

"This came today," he said.

She looked down on his desk and saw that the long sheet of paper was a xeroxed copy of her police record. Fortunately, most of it wasn't news to Lou. Most of it. She reached down to snatch it, but he blocked her hands.

"You don't seem that surprised," he said.

She told him about the incident at the ballpark and then gave him a brief rundown of Noreen Ramsey's escalating attempts to make her life miserable. "She even stole my trash, I think."

"Stole your trash? What a nut." Lou picked up a pencil. It snapped between his fingers. "We've got to stop her."

"I don't know what's left to do, short of doing her grave bodily harm." She was only half-joking.

"I'll call a guy I know," he said. "Jim McManis. You remember him. The guy with the black Jaguar."

"The guy who always bitches about the bill?"

"Yeah. He's a lawyer."

"I thought you hated lawyers."

"That's not the point. McManis practices criminal law and he's good at what he does. Let me see what he says."

"Don't run up a big bill."

"Don't worry about it. He owes me."

And I owe you, Munch thought.

Lou made the call, explaining the situation without bringing her name into it. Two minutes later he hung up and turned to Munch. "He says it's a felony for any law enforcement personnel to access your records without cause."

"What makes him think someone in law enforcement did this?"

"They're the most likely candidates, the people with access to the computers. Cops and probation officers. The good news is that anytime someone uses their terminal to request information, they have to use their access number."

"Why is this good news?"

"We can nail the bastard," Lou said. "McManis said to call the cops and register a complaint. That'll make them investigate. I think he's right. You've got cop friends. Use them. Call that St. John guy. I know he's on medical leave, but he's still got some juice and he owes you."

"He's still out of town," Munch said. "I know someone else, though."

Lou folded the rap sheet back into thirds, using the

original crease marks. He put it back into the envelope and handed it to her. "You want to use the phone in here?" he asked. "I was just leaving. You could have your privacy."

She half-smiled, thinking, *Boy, you can run, but you can't hide.* When and what to tell Rico about herself had been on her mind all morning. One half of her internal committee said to come clean with the guy before the relationship progressed any further. The other half voted to wait until he was in love and wouldn't care as much. A few more nights like last night should do the trick. Only now it seemed she no longer had the luxury of time. If Rico was going to learn about all this, then she wanted it to be from her and she wanted it to be face-to-face. Surely after last night's magic he would be on her side.

She pulled his card from her wallet and dialed his number. A woman answered, "Pacific Division."

"Detective Chacón, please."

"He's not in at the moment. Would you like to leave a message?"

"Tell him I have something I need to show him," Munch said. She left her name and number and then went back to reassembling the carburetors that were spread out in a hundred little pieces across the workbench.

Chapter 24

Ellen coasted her dad's sedan into the driveway with the motor off. She let herself quietly into the house and went directly to the bathroom. Minutes later she had removed the short dark wig. She almost laughed out loud when she read the cash receipt Noreen Ramsey had insisted she take. It was made out to Georgette Feinstein in the amount of nine thousand dollars. Of course, Georgette Feinstein had been no more real than the money itself.

Noreen had not wanted to take the cash at first, though Ellen had seen the greed light up the old witch's eyes as soon as Ellen had shown her the bundles of hundreds. Cold hard cash, especially large piles of it, made people do all sorts of out-of-character things. The desire was there. Noreen just needed a few well-placed nudges to her psyche to make the final plunge. And Ellen had known just where to hit.

The fictional Georgette Feinstein was getting back at her good-for-nothing husband. It was his cash,

Ellen/Georgette explained, skimmed from the profits of his fiberglass-manufacturing plant. The bum was cheating with his secretary, and his wounded wife needed a place to call her own. What better justice was there than for the injured wife to spend the lout's unreported cash?

Noreen had agreed and taken the bait like the fish she was. The personal mayhem to Noreen as a result of that decision was going to be fun to watch. Very fun indeed.

Ellen flushed the receipt and then went out into the kitchen to make her daddy a nice big breakfast. *Fiberglass-manufacturing plant,* she thought, chuckling. What hat had she pulled that one out of? There were times she just flat-out amazed herself.

Rico parked in a considerate spot on the lot, Munch saw, away from the flow of business. He had another man with him. A real cop-looking guy with a rough complexion and a big gut. *Must be his partner,* she thought. She finished removing the intake manifold bolt she been working on and dropped it in the sturdy cardboard box she used to store parts.

From under the hood she saw Rico stop and ask directions from a pump attendant who pointed in her direction. *Okay,* she told herself, *just get this over with.*

She came out from under the hood and he spotted her.

"Munch," Rico said, "this is my partner, Detective Becker."

She couldn't help but wince at the introduction—his first between her and one of his associates. She was "Munch," but his partner was "Detective."

Becker extended his hand.

Munch held up her own greasy ones. "Hi," she said. "Let me wash up."

Rico followed her over to the sink. She scooped a handful of waterless hand cleaner and worked the blue goop over her fingers. Rico stood over her and spoke in a voice only loud enough for her ears. "Your message said there was something you wanted to show me?"

"It's in the office," she said.

He grinned. "Is it, now? Should I tell Becker to go grab a cup of coffee?" His knuckles stroked her belly just above her waistband. Even through the fabric of her uniform shirt, the effect on her body was immediate.

"No," she said. "It's not that. It's something else. Police stuff."

"Something about Ellen?"

"No. Something about me." She rinsed off the soap and grabbed a paper towel. "Eight years ago I was a different person."

"Eight years ago, so was I."

"No, I mean completely different." She took a deep breath for courage. "I used to do drugs. I don't anymore."

"You had to be just a kid then."

She wished he would stop interrupting. This was already difficult enough. "I was twenty-one when I stopped."

"So what's the problem? How bad could you have been?"

"You know that expression, 'Couldn't get raped in Watts'? That was me." The words came out of her mouth before she had a chance to review them—half joke, half challenge.

"Why are you telling me this?"

Why *did* she always do this? she wondered. Ruby called it self-sabotage, a form of control, she said, beat those Munch feared would judge her to the punch.

"Follow me." She led him into the office. She noticed Becker watching them and wondered if Rico had told his partner how he had spent the previous evening. Lou looked up when they walked in.

"Lou, this is Rico Chacón. He's a cop."

"You tell him?"

"I was just getting to it," she said. "Would you mind if we were alone?"

Lou grabbed his ever-present cup of coffee and left.

Munch reached into her back pocket and pulled out the letter that had arrived in the day's mail. He reached out to touch her hand, but she pulled away.

"Does this have to do with Noreen Ramsey?" Rico asked. "We stopped by her office today and had a word with her."

"You did? Think it's going to do any good?"

"Truthfully?"

She nodded.

"I doubt it. But at least we're building a case."

"Well, add this," she said, handing him the letter. "It came this morning." She watched him unfold the paper, start to scan it. As he read, his mouth clamped shut. She expected him to look at her, but his eyes wouldn't leave the page. Her only clue to his reaction were the muscles in his jaw giving an occasional twitch. He said nothing.

"On Sunday," she told him, "one of these was

posted on the bulletin board at the park where Asia and Lindsey play softball. She picked up Lindsey before I got there and apparently left it."

He refolded the paper and put it back in the envelope. His eyes were a darker brown than she remembered when he finally looked at her, and his voice was huskier when he spoke. "What did you want me to do?"

"A lawyer told Lou that you could use the police computers to trace the person who requested this document. That it was a felony to misuse people's records like this."

"I'll need to take this with me."

"Is that all you have to say?" she asked.

"You should have told me about this sooner," he said.

She wanted to ask him why, if it would have made a difference, but the words wouldn't form on her tongue.

A knock on the doorjamb interrupted the moment. Becker stuck his head around the half-open door. "Sorry to intrude," he said.

"Not at all," Munch said. She folded her collar up to hide the love bites on her neck. "Come in."

Rico slipped the envelope into the breast pocket of his sports coat.

"I'm looking for your friend Ellen Summers," Becker said. "According to her building manager, she's not been at her apartment."

Munch shot a look at Rico, wondering how much of their pillow talk he'd passed on. She decided to assume pretty much everything that pertained to Ellen and tried to remember exactly what she'd said. "Ellen is staying with her dad for a couple of days."

"How's she doing?" Becker asked, as if he really cared. He looked her in the eye when he talked to her. She also liked that he wore a thick gold wedding ring that looked as if it didn't come off easily.

"She's coping," Munch said.

"My wife was just saying something about the grief process the other day," Becker said. "There's four stages. Denial, bargaining, anger, acceptance."

"How long have you been married?" Munch asked.

Becker blinked. "Twenty-eight years."

"Congratulations," Munch said, but she wasn't surprised. He seemed the type. Probably had grand-kids too.

"So Ellen is staying with her father?" Becker said.

"For the time being anyway," Munch said. "I know they're working together on the funeral arrangements." Munch felt tears well in her eyes. She wiped them away with her sleeve. The words "funeral arrangements" suddenly made Lila Mae's death real all over again.

"Tragedy in a family sometimes works to bring everyone closer. Do you have a phone number or address?"

"Sorry, no. Somewhere inside the VA."

"Can you take us there?" Becker asked.

Munch was in a quandary. She wasn't comfortable leading the cops to Ellen unannounced. What if they found her in violation of her parole? Ellen wasn't a suspect. Her dad hadn't even been in town when the murders happened. These cops were just trying to gather information. She wanted to help, but not at Ellen's expense. Her stomach growled loudly. She stuck her fist under her rib cage to quiet it. "Even if I remembered which house was his, I don't have the time right now. I'm sure Ellen will be calling me later. As soon as she does, I'll let her know you want to talk to her."

Becker handed her a business card. "Has she discussed her mother and stepfather's murder with you?"

"It's all we talk about," Munch said. "I knew them too, you know."

"Where do you think we should be focusing our investigation?" Becker said.

Munch affected a thoughtful expression, as if she needed a moment to think that one over. In reality, the answer was obvious. If she were the cop, she'd zero in on Ellen and not let up until something broke. But she couldn't very well say that. Not only would it screw up her plan to set things right, but she also didn't want either of these two men to think she was the kind of person who didn't back her friends. He waited for her to say something. She felt her eyes roll upward as she tried to remember how much she should know.

She sneaked a look at Rico. He wasn't looking at her. She hoped it was because he was worried she would reveal knowledge of the case she shouldn't have. That she might let slip to his partner some of the stuff he had told her. The alternative was that he was too disgusted with her to look at her. *Screw it,* she thought, *I am who I am.* She looked Becker in the eye. "I still can't believe it happened," she said.

"Tell me about Lila Mae Summers," Becker said. "What sort of person was she?"

"Nice," she answered immediately. She conjured up an image of Lila Mae in her kitchen, dressed in a shapeless cotton print dress that buttoned up the front, hair going gray, feet stuck in fuzzy slippers. Shoulders slumped and mouth grim. "She had it hard, you know?"

"How's that?" Becker asked.

"Putting up with us for one thing." Munch saw another image of Lila Mae from ten years ago. This time it was outside the emergency room of a hospital, a thin blue cardigan sweater over her pink Denny's uniform, the straps of her black patent leather purse looped over her folded arm, her eyes red from crying. Ellen was inside, having her stomach pumped.

"And by 'us' you mean?"

"Me and Ellen, whoever we were hanging with. Lila Mae would try to keep the household under control, but she was always tired. Worn out and just sort of resigned to her fate."

"What fate was that?" Becker asked.

Not to be beaten to death by some asshole biker, Munch wanted to say. *Not to be found in a pool of her own blood.* "She worked as a waitress at Denny's. That's a hard job for an older woman, to always be on her feet. She worked the night shift. I used to work a night shift at a cab company in Venice. In some ways the night is great. Quieter. Less people bugging you when you're trying to concentrate. But it also brings out a lot of weirdos and your inner clock gets all screwed up."

"What about Dwayne?"

"He was pretty worthless," Munch said, the words slipping out, greased by truth, yet still unkind. Sometimes she was a jerk, a big-mouthed jerk. She'd been raised better than to speak ill of the dead. "Uh, sorry. I shouldn't have said that."

"Why?"

"Because whatever he was or wasn't isn't for me to judge."

"Right now," Becker said, "it's too soon to rule out anything that might matter. How did Ellen feel about her stepfather?"

"You'll have to ask her that."

"Do you know a woman named Suki Monash?" Becker asked.

The change of subject caught Munch off guard. For just a moment she wished she still smoked. Pulling out a cigarette and lighting it would give her a few moments to think. "Hmm, Monash, did you say?" She picked up the work orders on the desk and sorted them. The phone rang, and she answered it before it completed its first ring. "Bel-Air Texaco."

It was Frank from the parts store needing the VIN number on the Buick she was working on. Midyear the manufacturer had changed the engine configuration on the engine. The VIN number would tell him which gasket set she needed. She cast the detectives an apologetic look. "I'll get it for you right now," she told Frank. She turned to Becker and said, "This'll just take a minute."

She walked out to the Buick and went through the glove box until she found the registration. While she was there she decided that she would just play dumb. She knew they hadn't spoken to Ellen. But maybe Suki had been nabbed for something and given up Munch. If that were true, then they would know about the money. Or at least that Ellen *said* she had a stash of thousands of dollars. The only thing either Munch or Suki saw on Sunday morning at her house were the five bills Ellen spread across the table. For all either of them knew, those were all she had. Munch was thinking corroborating witnesses now, thinking like a goddamn criminal instead of a good citizen.

And as to knowing who Suki was? Munch could always say that she had only met the woman once and she never got a last name. All true enough. She returned to the office at a slow walk, lifted the receiver, and read Frank the Buick's VIN number. He said he'd have her her gaskets by the afternoon, three at the latest. He had to pick them up from the other warehouse. She thanked him for his efforts and turned back to the detectives.

"Where were we?"

"Suki Monash?" Becker said.

"I don't think I know anyone by that name," she said.

"You're sure?"

"Maybe if I saw her."

"All right, just taking a shot," Becker said, but he gave her a long speculative look before continuing. "Don't forget to have Ellen call me."

"As soon as I hear from her." Munch held Becker's steady gaze. "I'll do everything I can to help you solve these murders."

"You've got my card," Becker said. Then he walked out of the office, leaving Munch alone with Rico.

She stood before him with her arms at her side. "So is that it?" she asked. The pause after her question seemed to go on forever as she waited for his answer.

"I'll call you later," Rico finally said, and then followed his partner out the door. She noticed that he had made no move to touch her. That said everything, didn't it? So much for denial. Bargaining probably wasn't worth the breath. According to Mrs. Becker, she should be all the way to anger by now. But she wasn't angry. All she felt was a weight in her stomach. A weight that was oddly empty, both oppressive and hollow.

After the cops cleared the driveway, she picked up the phone and called information. There was no listing, new or otherwise, for an Elliot Dane in Westwood. And why would there be? He was only passing through.

Before leaving the office she took the lawyer's card out of Lou's Rolodex. She was glad to see McManis's home number written on the back. When you needed one of those guys, it usually wasn't during office hours.

Chapter 25

Ellen scrambled up some eggs and sliced cheese. In another pan she fried bacon.

The Colonel emerged from his room fully dressed. "Something smells good," he said.

"I'm making you an omelet. How do you take your coffee?"

"Black."

He went behind the bar and came up with an unopened fifth of Jim Beam. She handed him a steaming mug of coffee. He cracked open the bottle and poured a generous dollop into his mug, then offered her the bottle. She declined, knowing that if she started now she'd lose the whole day.

"Did you get the paper?" he asked.

"On the table." She'd even put the sports page right on top.

He sat down and began to read. She added the cheese and bacon to the cooking eggs and popped two slices of bread into the toaster. Her senses took in everything. The smell of his aftershave, the gentle rustling of the paper as he turned the pages, the sizzling pops of the cooking food. How different her life might have been if she could have grown up with memories of a real father. Not Dwayne, in his T-shirt, fat gut hanging out the bottom. Telling Lila Mae, "Yes, Mother," as he dragged his ass out of the Barcalounger to fetch her a soda or check the sprinklers. Not that, a real man. A strong man who took control of his household, went to work every day, and sometimes brought his little girl presents just because he loved her and was thinking of her.

"Daddy," Ellen said, setting his plate of food in front of him, "I think I know who killed Lila Mae."

The Colonel paused in the buttering of his toast. "You do?"

"Yes. It was this guy I used to work for. A real mean son of a bitch. Big guy."

"Do you want to go to the police?"

"Well, that's the thing." She picked up his second piece of toast and spread it with butter, matching his movements, trying to make it exactly how he liked it. "I can't go to the police without, um, you know, uh . . ."

"Implicating yourself?" he asked. "How can that be? You were in prison when it happened. You couldn't have been involved." He poured another dram of whiskey into his coffee. This time when he offered, Ellen did accept just a smidgen in her own cup, only enough to take the edge off her hangover.

"This has more to do with the why of it than the how of it," Ellen said, taking a healthy swallow and glad to see he was willing to hear her out.

"So what do you want to do?" he asked. "You can't

let this guy get away with murder. We owe your mother that much. What's this guy's name?"

"Billy Vega," Ellen said, and as she could have predicted the Colonel's little black notebook came out of his pocket. She handed him a pen and poured herself just a speck more of the booze. "And then there's this other fella. Fred Purcell. He says he's some kind of private investigator. He threatened me the other day, said he'd do the same thing to me he did to Lila Mae."

"He said that?" the Colonel asked, pausing in his writing, but not looking up.

Ellen hesitated only a second. That skinny little geek had all but said it. "Yes."

"You said you knew the why of it."

"They're after money." She paused for a moment. "Some money I fell into."

"Did you steal it?" he asked.

Now here is the tricky part, Ellen thought, *how much of the whole truth to tell.*

"I was in a car wreck last summer. This guy kidnapped me, and then the car we were in crashed."

Crashed because Munch rammed it.

"I was dazed, and the fireman gave me this bag he thought was mine."

The fireman fetched me the bag when I asked for it.

"What happened to the kidnapper?" Dane stopped writing.

"He died before he got to the hospital."

From injuries sustained before, during, and after the accident.

"When I looked inside the bag, I saw it was full of money, but it was so long after the fact. The cops were gone already, and no one ever asked me about it, so I kept it."

"How do you get yourself in these predicaments?"

"I wish I knew," Ellen said, lifting her coffee to her mouth.

"And these two men," he consulted his notes, "this Billy Vega and Fred Purcell, want to force you to give them the money."

"Right," Ellen said. "They knew I couldn't go to the police because then I would have to explain where I got the money."

"And they killed your mother looking for it."

"That's what I think."

"Well," he said, "that's some story, all right. But it does all seem to fit."

"There's one more twist," she said. "Something old Billy doesn't know. The money turned out to be queer."

The Colonel chuckled, shook his head, and lifted his mug to her as if to offer a toast. His reaction to her confession surprised her. She thought he would be more upset. But then he was a military man, she reminded herself, and those types were probably trained to keep cool in action. She felt so much better getting the whole mess off her chest. If only she could have grown up with a parent she could confide in—one who didn't fly off the handle at every little thing.

"Now don't go blaming yourself for what happened to your mother," he said. "What happened to her was horrible, but nothing you made happen. There must be some way you can put the police on the right track."

"We have a plan," Ellen said.

"Who's 'we'?"

"My friend Munch, the one who brought me over here last night."

"What's her involvement with all this?"

"She's on our side. She wants to make those suckers pay for what they did."

"And how does she propose to do that?" He tipped the bottle of Jim Beam toward her cup. She let him top her coffee off with the whiskey. It was a good mix, the caffeine and booze, the effects of the one offset the other.

"We're going to set the suckers up," Ellen said. "I'm going to give them the money and then drop a dime to the feds."

"But won't they just point the finger right back at you?"

"We weren't planning on telling the feds immediately. We're going to give Billy and Freddy-boy a chance to spend a little, get themselves in good and deep."

"Sounds like you're working all the angles. But how is that going to get them arrested for your mama's murder?"

"Munch says we'll just have to take what we can. She knows a homicide cop. She's going to point him at Purcell and Billy; hopefully other evidence will tie them to the scene. You know how the cops always gather little fibers and make casts of footprints just hoping they can link it to someone later. Or maybe Vega and Purcell still have something with her blood on it, or her fingerprints. Something they took from the house."

"Maybe they'll find the gun that shot Dwayne."

"That would do it," she said. "Can I use your phone?"

"Baby, you don't have to ask. Who are you going to call?"

"Munch."

"Let's leave her out of this," he said. "I don't want you taking any more risks by yourself. I'm here now."

"Shouldn't I tell her what's going on?"

"The less people involved in this, the better. I'll help you bring your mama some justice. Let me just think a minute."

"What do you want me to do?"

He handed her the classifieds. It was opened to the employment section. "Shouldn't you be looking for a job?"

"Absolutely," she said.

"You line up some prospects and I'll drive you."

She was too overwhelmed to speak, only nodding her head. He patted her hand and left the room. She took another sip of her coffee and squinted at the paper through her tears, circling jobs she thought she had a shot at.

"Activity Assistant for Santa Monica Hospital, great benefits, will train." Sounded promising.

"Answering Service." Another "will train."

"Assembly." No thanks.

"Auto. Parts Driver. Must bring DMV printout. Many bnfts. Apply in person." Possibility. Wouldn't that just be something else again if she could get a job where she'd see Munch every day?

"Beauty. Stylist with strong hair-cutting skills. Busy Beverly Hills shop." She circled that one twice and then dialed the number. There would be good money in tips from a place like that. And if there was one thing she knew, it was hair.

"Beverly Hills Beauty," a woman answered.

"I'm calling about the . . ." She looked again at the ad, realized she had trouble focusing on the tiny print.

"Yes?"

"Uh, you know, the stylist job." The word came out "shtylist." Great first impression. *Damn,* she thought, *it's gotten a bit tipsy out.* "I'll call back," she said and hung up the phone.

The Colonel emerged from his bedroom.

"Anything look promising?" he asked.

"A few."

"Where do you want to start?"

Ellen knew what she had to do, what would get her right for the day. She needed to be sharp, to wake up. She really didn't want to go back to Lenny's and put up with that dog of his. Not to mention that she didn't want to take the chance of running into Roofer Russ. Maybe Suki could fix her up with a little wake-me-up.

"There's a part store," she said, "looking for a driver. I'll have to stop by the DMV and get a printout first. I think there's one in Culver City."

"All right then," he said. "Let's get cracking."

The Colonel drove her to the Department of Motor Vehicles. Before she got out of the car, he handed her a mint and winked at her. She told him it would take a while so there was no point in waiting.

"I'll pick you up in a hour," he said. "You think that will give you enough time?"

"Sure, sure. You go on and I'll see you in a bit." She

waved good-bye, waited a couple minutes, then headed off for Suki's place.

At one o'clock Munch grabbed the keys of the Volkswagen Rabbit on which she was supposed to run a smog check.

"I'm going to pick up some lunch," she told Lou. "Want anything?"

"Where you going?" he asked.

"Up to you. You want chicken or burgers?"

"Surprise me."

The Rabbit belonged to an older lady named Mrs. Stuart. The mileage was low for the year model, and the black soot collected in the end of the exhaust pipe told Munch that Mrs. Stuart only did occasional short-trip driving. The VW had an oxygen sensor that controlled the fuel injection. Oxygen sensors didn't kick in until they were good and hot. Munch knew she'd improve the car's chances of passing by taking it for a quick run on the freeway and burning off the built-up carbon in the exhaust. At least that was the part of the truth she told Lou.

She jumped on the freeway at Sunset and headed north. At Mulholland she got off the freeway and came back down Sepulveda. When she got to the entrance of the VA, she turned in and found Ellen's dad's rental bungalow with little trouble. The Ford wasn't in the driveway. She parked in front and got out. The street was empty of traffic and people. She walked up to the door and knocked. No answer. She rang the bell. While she waited, she looked around. The coffee can by the door was full of cigarette butts. She shuddered. The guy must be a chain-smoker.

She looked in through the window and saw a half-empty bottle of Jim Beam on the kitchen counter. Munch wondered briefly if a nonalcoholic might see the same bottle as half full. Either way, it appeared that Ellen and her dad had wasted no time finding common ground. Guess it was obvious from which side of the family she'd inherited her addiction-prone personality. There was a newspaper folded neatly on the coffee table. Ellen's luggage was stacked against one wall.

Munch shaded her eyes against the sun's glare and continued to study the room. She was deciding to leave a note when she spotted the Colonel's little black notebook on the floor. It must have fallen out of his pocket on his way out. She wondered what else he had written in there about her. Truth be told, there was nothing as irresistible as reading a person's private notes to himself in longhand. She had once dated a guy who wrote a pro and con list of their relationship on lined notebook paper. She found it in the trash. In the "pro" category he had written that his truck needed a tune-up. For "con" he wrote "Goes to AA, damaged goods."

Right after reading that, she wrote her own list and decided the guy wasn't so great a catch. His good points were that he was cute and funny. They didn't quite outweigh the fact that he was unemployed and talked to himself when he thought he was alone.

She tried the door. It was locked. She walked around to the side of the house to the kitchen door. There was a decal of the American flag pasted to the window with the caption THESE COLORS DON'T RUN. The door was locked, but the window in the center of the door slid open with only a little encouragement from her pocket screwdriver. From there it was a simple matter to jiggle the screen free, reach inside, and unlock the door.

She walked in without looking around, acting as if she belonged there. Already her uniform made her partially invisible. Working stiffs such as water-delivery guys or fire extinguisher–service people could walk into just about any business unmolested. They just blended in.

Munch kept her posture erect and attitude positive yet casual. The first thing cops always asked possible witnesses was *Did you see anyone acting suspiciously?* Hunched shoulders and furtive looks set off warning signals in people's brains. Even if they weren't aware of it at the time, it made them remember.

Just to be on the safe side, she rehearsed excuses. She could always say she was worried about her friend. That they had agreed to meet, and Munch thought something might have happened to her. She'd even play the distraught-daughter-of-a-murdered-mother card if she had to. All valid reasons for her to check up on Ellen.

Munch walked through the kitchen with its lingering odors of bacon fat and coffee. She smelled the whiskey too. Sickening sweet. She picked up the black book and leafed through it, looking for references to her and hers.

She discovered that and more. She only half-heard a car pulling into the driveway. Its significance didn't register until she heard the key in the front door.

Chapter 26

"May I?" Rico asked, walking over to the black chalkboard and picking up a piece of chalk. He and Becker were back in their office.

"Please do," Becker said.

Rico divided the chalkboard into a three-by-three grid. He wrote the names of the murder victims into the four corner squares and the dates of their deaths. *Corinne Adams, January 10; Lila Mae Summers, January 17, Dwayne Summers, January 17; Suki Monash, January 22.* He drew a line between the first two and wrote *broken fingers, females.* Between Suki Monash and Lila Mae Summers he drew a line and wrote *twisted necks.*

In the remaining squares he wrote the names of all the other players. In the middle square, between Lila Mae and Dwayne, he wrote Ellen Summers, and made a note of their relationships to each other. Then he added the name Elliot Dane between Lila Mae and Ellen Summers with the notation *ex.*

"All right," he said. "What next?"

Becker took the chalk from him and wrote two more names: *Lawrence "Animal" Whitley* and *Billy Vega.* After a moment's hesitation he added one more: *Miranda "Munch" Mancini.*

Rico drew the lines connecting Whitley and Vega to Corinne Adams and wrote *Spearmint Rhino.* He then added *Darlene "Ba-Boom-Ba" Tarrel.*

Now the board was complete with victims, suspects, witnesses, and accomplices. When all the lines were drawn and connections filled in, the chalkboard resembled a morbid game of cat's cradle.

"Let's consider motive," Rico said. He picked up a stick of green chalk and wrote *1) $* followed by *2) Revenge.* He paused for a moment then added, *3) Self-protection / fear of discovery.*

"Now we speculate," he said. "The feds have a counterfeiting case they're working on. Ellen is involved." He drew a dotted line between Ellen's name and the money symbol. "Suki Monash has a forgery jacket and was in prison with Ellen. Let's call up to CIW and find out if the two of them were known associates." He made a note to himself to do that.

"And while we're at it," Becker said, "let's run a TRW credit history on the Mancini woman. Didn't you say she just bought a house?"

Rico nodded. "I'll do that." He pulled an envelope from his pocket. "I've got one other thing to check."

"What's that?"

"Someone's been distributing copies of her rap sheet. I want to run a trace and see who's been accessing her court records."

"Besides us," Becker said.

Rico didn't look up. "Right."

"Okay, I've asked Firearms to run a comparison on the bullet we dug out of Dwayne Summers and the bullets recovered from Purcell's car. I also sent the Spearmint Rhino flyer we found at the crime scene to Questioned Documents to see if they could come up with something. We should know by tomorrow."

The phone rang. "Or maybe that's them now."

It was Josh Greenberg from the DA's office with an update on his request for a warrant on Billy Vega. The search warrant request was being denied. There was an operation in progress, a multiunit task force involving Vice and Organized Crime, formed under the auspices of the U.S. Attorney's office. They were investigating a syndicate of exotic dance clubs and didn't want their efforts compromised by Becker's intrusion.

"Great," Becker said and took the names of the detectives involved. One name was familiar, Abe Hymen. He'd gone through the academy with Hymen a million years ago.

"I'll send you what files I can on the case," Greenberg said.

Becker thanked the state's attorney and hung up. As he waited for his call to Hymen to go through, he looked down at his desk. It was piled high with other cases and hours of backlogged paperwork. He'd let this Summers case get under his skin, and the rest of his work was suffering. But what choice did he have when the body count on this investigation was still rising?

Ellen saw the four police cars parked in front of Suki's building. Thank God she had avoided what had obviously been a raid on the premises. She turned around and walked away. Half a block down she spotted Kenny, the skinny junkie who lived in the unit next to Suki's.

"Hey, Kenny," she said. "What is going on?"

"It's Suki, man," Kenny said through his tears. "Someone wasted her."

She grabbed Kenny's arms and shook him. "Are you sure?"

Kenny twisted away from her. "Of course I'm sure. Suki's dead. Sweet little Suki."

"When did this happen?"

"I don't know," he said. "Sometime during the night. I saw her this morning. Her head was all bashed in and twisted around. Who would kill Suki? She never hurt a soul."

Ellen pushed him away and ran. She could hardly see for the tears. A car honked and barely missed her as she crossed Sawtelle. Her heel caught in the gutter's grating. She felt her ankle twist. Hands reached out to catch her.

"Are you all right?"

Her benefactor was a man in a priest collar.

She let him help her up. "Ouch," she cried, when she put weight on her twisted ankle.

"Did you hurt yourself?"

She tested her ankle. It was sore, but not really injured. She faked a collapse in his direction. He caught her again. "Oh, Lordy," she said. "Now look what I've done."

The priest helped her to the bus bench. She wiped her eyes and smiled at him, wondered if he was the celibate kind of minister and then decided to take no chances.

"Where's the fire?" he asked.

"Oh," she said, wincing as she rubbed her ankle. "I'm running late as usual. Now what will I do?"

The priest looked around, as if trying to find a solution to her dilemma. She decided to help him out.

"Father, you wouldn't be able to give me a lift, would you?"

"Where do you need to go?"

"The DMV. I'm leaving town this week and I have just got a million things to do. Funny, I thought joining the Peace Corps would simplify my life."

"You joined the Peace Corps?"

"Yes, we leave next Monday for El Salvador."

"Let me get my car," he said. "You wait right here."

"Thank you, Father. You are heaven-sent, for sure."

The priest dropped Ellen off at the DMV and helped her limp inside. "Are you going to be all right from here?" he asked.

"I have a ride picking me up, but if you want to say a little prayer for me I would be much obliged."

Chapter 27

Munch heard the front door start to open. She clutched the Colonel's book and dashed for the kitchen. There was no time to get out the back without being seen. She opened a set of louvered doors to what appeared to be a pantry and discovered they sheltered a water heater. It was a tight squeeze but she managed to conceal herself just as the Colonel walked into the house. She could hear the sound of his footfall. He crossed into her view as he walked past the kitchen counter and then into his bedroom. He opened drawers. Several minutes later she saw him pass again. He was carrying something wrapped in a towel. He stopped in front of her. She held her breath. Ten long seconds passed and then Dane picked up his telephone.

"It's me," he said. "She's got it."

He was quiet, then, "I'll call you when we're set." He hung up. A moment later she heard the front door open and close, and then his car started in the driveway. She waited several more minutes until she was sure he was gone and then let herself out the way she had come in.

Her first thought was of Asia followed immediately by Rico. What if she had been caught and had not been able to talk her way out of the situation?

She got into Mrs. Stuart's little Volkswagen. She was doing pretty good until it came time to fit the key into the ignition and she had to use two hands. One to hold the key and one to steady the hand holding the key.

She drove away thinking about the contents of Elliot Dane's little book. She set it on the seat next to her. It was filled with names, phone numbers, and annotations. Ellen's known acquaintances were listed along with phone numbers and brief notes. Several of the names had lines through them, including those of Lila Mae and Dwayne Summers. Munch guessed that meant that those were two who didn't matter anymore. She made a stop at Pioneer Chicken, and then returned to work.

"Anybody call for me?" she asked Lou as she handed over his box lunch of impossibly orange fried chicken.

"Nah," he said. "Who are you expecting? Lover boy?"

She looked at him and tried to think of a response with the appropriate amount of sarcasm, but then to her horror tears sprang to her eyes. Lou, for once, was speechless. She turned away from him, wiping the traitorous tears. She hadn't survived in this world by wearing her heart on her sleeve. His teasing would be relentless now that she had shown him a vulnerability. He surprised her by returning to the office without saying another word.

She went back to work on the Buick. The gaskets still hadn't arrived but she took extra care in scraping all the mating surfaces clean. She called the parts store again and discovered that she wouldn't get the gaskets until late in the afternoon, which meant there was no way the job would be done today. She called the customer and gave him the news. While she waited, she organized her toolbox, cleaned sockets, wound loose coils of wire, and squirted Marvin's Marvel Mystery Oil into the fittings of her pneumatic tools.

She supposed she could call Rico and ask him if he had any luck discovering who had run her record, or better yet, invite him to dinner. Bachelors always liked home-cooked meals, didn't they? The least he could do was talk to her, give her a chance to explain to him that she was not the person she used to be. But she'd told him that already. He could see for himself. Or did he think she was the kind of woman who was casual about who she had sex with? Why wouldn't he think that? She hadn't been that much of a challenge, had she? The hell with him if he wanted game playing, she thought angrily. She wasn't into that. With a cringe she thought of her own words from eight years ago. *I ain't like that*. Had she really changed as much as she liked to think?

When the phone rang an hour later, she made a point of not rushing to answer it. And when Lou paged her, she took her time picking up, even though her heart was doing double-time. She wasn't going to appear anxious.

"Hello?" she said, as casual as she could.

"Something terrible has happened," Ellen said.

"Where are you?" Munch asked, swallowing her disappointment.

"I'm at your house. We've got big trouble."

"No we don't," Munch said.

"It's the you-know-what," Ellen whispered. "It's gone."

"You're damn straight," Munch said. The button for the second line lit up followed immediately by ringing. Typical. No calls for an hour and then two at once. She heard Lou answer his extension in the office. "You and me need to talk," she told Ellen.

"But not on the phone," Ellen said.

Munch rolled her eyes skyward. Did Ellen really think the phone was bugged?

"Munch!" Lou called from the office.

She cupped her hand over the mouthpiece and yelled back to him, "Just a sec. I'm on line one." She turned her back to Lou and the office. "I've got the *groceries,*" she told Ellen. "I thought we were going to wait a day to get ready for our *picnic.*"

"I know that's what we said," Ellen said, "but my dad said he'd help with the *cooking.*"

"Your dad? You told your dad?"

"He wanted to help."

"You sure he can take the heat?" *Why am I fighting this?* Munch thought. She looked down at the phone, saw the light lit but not blinking, which meant Lou hadn't put whoever it was on hold. If it was Rico, then what could Lou and he be talking about?

"Munch?" Lou called again.

"Ellen, I have to go."

"And I need those groceries now," Ellen said.

This was getting ridiculous. "Go back to your dad's house," Munch said. "I'll call you there in a half hour. Give me his number." She wrote as Ellen recited the number and then hung up before Ellen could say another word. Line two went dead at the same moment.

Lou came out of the office waving a piece of paper. "You got a service call," he said. "Some guy locked his keys in his van over on Church Lane. I told him fifteen bucks. Cash."

"All right," she said.

"Hey, cheer up," he said. "Money is money, right?"

She laughed out loud as she took the address from him and then went back to her toolbox to grab her Slim Jim. At least she had something to do. She took the keys to the station wagon they used for service calls and left without looking back.

"Chacón," Becker said, "someone I want you to meet."

Rico put down the papers he was reading and stood.

"Abe Hymen," Becker said, indicating a gray-haired man with a detective shield clipped to the waistband of his suit pants, "Rico Chacón."

The two men shook hands.

"What's up?" Hymen asked. "I got a message from my dispatcher you wanted to talk to me."

"We're working a double homicide. The victims were Lila Mae and Dwayne Summers, happened in Culver City last Thursday."

"Married couple?" Hymen asked. "Did the guy outside and the woman in the house?"

"That's the one," Becker said. "What you don't

know is that the woman was found with her fingers broken, and her daughter used to dance at the Spearmint Rhino."

Rico brought over the murder book and opened it to the pictures of Lila Mae's dead body, with close-ups of the damage to her neck and fingers.

"*Chingow,*" Hymen said, with no apology to Rico for his approximation of the Spanish swear word. "What do you need from me?"

"We picked Vega up yesterday, and when we applied for a search warrant of his workplace, we were denied and your name came up. Tell me what you know about Vega, Lawrence 'Animal' Whitley, and the murder of Corinne Adams."

"Whitley had a controlling interest in three strip clubs. He had one in Inglewood, another in Lynwood, and then the one in City of Industry. We had a damn good case against him, been building it for months. I mean we had it all. Receipts, phone conversations, surveillance videos, couple girls willing to talk. We had him for pandering, narcotics, money laundering. Even the IRS had charges forthcoming. Then it all went to shit two weeks ago. One of our informants warned us that Animal's kingdom was crumbling."

Becker groaned. Hymen always liked stupid puns, and him with a name like that. "Animal's kingdom?"

"Law of the jungle," Hymen said. "A guy does too good, someone's going to want to take him down. The Heathens motorcycle gang targeted him, and he had money worries, big time. He was into loan sharks for six figures, and they don't like to ask twice."

"How does Billy Vega figure in?" Rico asked.

"Vega was Animal's lieutenant. They've known each

other since they were kids. Animal was the brains. Billy was the muscle. About a month ago they were observed arguing by our surveillance teams. Then two weeks ago one of the dancers, Corinne Adams, was found dead in Downey with her fingers broken, which we've learned was one of Lawrence Whitley's trademarks."

"No shit?" Becker said. He and Rico met eyes.

"That's right. Are you looking at Whitley for the Summerses' murders?" Hymen asked.

"I'd like to talk to him."

"We all would. Was there robbery involved in the Summerses' homicide?"

"Looked like someone had been looking for something and honed in on the daughter's stuff. Like I said, the daughter, Ellen Summers, used to dance at the Spearmint Rhino. I interviewed a dancer there named Darlene Tarrel. She said Vega was Corinne Adams's man."

"Yeah, we spoke to the Tarrel broad too." Hymen cupped his hands in front of his chest in pantomime. "She wasn't particularly broken up about Corinne Adams's death. In fact she was a suspect for a while."

"Oy vey," Rico said.

Hymen turned and appraised Rico. Then to Becker he said, "You got yourself a comedian here."

"You should see him juggle," Becker said.

Color rose to Rico Chacón's cheeks.

"Yeah," Hymen said, "some sort of love triangle between Darlene Tarrel and Billy Vega and Corinne Adams."

Speaking of love triangles, Becker thought, watching Rico's reaction. "You still looking at Tarrel?"

"Her alibi checked out, but we're not ready to rule out anybody yet."

"What about Vega?"

"Get this," Hymen said, "he was visiting his dad in Folsom. But now we're looking at him for involvement in Lawrence Whitley's death."

"Whitley is dead?" Becker asked.

"Found his body this morning at a recycling plant in Downey. Guy working the conveyer belt found him. Looks pretty gangland. Hands tied with duct tape, took two rounds in the temple point-blank."

"How long had he been there?" Rico said, moving toward the chalkboard.

"I talked to the foreman. They have a regular processing routine. The trucks unload the glass and aluminum cans to be recycled into their various containers. Each night the day's load is tamped down. Twice a week the full receptacles are dumped on conveyor belts that take the glass or whatever to the furnaces. The container Animal's body was in had been emptied last Monday. It was compressed Wednesday afternoon and then not touched again until Thursday morning. Shift started at five A.M. So we figured the dump was made the night before. The body wasn't crushed and none of the morning crew saw anyone go near the dump site. Do you still have Vega in custody?"

"No, I kicked him loose this morning." Becker said.

"We're going to want to talk to him. Billy Vega was seen meeting with one of the Heathens. Supposedly an enemy, but according to surveillance teams these guys were all buddy-buddy. Obviously there was a breakdown in Animal's security structure. We think that was orchestrated by someone close to him."

"Like his lieutenant?" Rico said.

"Good possibility. And we got the revenge factor. Animal was our number-one suspect in the murder of Corinne Adams. Turns out Billy Vega and Corinne Adams were planning to get married."

"That explains why Vega was so willing to give up his buddy," Becker said.

Hymen chuckled. "Some of my best informants have been Hell's Angels. They'd roll over on their own mothers for a buck."

"Yeah, I've had a few myself like that," Becker said, although he held the belief that assholes like the Angels didn't snitch so much out of an absence of moral code as that they used the cops to help them neutralize their enemies and competition. What the hell, he figured, it all came out in the wash. "Thanks, Abe."

"You be sure to stay in touch now."

"I'll do that," Becker said. "Give my best to Irene and the kids."

They all shook hands again, and then Hymen left.

Rico went back to his desk, retrieved the paperwork he'd been reading, and set it down in front of Becker. "This is the list of who else has been accessing Munch's records. There've been three background requests in as many months, two last week."

"One of which was us," Becker said.

"Yeah. That leaves just the two other instances then." He stabbed at the printout. "The other hit last week was traced to a probation officer in Van Nuys. Perry Wood. And then there was one on November ten of last year."

Becker stared at where Rico pointed. "Perry Wood. Isn't he that guy that got busted last month for selling information to some private dick?"

"The very one," Rico said. "Too bad the PI's name wasn't Fred Purcell."

"Purcell? That was the mope whose ride got all shot up outside the Century Club. Yeah, I had a bad feeling about him too."

Rico nodded and read from his paperwork. "I've already contacted West Valley, and we're welcome to come by and sift through Wood's seized records to see what else might pertain to our case. I bet we're going to find the brother-in-law was hired by that Noreen Baker bitch."

"And the other instance?"

"This is where it gets fascinating. The agency that made the request in November was the State Department."

"Got to be tied to the funny money."

"Which means we're shut out," Rico said. "Questioned Documents also sent us this." He laid down a photocopy of the flyer from the Spearmint Rhino found at the Summerses' murder scene—the one with Ellen Summers's face and scantily clad body. QD had been able to lift some impressions of indented writing across the back. It was the Summers address, written in block letters across the middle. "Looks like this arrived in the mail," Rico said.

"Any return address?" Becker asked.

"No, but they lifted another message, apparently written on a separate piece of paper that was on top of the flyer."

"What'd it say?"

"'I blame you.'"

"The father?"

"I'm thinking."

"Let me run another scenario by you." Becker grasped his chin for a moment and then pointed at all the names on the board. "Suppose someone had a hit in mind and they figure to put the blame on Whitley for the murder by using his technique, maybe planting some other clues that lead us back to the club."

"Possible, sure. But Vega?"

"Maybe he's smarter than he looks," Becker said.

"Or maybe he wasn't acting alone."

Becker nodded. "So Vega and/or this accomplice do the Summerses and leave us with a solid suspect. And then to make things really tidy, our suspect shows up dead. Only, unfortunately for Vega and company, they got a little too cute on their timing. By the time the Summerses were getting killed, Animal was already sleeping with the bottles."

They both walked back to the chalkboard with its lists of victims and suspects. Becker picked up the chalk, amended Animal's status to victim, and added the name Fred Purcell.

"What do you think?" Becker asked.

"I think we need a bigger board."

Rico pointed to Suki's name. "I talked to a Corrections Officer at CIW. Suki and Ellen shared a cell for a while."

"And who knows what else, huh?" Becker said. "What was Suki's job at CIW?"

"She clerked for the warden. The woman I spoke to said she had beautiful penmanship."

"So maybe Suki was working with these guys, supplying information."

"It follows," Rico said. "If this is a conspiracy gone wrong, then our guys are going to want to cover all their tracks." Rico picked up the phone.

"Who are you calling?" Becker asked.

"Munch. She might know just enough to get her killed." He dialed the number from memory, identified himself, and asked to speak to Munch. He listened for a moment, placed his hand over the mouthpiece, and said to Becker, "She's out on a service call."

"Leave a message," Becker said.

Rico was already speaking into the phone again. "Can you have her call me when she returns? It's urgent." He left his direct number and hung up. "Guy said she should be back within fifteen minutes."

"Let's hope we're not too late."

Rico dialed another number.

"Who are you calling now?" Becker asked.

"CIW. I think we'd better find out who all visited Suki Monash while she was a guest of the state."

Chapter 28

Munch knew Church Lane well. She often used the quiet tree-canopied street south of Sunset Boulevard for test drives, especially when she was trying to determine if a bearing howl was coming from the differential or one of the axles. A thirty-foot ivy-covered concrete wall that sheltered the street from the San Diego Freeway worked well to echo problem noises back to her trained ear.

Lou said the customers were in a Dodge van in the 300 block of Church, just north of Montana. There was a church on the corner of Elderwood, then only the fences of side yards. Munch cruised slowly past a hodgepodge of bougainvillea, bottlebrush, and verbena bushes, looking for the address Lou had written down. The customer, some man, had indicated that he would be on the street and waiting for her. The address turned out to be a phantom also—335. Lou must have misheard.

Finally, she spotted a brown Dodge van. She pulled next to the curb and looked for the driver, but saw no one. Maybe he had gone to make another call. She walked over to look in the window. She looked in the driver's side first and then realized the ignition switch was mounted on the column and impossible to see from her vantage point. According to the customer, he had locked the doors with the power switch, realizing one second too late that the keys were still dangling from the ignition. That was the problem with all those electronic bells and whistles; sometimes they outsmarted the drivers. She walked around to the passenger side, her Slim Jim in hand, hoping this year's model didn't have those antitheft plates protecting the lock mechanisms.

She peered in the window, but didn't see the keys. Suddenly a hand pressed into the back of her head, crushing her face against the glass. A second hand gripped the wrist of her hand holding the Slim Jim and twisted it behind her back. The thin steel burglar tool clattered to the ground.

"How ya been, Munch?" a man's voice asked.

"Better," she managed through squished lips. Her cheek moved against the wet spot her mouth made on the glass.

She heard the side door of the van slide open. Her captor lifted her by her belt and the back of her collar and then shoved her roughly into the back of the van. Her hands skidded across the steel floor as she did the best she could to soften its impact. She spun around and kicked at her assailant, recognizing him immediately. Billy Vega. She wished she was wearing steel-toed boots instead of black tennis shoes with grease-resistant soles. Still, Vega grunted as her heel found his knee. He slammed his fist at her, not connecting entirely, but enough to make her ears ring. She screamed. Billy clamped a hand over her mouth.

Someone else had come around to the driver's side of the van and opened the door. "Keep her quiet," the guy said.

"I'm trying," Billy said.

She heard the van start and struggled anew. Mace St. John told her that if she was ever attacked, whether to be robbed or raped, that no matter what else, she shouldn't allow her assailants to take her someplace else.

Billy's hand covered her nose and she felt new panic. She couldn't breathe. She looked up and saw the driver's face in the rearview mirror. It was that skinny guy from Century Entertainment. The one whose car Ellen had shot up. Fred Purcell.

Her lungs felt tight. She forced herself to relax. Struggling would just use up more oxygen. The smart thing to do would probably be to get eye contact with the driver and hope to evoke his sympathy. But she was too angry to do anything but glare at him. He looked away and she felt the van pull into the street.

Her throat ached for air. How long would it take for them to kill her? Five minutes? Ten? She couldn't die. She couldn't do that to Asia, although Mace and Caroline St. John would give her a home. She would be loved, Munch had seen to that. The one losing out would be Munch.

Vega straddled her now. She stared into his face, wishing him dead.

He chuckled. "That's what I always liked about you, Munch," he said. "You've got the heart of a pit bull."

He released her mouth, and she took in one shuddering breath after another. She considered screaming again, but doubted if that would help her.

"What do you want?" she asked.

"We're looking for Ellen."

"I don't know where she is."

He put his knee in her chest and jerked her left hand up. Holding her wrist with one hand, he closed his other around her middle finger and jerked it back. She felt a sharp pain, and knew the bone had broken. Tears filled her eyes.

"Wrong answer," he said. He grabbed her index finger. "Where's Ellen?"

"Okay, okay," she said. "Wait a minute. Please."

He pulled the finger back. Pain radiated down her wrist. She had to put the fiery ache aside. To think. Vega didn't want to hurt her, he wanted the money.

"She said she'd call me this afternoon."

He pulled it back further. She felt tendons and ligaments stretch beyond endurance.

"Fuck!" she yelled at him. He wouldn't buy her act if she gave in too easily. "That's the best I can do. She's been all freaked out, scared about something. Last time I talked to her, *she* didn't even know where she was going to wind up."

A drop of sweat fell off Billy's nose and landed on her lower lip. Munch knew Billy was capable of murder, but it was Purcell's complete lack of agitation that had her worried. The cold-blooded ones were much harder to play, and she needed to give them a way out of killing her.

Billy released her finger and looked at Purcell. "What do you think?"

"This is about your car, right?" she said, also directing her attention to the man in the driver's seat. "Look, you know the woman is nuts. She's always pulling shit and dragging her friends into it. I didn't even know she had a gun. I'm an innocent bystander here."

Billy's eyes darted nervously to Purcell's. His knee eased off her chest.

"I don't want any more problems," she said, feeling encouraged. "Not with you guys. Not with anyone. You don't tell the cops I was driving, and I'll say I fell." She held up her damaged hand. The middle finger was misaligned and her knuckle had disappeared into a mass of purple swollen bruise. "I've got like fifty bucks in my wallet. You can have it."

"She's lying," Purcell said in a flat, almost bored voice.

Billy slapped her face. She tasted blood.

"Shut up and listen," Purcell said. "We want the money, you want to live." He looked at Billy. "Give her the pager number."

Billy rummaged around in the debris on the floor of the van and came up with a brown paper bag. She handed him her pen. He wrote down a phone number and stuck it in Munch's shirt pocket. She flinched as the back of his fingers rubbed against her breast.

Purcell didn't turn around to speak to her. "Tell Ellen she has today to call us. She can play this smart, you tell her, or the world isn't big enough."

"I'll make sure she gets the message," Munch said. In that moment, she hated Ellen, and then she was glad for her pain. She deserved it all. She was an idiot for ever opening the door to Ellen, and now she would have a permanent reminder.

They had made a large circle of the neighborhood and now were back on Church Lane. Purcell pulled alongside the shop's station wagon. Billy opened the door. Munch climbed out. As the van pulled away, she memorized their license plate number, already knowing that it was stolen. Vans, trucks, and limos were issued commercial plates, and the one bolted to the bumper of the brown van belonged on a car. She wished she'd paid attention to that sooner.

She got back in the station wagon, cradling her hand against her chest. She was too angry to feel pain as she drove herself to the hospital. But one thing she was certain of: Billy Vega and Fred Purcell were going to pay. All these sons of bitches were going to pay.

Chapter 29

The emergency room of Santa Monica Hospital was having a slow day, Munch was glad to see. She walked up to the front desk and showed the woman in charge her injury. Within minutes Munch was sitting across from an admissions nurse, reciting her financial and personal information. When she finished that process, another nurse brought her a bag of ice and told her to take a seat in the waiting room.

"How long do you think this will take?" Munch asked.

The nurse checked her watch before saying, "Two hours minimum. We've paged the orthopedic surgeon."

Munch looked up at the big clock on the wall. It was already almost four. She usually picked up Asia no later than five-fifteen.

"Can I call someone for you?" the nurse asked.

"You wouldn't mind?"

"I think I can manage it," the nurse said with a wry

smile, her gaze encompassing the empty waiting room. "C'mon over to the desk."

Munch followed. The nerves in her hand and wrist were beginning to wake up and scream. She let out an involuntary "Ouch."

The nurse had walked around to her side of the workstation and gave Munch a sympathetic look. "Who first?"

She recited Sally Bradbury's number, thinking how someone like Sally would never be responsible for bringing crazy bikers and suspicious homicide cops into her life.

The nurse dialed and then stretched the receiver across the desk. Sally was happy to take Asia one more night, she said, and would explain the situation in a way that wouldn't upset her.

"Oh, shoot," Munch said as she remembered. "I'm watching my friend's dogs. I almost forgot about them."

"You want me to swing by and feed them?" Sally asked.

"I hate to ask. They're friendly, especially if you have Asia with you. She knows where the house key is."

"Don't give it another thought," Sally said. "We all get more than we can handle every once in a while. That's what friends are for."

Munch thanked her with a thick voice. It always caught her off guard when someone she knew and admired claimed friendship. She said she would call again when she was through with the doctor. And when she got her life back.

Lou took the news a little harder, demanding to know how serious the injury was, and what he could do to help. She assured him it wasn't too bad and promised to let him know more as soon as she did. She couldn't tell him how she got the injury. Dragging him into this would only complicate things and maybe even get him hurt. "If my friend Ellen shows up, tell her . . . tell her our picnic plans have changed."

She handed the nurse the phone and thanked her.

"Just have a seat, hon. We'll get to you as soon as we can."

Munch stepped into the waiting room. A television mounted in one corner was tuned to an after-school cartoon show. The show broke for commercial. Business Barbie modeled her suit and attaché case. A news update followed the commercials. Munch's attention riveted on the face of the smiling anchor-woman as she led with her local report.

"A well-known West Side Realtor is being held on counterfeiting charges." The scene cut to video footage, and Munch watched Noreen Ramsey being led out the doors of the Bank of America on San Vicente Boulevard. She was being escorted by two men in black suits and sunglasses. The scene cut back to the studio. "We'll have the full story for you at five," the anchorwoman said.

Munch felt her mouth drop open as she stared up at the screen. Ellen had outdone her again. Munch had only called the local child welfare services and the police; Ellen had brought in the federal government. Munch laughed out loud seeing the witch in hand-cuffs. Then that first feeling of gratification quickly dissipated to be replaced with dread. Was another of Ellen's misguided attempts to help going to backfire? Would Rico see this same newscast and make the connection back to Munch? Her hand throbbed with each pulse of her heart. She rolled her head back to rest on the top of the padded waiting-room furniture and thought, *Fuck it. It's already done.* She didn't feel a bit sorry for Noreen Ramsey. With any luck, and Munch was due some, the feds would keep Noreen tied up and distracted, maybe even give her a new direction to focus her mania. No, if Munch pitied anyone, it was those poor Secret Service agents.

She looked over at the pay phones and thought of Rico and Ellen and which one deserved to be called more. What she wanted was a big time-out before the next round. She drew a quarter from her pocket and flipped it in the air. Heads she'd call Rico, tails Ellen. As the coin circled in the air, she realized she was hoping it would come up heads. She caught it midair, deposited it in the coin slot, and called Rico's private line. After twelve rings, she got an answering machine that cut her off midsentence.

A nurse dressed in green surgical scrubs and holding a clipboard stepped into the waiting room.

"Miranda Mancini?" she called out.

Munch held up her hand. "That's me." She didn't think this news would come as any big surprise to the woman, since she was the only one in the waiting room.

"Come with me," the woman said, and installed Munch in one of the examination rooms. "Dr. Yuen, the orthopedic surgeon, is on the way."

While Munch waited for the specialist, she pulled Elliot Dane's book out of her back pocket and leafed through it again. Suki Monash's name was near the front. Next to her name Dane had listed three different sums of money: $50, $75, and $125. Escalating payoffs? Munch wondered. But for what? Suki's name had been circled and crossed out with a different color pen with today's date written next to it. Dane also had the address and phone number of the Spearmint Rhino, and below that were several names: Billy Vega, Lawrence Whitley, aka "Animal," and Darlene Tarrel, aka "Ba-Boom-Ba." Ba-Boom-Ba had also received several payments, it seemed. Elliot Dane really took the informed father role to its limit.

Twenty minutes later, the door opened again, and a tall brunette woman in a white lab coat bustled in. Her name tag identified her as Dr. Yuen.

Munch brightened at the surprise of a woman surgeon. Dr. Yuen also took in Munch sitting on the examination table in her Texaco uniform. They exchanged half smiles.

"What have we got here?" Dr. Yuen asked.

Munch lifted the ice.

"I see," the doctor said, looking down at the swollen finger. "How did this happen?"

"I fell."

"At work?"

"I was out on a service call and I tripped. I stuck out my hand to break my fall and my finger caught the curb."

"Hmm," the surgeon said, prodding gently. "Looks like a mid-shaft break. How's the pain?"

Munch shrugged. "Getting there."

Dr. Yuen made a note on her chart. "I'm going to send you for an X ray before we reduce this."

"Reduce it?"

"Set the break. Who's driving you home?"

"I'm driving myself."

"Then I can't give you a shot of Demerol."

"A local is fine, Doc."

"I'll write you up for something stronger once you get home."

Munch followed the nurse to the radiology lab. The technician had her stretch out her hand the best she could on a glass-looking plate.

"Are you pregnant?" he asked.

"Not a chance," Munch answered.

The tech aimed the lens of the X-ray machine over her hand and left the room. The machine clicked and flashed bright white. The X-ray guy came back in the room.

"This will just take a few minutes," he said. "You can have a seat in the hallway."

She put the ice pack back in place and went outside to wait.

The same nurse from the waiting room came by and told her she had a visitor. Munch looked up and saw Lou's worried face.

"What happened?" he asked.

"I tripped. Came down on the curb and caught my finger."

She lifted the ice pack. He winced in sympathy.

"I need you to put my tools away and lock my box," she said.

"Sure, anything else?"

"No, that should do it."

The X-ray tech opened his door. "I've got your pictures ready," he said.

Lou insisted on being in on the consultation with the doctor.

"This all could take hours," she said. "I'll be all right. You go on."

"You're sure?"

"No problem. When I'm done here, I'll stop back at the station and trade cars."

"What about your kid?"

"Already handled. She's going to stay over with her friend for another night."

"Call me tomorrow," he said.

"I'll see you tomorrow," she said. "Now go."

"Oh," Lou said, "I almost forgot. That cop called you. Rico Chacón. He said he needed to talk to you."

"When did he call?"

"Right after you left on your service call. He said it was urgent."

"Okay, thanks. I'll call him from here. I'm feeling a little urgent myself." Lou left and she fished in her pocket for change. She had to look up the number in the phone book one-handed. It was an awkward business. She started to get an inkling of how difficult life was going to be for the next month or however long it was going to take to heal.

The recorded message for the police station told her to hang up and dial 911 if this was an emergency. She waited to speak to a live person. Finally a woman came on the line, and Munch asked for Rico Chacón in homicide.

"Is this Kathy?" the woman asked.

"No," Munch said, wondering who the hell Kathy was and not liking how hot she suddenly felt.

"I'll transfer you," the woman said.

Munch was listening to a Muzak version of "These Boots Are Made for Walkin'" when the doctor came back into the hallway and motioned for Munch to join her. Munch hung up and followed the doctor into the treatment room.

Dr. Yuen had the film of Munch's hand, which clearly showed the break. She explained how she was going to set the finger and then splint it. Before she left the room, she gave Munch a small manila envelope full of codeine pills and a prescription for twelve more.

Munch studied the surgeon's precise scrawl on the white slip of paper in her good hand, knowing what she held was a get-out-of-sobriety-free card. Limited time offer. Act now. She opened the small envelope and shook out two pills. They were Tylenol, codeine number 3's.

Hello, darkness, my old friend.

After a brief inner debate, she took one. She wasn't one of these militant sobriety freaks who swore to never take another pill no matter what. God had made drugs for a reason. She was in legitimate pain. Codeine was for pain. A doctor had given it to her. There was no law that said she was absolutely not to appreciate the effects of this medicine.

Of course, she knew she shouldn't like it *this* much.

Within minutes she was savoring the rush of being transported from a state of pain to a state of indifference to the pain. She could feel her dormant junkie cells breathing tiny sighs of relief, like little dehydrated creatures getting a drop of rain after a long drought.

Old thinking kicked in, and she indulged herself with idle speculation. How many minuscule grains of the drug had brought on this blessed release? And if taking one pill felt this good, how much better would three pills feel? One every four to six hours as needed, the prescription said. Munch knew she'd be watching the clock for her next dosage. She wouldn't take a second pill a minute under four hours, but it was highly unlikely she'd wait six. That's what separated her from the "normies" of the world—the non-addicts. She'd talked to them, even dated one or two. He didn't like the sensation, Garret told her once, of being separated from his thoughts, his feelings. She tried to explain to him that for an addict that distancing, that anywhere-but-here feeling was exactly the point.

A slight knock on the door interrupted her thoughts.

"Come in," she said.

It was the good doctor carrying a bowl and scrub brush. She had Munch lie back on the examination table, then pulled up a chair. The table had an extension that lifted out to the side where Munch rested her arm.

"You mind needles?"

"Not especially."

"This is a local anesthetic," Yuen explained. "Before I get started, I'm going to need to clean the area."

"All right." Munch's good hand clenched her belt buckle as Dr. Yuen administered the shot.

"I'm going to give that a few minutes to take effect," Dr. Yuen said. "How are you doing?"

"Just ducky," Munch said. She started to think about the next month and all she had to do. Everything required two hands and ten fingers. How was she going to get her house in order, finish the job at the shop, take care of herself and Asia? She felt tears trickle down the sides of her face.

Dr. Yuen applied the scrub brush. Sweat soaked the

back of Munch's shirt as the surgeon scoured Munch's damaged finger for what felt like twenty minutes. The clock on the wall reported only three minutes had passed. Munch closed her eyes and tried to put herself elsewhere.

"All right," Dr. Yuen's calm voice said. "You're doing great. You're lucky the break was so clean."

Munch rolled her head to watch. The doctor pulled her finger in one deft move and said, "There you go. That wasn't so bad, was it?"

"No, you did great."

"Keep your hand elevated above your heart, and it won't throb as much." She affixed a padded splint and taped it in place. "When the swelling goes down, we'll fit you with a cast."

Dr. Yuen also told her she couldn't work for three weeks. Munch knew she was wrong about that. There was always a way to get around things if you wanted to badly enough.

She walked out through the waiting room. The television was still on and tuned to the same channel. A logo flashed by announcing the five o'clock news show. She hung back and watched, wondering if there would be an update on the big counterfeiting bust, but the story on Noreen was preempted.

The scene on the screen was some industrial building, and the station's roaming reporter was on live with a late-breaking story. "Workers at this recycling plant in Downey," he said, holding a microphone close to his mustache and using the other hand to cup his ear, "made a grim discovery this morning. The body of a man whom police have identified as Lawrence Whitley was found in one of these large recycling vats behind me, dead of an apparent gangland-style execution. Police are speculating that the body has been here several days. Whitley, known on the street as 'Animal,' was the suspected kingpin of a widespread criminal ring that included prostitution and drug dealing."

"Are any suspects in custody?" the anchorlady's voice-over asked.

"Yes, Connie," the reporter said, looking down at his notepad. "In this case, justice has been swift. A warrant was issued this morning for another member of Lawrence Whitley's crime syndicate. An anonymous phone tip led police to this Lawndale residence."

Munch stared at the television and watched as a tousled Billy Vega was led, handcuffed, to a police car. The scene switched back to the reporter.

"This man, William Vega, is expected to be arraigned tomorrow sometime. Back to you, Connie."

Whoa, Munch thought, *what the hell was going on?* Bad guys were dropping like flies, but she had no illusions that it was safe outside yet. She considered calling Rico again, but the waiting room had filled up, and now all the pay phones were in use. Work was only ten minutes away; she could use the phones there for free.

As she drove from the hospital, she rested her elbow on the sill of the car door. There were still too many unanswered questions. What had Elliot Dane's notes about talking to Ellen's coworkers at the club and to Suki meant? What did that phone call that Munch had heard mean? What was he after? How did he even know whom to contact? And who the hell was Kathy?

Her splinted middle finger wrapped in a white bandage, elevated and extended, Munch couldn't help but smile. It looked like she was flipping off the world.

When Munch got back to the station, Lou was gone for the evening. Her toolbox was locked. The lube bay had already been hosed down and the big paneled doors pulled shut. The shop's phone was ringing, but quit before she got to the office door. The crew of gas attendants were all busy at the pumps with the going-home traffic's nightly rush of business.

Elliot Dane's big white rental car was parked in front of the office. A black garment bag hung from the hook over the rear driver's side window.

Ellen rushed out to greet her. She was wearing a wig of brunette hair, styled in a perm of short curls. She'd gone light on the makeup too. Munch was struck by how much she resembled Lila Mae. Adding some gray to those curls would have completed the image.

"I called back when you didn't," Ellen said, "and Lou said you hurt yourself."

Munch held up her damaged hand, figuring that said it all.

"Oh my God. How did that happen?"

"What do you think?"

"Billy?" she whispered.

"And that Fred Purcell guy." Munch produced the scrap of paper with his pager number on it from her pocket. "He'd like to hear from you."

"Oh, he's going to hear from me, all right," Ellen said. "Daddy, look what they did."

Munch looked up to see the Colonel come out of the driver's seat of the rental car. His expression was grim.

"You got the you-know-what?" Ellen asked.

"Yeah, I'm going to need some help." Ellen and her dad followed Munch to her car. She opened the trunk and hefted out the spare tire with her right hand. The Colonel reached out to help, but she already had it out on the ground and was rolling it toward the lube bay. Munch leaned the wheel against the tire machine and turned to Ellen. "I need you in the bathroom before we start."

"Oh, okay," Ellen said, following.

As soon as they were through the door of the bathroom, Munch said to Ellen in a low voice, "What's your dad doing here?"

"He's going to take me to the meet."

"You told him everything?"

"Yeah, he's cool. He wants to help. In fact, he doesn't think I should involve you in this anymore."

Despite herself, Munch felt offended. "He wants to cut me out?"

"It's not like that."

"Ellen, we should rethink this whole deal. Billy's in jail."

Ellen pointed to Munch's hand. "For this?"

"No, for killing Animal."

Ellen stared at her wide-eyed. "Killing Animal?"

"I know," Munch said, "it's crazy out."

"Sounds like we're almost home free."

"Not by a long shot. There's still the other one, Purcell."

Rico hung up the phone in frustration.

"No luck?" Becker asked.

"No. I left messages on her answering machines at home and for her limo business."

Rico's direct line rang. He lifted the phone. It was his CID contact.

"Tony DeSiderio," he said out loud for Becker's benefit.

"I got the information you wanted on Elliot Dane," DeSiderio said.

"Let me put you on speaker." Rico pushed the appropriate button on his telephone and said, "Go ahead."

"It's impressive," the CID agent said. "Dane made a quick rise through the ranks. Colonel in less than twenty-five years. His Duty Station is command of the Q course at Fort Bragg. He was a Green Beret, twice decorated for valor. Planning to retire in a couple of months. Twenty-five years in. Healthy pension. Nothing funny with his finances. No big debts, no liens, no outstanding loans. But I did find one thing of interest. There was a fifteen-six launched last year and then buried."

"What's a fifteen-six?" Becker asked.

"Administrative Investigation. It should have been reported to the CID office, but it wasn't. Base command was probably trying to keep it in-house. Word is this Dane fellow has some serious pull, class-four security clearance, friends in high-high places."

"What was the nature of the complaint?" Rico asked, looking at Becker.

"Some civilian woman claimed that Dane had tortured her."

"Tortured?" Rico raised an eyebrow.

"Dane contended that they had a relationship of consensual sex and that the woman was bitter when it ended," DeSiderio continued.

"What kind of torture?" Becker asked.

"She said he burned her with cigarettes. She had fresh wounds, so it was pretty much a case of his word against hers. I talked to the Fort Bragg CID agent, a guy with no love for commissioned officers, I might add. He said the woman had a sudden change of heart and recanted her entire testimony."

Rico pulled the autopsy photograph of Lila Mae Summers's back out of its folder. He stared down at the array of burn scars between her shoulder blades, then held it up for Becker to see. "Where were the burns?"

"Across her back, I believe."

"When did all this happen?"

They heard papers shuffle on the other end of the line.

"The beginning of November, last year," DeSiderio said.

"You have this woman's phone number?"

"Won't do you any good. She died New Year's Eve. Drunk driver."

"They catch the guy?" Becker asked.

"No, it was hit and run."

"Lucky break for Dane, though," Rico mused, "in case she changed her mind again. A conviction of an assault like that would earn him a court-martial, undesirable discharge—"

"A bust to private, ten hard years in military prison, and bye-bye, pension," DeSiderio finished.

"Dane's name didn't by any chance show up on a military transport's passenger list, did it?"

"No. But he could have hitched a ride with an Agency transport from El Segundo Air Base. The bad news is that you'd have a hard time proving it unless you could show some threat to national security."

Rico thanked him, hung up, and then picked up his chalk and wrote another name on the chalkboard. While he was writing, Becker handed him a piece of paper.

"What's this?"

"Bail receipts for Billy Vega's last three busts. I thought it was interesting how her name kept coming up."

"Huh," Rico said. "I'll be damned."

Chapter 30

Elliot Dane lifted Munch's spare onto the tire machine and centered it on the spline. Munch centered the rim into position with the spinner nut, tightening it by hitting the ridged center of the nut with a large slotted tire spoon. This was an action she usually did without thinking, but one-handed it was awkward and required much more concentration. She then unscrewed the core of the valve stem and waited impatiently for the air inside to escape. Behind her, Ellen used the shop's phone to call the pager number. As prearranged, she left the station's pay phone as the return number.

"How are you going to get the money to Purcell?" Munch asked Ellen when she returned to supervise the operation on the tire.

"I suppose I'll just hand it over," Ellen said, looking none too pleased at the prospect.

"You're better off without it," Munch said. "We'll all be."

"I know. It's just I spent the last six months thinking about all the great things I was going to do, and nothing worked out like I thought."

"Nothing usually does. But that doesn't mean things can't still turn out all right."

"Munch is right, baby," the Colonel said.

Munch looked at Ellen. "What's to stop them from pointing the finger back at you when they get busted with it? You going to say it's their word against yours?"

"I'll say I got it from Suki to give to them, but I didn't know what it was or where it came from."

"Why do that to her?" Munch asked.

"Suki's dead," Ellen said.

"She is? How?"

"Killed. Somebody beat her to death in her bed."

Munch looked at the Colonel. His face was completely void of expression. "When did this happen?"

"Last night sometime."

"Okay, that's it," Munch said. "It's getting way too heavy out here. Let's forget this plan. You know how guys are who kill. Once they start, it just gets easier for 'em. Why don't you talk to a lawyer? Play this straight up. Maybe you can work out some kind of immunity deal."

"Lawyers cost money," Ellen said.

Munch turned to Elliot Dane, hoping he wouldn't pick up on the suspicion forming in her mind. "Maybe your dad can help with that."

"No," the Colonel said. "We've come this far. We have to go through with it."

"Listen," Ellen said, "if you want out, that's cool. We can handle it from here."

Munch wanted nothing more than to get out, go home, take a pill, a hot bath, climb into bed, and pull the whole fucking mattress over her head. But she knew she couldn't.

"Let's get our story straight anyway," she said.

"I'll just stick to the truth," Ellen said. "Purcell and Vega have been after me because they think I have a bunch of money. In fact, I suspected they killed my mama and Dwayne as some kind of message to me."

"But you didn't tell the cops because you were in fear for your life," Munch said.

"That's good. And I went to Century Entertainment thinking Billy was my friend—"

"I'm not sure you should mention Century Entertainment." Munch made her good hand into a gun to remind Ellen of *that* felony.

"Oh, right," Ellen said, smacking her forehead. "What was I thinking?"

"I need you to focus," Munch said. "This is some serious shit."

"I hear you."

"Remember, keep it simple. The less you say, the better." Munch pressed the foot lever that operated the tire machine's pneumatic bottom spoon. It lifted with a whoosh. The bottom bead of the tire broke with a dull pop. She released the foot lever, swung the upper spoon into place, nestled the shovel attachment under the lip of the rim, and pressed. The top bead broke free. She picked up the slotted tire spoon and worked the curved end inside the tire, then she fitted the slotted handle over the corresponding flattened top of the spline.

"You want me to do anything?" Dane asked.

"Not yet," Munch told him. She held the spoon in place with the palm of her left hand and then pushed the foot lever once more. The spline turned, rotating the spoon under the lip of the tire and lifting it over the edge of the rim. She released the pedal, and the spline returned to its original position with a sigh of escaping air.

"This is where I need your help," she said.

"What do you want me to do?"

"Reach inside here and pull the pillowcase out."

"What should I do?" Ellen asked.

"Keep a lookout."

Dane found a corner and tugged. Five minutes later he had successfully freed the bag of money. Munch talked him through helping her remount the tire.

"If you want to wash up," she told him, "there's a sink in the corner. The hand cleaner is in that white tub on the floor."

He went off to clean up while Munch rolled her tire back out to her car. Ellen followed, the bag of money slung over her shoulder.

Munch reached into her coat pocket for her keys. The lining pulled inside out, and she realized for the first time how she usually used her left hand to hold the bottom of her pocket from the outside. How many other simple gestures had she always taken for granted?

"What's this?" Ellen asked, pointing at the hickey on Munch's neck.

"What does it look like?"

"Anyone I know?"

"Don't change the subject. You have other problems. The cops were here today. Becker and Rico, the same ones investigating Lila Mae and Dwayne's murder. They're looking for you. Wanted to talk to your dad too. They asked me to take them over to his place, but I said I was too busy. Before they left, Becker asked me if I knew Suki Monash."

"What did you tell him?"

"I played off like I didn't know her. What did your dad say about Suki getting killed?"

"She wasn't anybody he knew."

"Did he say that?"

"No, why?"

The pay phone rang. Ellen's eyes widened. "I guess it's show time," she said.

Munch followed Ellen out to the pay phone mounted on the wall by the bathrooms, rolling her tire with her right hand, and holding her broken finger shoulder-high. The Colonel had finished cleaning up and had put on a pair of leather driving gloves. He walked over to the service counter and picked up the phone. "Do I need to dial nine?"

"Not if it's local," Munch said, wondering who he needed to call right this minute.

"I'm just going to check on my flight," he said, and then turned his back to them and made his call.

"Hello?" Munch heard Ellen say into the phone. Then, "No, I don't have it. But I know who does."

Ellen looked at Munch and winked. Dane finished his call, took the sack of money from Ellen, and headed toward his rental car.

"No, you asshole," Ellen said into the phone. "She had nothing to do with it, and I don't appreciate what you did to her either." Ellen pointed to Munch when she said "she."

Munch balanced the tire against her knee and made a rolling motion with her good hand, a stage direction to Ellen to just get it over with. Ellen held up her hand as if to say, *I know what I'm doing*.

The Colonel opened his trunk.

"I want twenty percent," Ellen said.

Munch felt her eyes pop in disbelief. She mouthed the words *What are you doing?*

"Just a minute," Ellen said into the mouthpiece and then covered it with her hand. "If I don't bargain a little," she told Munch, "they'll get suspicious."

Munch shook her head in disgust. "Don't play around with this guy."

"I know what I'm doing." Speaking back into the phone, she said, "That's right. No. Bullshit. Ten ain't gonna do it."

Ellen listened for a moment, rolling her eyes.

"Well, darlin', I have my expenses too."

Munch smacked her friend's shoulder.

"All right, all right," Ellen said. "I'll meet you there in twenty minutes. Out by the bumper cars." She hung up.

"Well?" Munch asked.

"All set," Ellen said. "We agreed on fifteen percent."

"Fifteen percent? Are you nuts?"

"I'm telling you, if I didn't ask, he'd think something was up."

"So then you'll call the feds as soon as Purcell has the money?"

"My daddy's taking care of that."

"Before or after he leaves town?"

"He has to go back to work for a spell, to settle his

affairs, like. He's coming back in time for the funeral."

Munch looked over at where Ellen's dad was still standing. She glanced up at the large concave parking mirror mounted on the corner of the building which gave her an angle on the Colonel's movements behind his open trunk lid. She saw him grab something wrapped in a white towel from the far corner of his trunk. She was reminded of what she had seen him carrying out of his house earlier in the day. He shook out the towel over an open nylon gym bag. Whatever had been inside dropped out. He dumped the money out over it and zipped the bag shut. Munch felt an awful prickling sensation rush up her back. The feeling increased as the the Ford's trunk closed with the finality of a coffin lid.

Ellen and her dad got into his sedan. "Wish us luck," she called out the window.

"Don't go," Munch said.

"We'll be fine," the Colonel said. "You just take care of you."

He started the car, put it in reverse, and backed out.

Munch watched them roll down the street, then ran to the phone and dialed Rico's number. While she waited for the connection to go through, she opened the Colonel's book once more, hoping she wasn't going to find what she knew was there. Each entry caused another chill. Especially when she saw that Lila Mae and Dwayne Summers's names were, like Suki's, annotated with the day of their death. Billy Vega's name was on page six and circled. On the last page to have an entry, the page with today's date, there was a statement: *Ellen admits possession of $$.*

Rico answered his telephone with a curt "Chacón."

"It's me," she said, "Munch."

"Where are you?"

"About to head to Santa Monica." The only place she knew that had bumper cars and was within a twenty-minute drive was the Santa Monica Pier.

"Have you heard from Ellen or her dad?"

"That's why I'm calling you. I've got an offer for you."

"What kind of an offer?"

"I want to trade you a killer for a friend. Can you do that for me?"

"Can you give me the details?"

"I can give you everything you'll need. In exchange, I'm going to need you to overlook a few things."

"I'm listening."

Munch told him what she needed him to do. "I'm also pressing charges for kidnapping and assault."

"On who?"

"One of my assailants is going to be at the Santa Monica Pier by the bumper cars in about twenty minutes. I'll be happy to point him out."

"Don't put yourself in danger. Wait for me."

"Just get there." She hung up. On the way out to her car, Munch grabbed a red one-gallon plastic gas can half full of unleaded.

Chapter 31

Fifteen minutes later, Munch pulled her GTO behind a motor home in the parking lot below the old Santa Monica Pier. She grabbed the can of gasoline and climbed the steep concrete stairway past the large plate-glass windows of the Boat House. The sun had set, and there were only a few stragglers on the pier's boardwalk. A couple of Mexicans in hooded sweatshirts and baseball caps had fishing lines cast into the murky green water. Light from the overhead lamps reflected dully off the stainless-steel sink and counter where they cut their bait. An old bag lady was rummaging through the trash cans farther down. The Ferris wheel and the other rides weren't running, but the arcade was open. She wished she had Ellen's talent for disguise as she waited for all the players to arrive. She hid along the side of the shuttered booth of the ring-toss game. From her vantage point she could see the street-level parking lot, the stairway leading up from the beach parking area, and anyone headed out to the bumper cars on the end of the pier.

The white Ford was already there, but no one was in it. If Purcell was still using the brown van, he hadn't arrived yet. There was no sign of the shot-up gray Mustang either. She spotted Ellen coming out of the rest room, gym bag in hand, and caught up to her at the end of the darkened ticket kiosk.

"Ellen," she hissed.

Ellen paused, but didn't look at her. Instead she bent down as if to tie her shoe and said, "What are you doing here?"

"This is a setup."

"No shit," Ellen said.

"No, I mean against you too."

"What are you talking about?"

"Come here."

"Purcell is going to be here any minute."

Munch reached out her good hand and pulled her friend to her. "Your dad put something in the bag. Check it out."

Ellen unzipped the bag and looked inside.

"On the bottom," Munch said. She pushed Ellen out of the way and dumped the bag out. One of the packs of money clattered as it hit the ground. Munch picked it up and peeled back the top layer of bills to reveal a dye pack.

"What in the world?" Ellen said, either not able to or not willing to comprehend its meaning.

Munch started picking up the bundles of money and throwing them in a wire-basket trash bin. She unscrewed the cap of the gas can, threw the nozzle aside, and dumped the raw gas over the money. "Give me a light," she said.

"But what about Purcell?" Ellen asked.

"Forget Purcell. He's not your problem. The cops are on their way. We've got to get rid of this stuff."

"Who called the cops?" Ellen asked.

Munch held up her splinted finger. "I did. I'm willing to press charges on Billy and Purcell for what they did to me. I'll say they were trying to get to you. And you say you agreed to meet with them because your daddy was going to tell them to lay off or else."

Ellen handed Munch her lighter.

Munch lit a stack of bills and tossed it in with the others. Flame whooshed out the top of the can. She looked up when she heard a man's voice say "No." It was Purcell, running up the ramp from one of the lower fishing balconies.

"Uh-oh," she said. "What was he doing down there?" She cast a quick look over the side and saw that the ramp below the landing continued all the way down to the sand.

The Colonel burst out of the arcade and ran at them, yelling, "Halt!"

Halt this, Munch thought, picking up another stack of bills and adding it to the growing inferno.

Purcell had shed his suit for Levi's and a black leather motorcycle jacket. His heavy boots clumped down on the wooden planks, sounding like battering rams as he closed the gap between them.

Ellen reached into her waistband and pulled out what appeared to be a cap gun. It looked woefully inadequate to the task of stopping the charge of a grown man.

Purcell must have thought so, too, because he didn't slow his pace and pulled out a gun of his own. His was bigger.

Ellen's dad yelled, "Stop!" and took a flying leap from six feet back, his arm straight out and aimed for Purcell's chest. The concussion knocked Purcell back. Munch saw the flash of the knife's blade in the Colonel's hand for one split second before he plunged it into Purcell's rib cage. Both men grunted and fell heavily to the ground. There was a sick gurgling sound as Dane's knife hand thrust upward. Purcell's booted foot kicked once and then was still. It all happened so quickly that Munch was still holding her arm up to ward off the attack.

The Colonel looked up at her with red-rimmed eyes and said, "It's over." He put out his hand for Ellen's gun.

Ellen looked from one of them to the other, her face crumpled in confusion.

"Ellen," Munch said, "he knew Suki. She probably supplied him with information about you. He knew all about you and the club, and he knew about the money. Ask him why now? Why did he take the trouble to find you now?"

Ellen looked like a little kid, small and helpless. "Daddy?"

The look Elliot Dane leveled at Munch was pure hatred. "You don't know what's at stake here. Now put that gun down, and you won't be in any worse trouble than you already are." He walked toward them with complete confidence. "You know, I had a feeling you were going to be trouble."

"The cops are on their way," Munch said. "Don't you make it worse."

"Daddy, what's going on?" Ellen had both hands wrapped around her little derringer. It was aimed at her father's feet. "Why are you talking like this? You didn't kill Mama, did you?"

"Of course not. Put that weapon down. Now."

"Explain this," Munch said, holding up his little black book.

"Where'd you get that?" Dane asked.

"Daddy?" Ellen asked again. The barrel of the derringer wobbled uncertainly.

Dane's eyes strayed to their right. Munch heard tires screaming on blacktop and turned to see a dark four-door sedan fishtail to a stop in the parking lot below, but whoever it was was too far away to be any help. There was no escape. The water below them was too shallow to risk jumping. The burning money crackled and sent up palm-sized ashes. She swatted away a cinder spiraling toward her eyes just as Dane lunged.

Chapter 32

Rico drove as Becker ordered backup. The magnetic beacon on the unmarked sedan flashed red as they weaved through going-home traffic.

"We've got two squad cars waiting for our word at the McDonald's parking lot across from Santa Monica Place," Becker said, holding a walkie-talkie with an open frequency to the backup units. He also had his .38 out of its holster and lying across his lap. This was only the second time in his career that he had drawn his weapon in a real-life scenario. The other time he hadn't needed to fire it.

"She said by the bumper cars," Rico said. They were still on Ocean Avenue when he pointed and said, "There she is."

Becker saw them all, lit eerily by the flames and black smoke of a fire raging next to them. He lifted his radio to his lips and said, "Two females and a white male on foot. The white male has a knife. Get ready." Becker had also heard the screeching tires in the parking lot, but put the distraction out of his mind. What mattered now was the other man. The one with the knife. Rico pointed the car's searchlight on the scene just as the man with the knife lunged.

They heard the unmistakable pop of gunfire.

"Daddy," Ellen screamed in a voice that cut through the hubbub of traffic.

The man with the knife staggered back as if an unseen hand had pushed him.

"Shots fired!" Becker screamed into the walkie-talkie. "It's going down now!"

Rico drove up on the sidewalk, glancing off a lamppost. The car stalled. He threw it in park and desperately cranked the starter as the surreal scene below them unfolded.

Munch watched Elliot Dane stagger back. A small hole near the bottom of his rib cage pumped dark, almost black blood. Ellen dropped the little derringer and screamed. Dane slumped to his knees and wove there drunkenly for a moment, his mouth open.

"What did you do?" Munch said.

Dane coughed wetly and tried to reach inside his suit pocket, his movements slow and uncoordinated, as if he were asleep and dreaming. Thinking he was going for a weapon, Munch easily stopped him and stuck her own hand in his pocket. She found two things: one was a slim leather billfold, the other was a black plastic device the size of a match box with a small red button in the center. She stood and opened the billfold. Inside was a silver shield that read SECRET SERVICE.

"It wasn't me," Ellen said, dropping to her father's

side and wrapping her arms around him. "Daddy, it wasn't me. I didn't shoot you. I swear."

Munch's ears were still ringing from the gunshot as she reached down and picked up Ellen's cold gun. The derringer looked like a toy.

"The pig is her daddy?"

Munch turned to the voice speaking from the shadows.

"Ba-Boom-Ba?"

"You point that peashooter at me," Ba-Boom-Ba said, "and I'll cap you."

Two Santa Monica PD squad cars, their beacons flashing, skidded to a stop at the base of the boardwalk. They were prevented from driving any closer by the concrete posts that were meant to separate the pier's foot traffic from vehicles. Munch knew they would see the gun in her hand, see two men down, and rush to conclusions. They had no way of knowing the shot fired had not come from Munch's weapon or that the threat to their lives was in no way contained. They would only be reacting to the huge dumps of adrenaline charging their fight-or-flight reflexes.

"Drop it now," one of the cops yelled over his loudspeaker system.

Munch looked back helplessly. The cops were positioned behind their open doors. Counting Ba-Boom-Ba's large black pistol there were five guns trained on her.

Ba-Boom-Ba's eyes reflected the light of the flames. Her cheeks were flushed red and her hair was blown back. Munch realized the Ba-Boom-Ba and Purcell must have arrived on a motorcycle, which explained why she hadn't spotted their car and how they had gotten here so fast in rush-hour traffic.

Ba-Boom-Ba's lips curled back in a small but heartless smile. "Better do as they say."

Munch let the little derringer clatter to her feet.

Ba-Boom-Ba pointed at Purcell and asked, "Is he dead?"

Munch looked at the mass of dark blood that had spilled from Purcell's body and said, "I'd say so."

"Where's the money?"

Munch gestured to the fire with one of the hands she now held high in the air. "You know, you did some job here, playing these guys off each other."

Ba-Boom-Ba kept the gun trained on Munch as she knelt down behind the cover of the burning barrel and scooped up the remaining packets of bills. She smiled as she began to stuff the money down her pants.

"Put your hands over your head," the cop's voice boomed from the base of the boardwalk. "Both of you, do it now."

Ellen, working desperately to seal the bullet wound in her father's abdomen, screamed, "We need an ambulance here!"

"Hands up. Now!"

"Let me see if I got this right," Munch said, her hands up and fingers spread. "You set up your buddy Corinne first."

Ba-Boom-Ba was still shoving the packets of money down her pants. "She wasn't my friend."

"No, that's right. That was the problem. She was Billy's friend, and then Billy took care of Animal for you. But what did you have against Lila Mae?"

"Some people just manage to get themselves in the wrong place at the wrong time," Ba-Boom-Ba said.

"Like Suki?" Ellen said.

"Why don't you ask her when you see her," Ba-Boom-Ba said, then she pointed her pistol at the nervous cops on the pier and fired off three rounds.

Behind her, Munch heard the cops guns racking their loads of ammunition. Ba-Boom-Ba disappeared down the stairs.

"Wait, don't shoot!" Munch yelled, using all her willpower to keep perfectly still.

"We surrender!" Ellen yelled, her hands glistening with her father's blood.

The world around them was full of color: red blood, orange flames, black smoke, green water. The stragglers at the end of the pier had all taken cover behind the concrete benches; red and blue lights bounced off the thick plastic sheeting around the carousel. The sirens had stopped. In fact, there was no sound at all—not the cry of the gulls, nor the roar of traffic on the Coast Highway, not even the constant crash of the surf. Munch waited for the hail of bullets to rip into her. Part of her mind wondered if they already had.

It's okay, she told God in her head. *Thy will not mine be done. Thanks for everything.*

Then the first bit of sound returned to the world. It was a man's voice shouting, "Hold your fire!"

What she felt next were rough hands pushing her to her knees. One cop kept shouting, "Keep down, keep down!"

"We're cool, we're cool," Ellen said.

"She's getting away," Munch said, as one of the uniformed cops kept patting her down, turning her pockets inside out, running his hands behind her back, looking for a reason to get more physical.

Becker said "They're okay" several times, but the patrol officers needed to convince themselves.

"Please," Ellen pleaded, "he's bleeding."

"We've got an ambulance on the way," Becker said.

Rico brushed the uniformed cops away and brought Munch to her feet. He put his hands on either side of her face and drew her close to him, so that the whole rest of the world dropped away. "Who's getting away?" he asked.

"Ba-Boom-Ba . . . Darlene . . . she went down, under the pier. She's got a gun."

Below them a loud rap-rap-rap echoed, the unmistakable roar of a Harley with straight pipes.

"Down below!" one of the cops shouted. "On the bike path!"

Ba-Boom-Ba, astride a large Harley-Davidson motorcycle, shot out from under the pier.

Becker ran to the railing and pointed his gun. Later he would admit that what he meant to shout was "Police, stop or I'll shoot!" in an authoritative voice. But what came out was a shrill "I'll kill you, motherfucker!"

Rico also had his weapon drawn and was shouting, "Halt! Police!"

Munch stood, aimed the small flat device she had found in Elliot Dane's pocket in the direction of the escaping motorcycle, and pushed the little red button on the top. There was a muffled bang and a red mist of escaping ink as the dye pack wedged in Ba-Boom-Ba's too-tight jeans exploded. The big Harley with the pink paint job slid on its side across the paved bike path below with a grinding shriek. Ba-Boom-Ba skidded into the sand amid a hail of sparks. She didn't try to get up, and within minutes she was surrounded by cops with drawn guns.

Up on the pier, Ellen cradled her father's head in her lap. Munch pressed the heel of her good hand to the wound on Dane's torso. She could feel his pulse against the skin of her palm as his life blood escaped through her fingers.

"How could you?" Munch asked.

The Colonel looked at Ellen when he said, "I'm sorry, baby."

Ellen just stared at him.

A dark sedan with government plates pulled up beside the police cars. They said a few words to the officers containing the crime scene and were allowed to pass.

"Now who's this?" Munch asked under her breath, as the two men jogged over to them.

"It's Agents Carter and Long," Ellen said. "The Secret Service guys who came to see me in the joint."

"Is that who you called from the station?" Munch asked Dane. "You're working with them, aren't you?"

"That's why you came back?" Ellen asked.

Dane looked at Ellen; his mouth was slack and didn't close completely as he formed his words. "I didn't know you," he said. His palm fell open as if in supplication.

"No," Ellen said, "and you never even tried."

"You still have a chance to do the right thing," Munch whispered into his ear. "Tell her."

The agents reached the trio. "We've got help coming, sir. Hold on."

"Who's that?" Dane asked, squinting as if he were peering into the dark.

"It's Carter, sir. Save your strength."

"Ellen?" Dane said, slapping a weak hand at the air.

Ellen took his hand. "I'm here. I'm right here."

"I love you, baby."

Munch watched as the last bit of light went out of Dane's eyes, to be replaced by the dull film of death.

"No," Ellen sobbed. "Please don't go."

Munch put an arm around her friend's heaving shoulders and pulled her close.

Behind them, Becker was on the radio ordering paramedics to the scene. Rico left Darlene Tarrel in the custody of two uniforms and went to check on Purcell. The man was dead, from what looked like a filleted heart. Rico stared at the wound, then looked up in time to see Munch spread her fingers over the burning drum. Munch stared back hard when she saw him observing her. He'd seen the same look before on gang kids caught in the act. He had the strange sensation that he and Munch were running on parallel tracks in parallel universes.

"We're going to need a coroner," Rico said. Becker nodded and relayed the information to dispatch.

Munch knelt down next to Ellen. Ellen's sobs were soon drowned out by the approaching sirens.

Rico knew he should separate the women and question them, but for now he didn't have the heart. There would be plenty of time to sort it all out later.

Munch whispered urgently into Ellen's ear. "Tell them you're not saying anything without your lawyer."

"But—" Ellen said.

"I already have one lined up. We'll see what he says is the best way to go, but if you don't come clean, this is never going to end. I'll back you one hundred and ten percent. We'll get through this. I promise."

Rico walked up to them. "Are you all right?" he asked. "Let's see that arm."

Munch let him help her out of her coat. The bullet that had felled Dane had raised a furrow across her forearm. Rico closed his big hand over the wound and said, "We've got paramedics coming."

"Thanks for getting here so quickly."

"You should have waited for me," he said, his tone angry. "One more minute and you might not have been so lucky. Never, I mean, never do this again."

"All right," Munch said. It seemed an easy enough promise. She liked his strength, his forcefulness, even the brusque tone that he used to order her around. He was macho, probably a chauvinist, and clearly expected his word to be the last. One day, she thought, she wouldn't like that about him. But now, she found it incredibly comforting, even sexy.

"What happened to your hand?" Rico asked. He sounded angry, and his grip on her arm tightened.

She motioned toward Fred Purcell's body. "He attacked me earlier this afternoon. Him and another guy named Billy Vega threw me in the back of a van. They were looking for Ellen. After Billy broke my finger, he told me to get ahold of Ellen. He thought she had a bunch of money." Munch paused and looked him directly in the eye. "But there is no money now."

"You should have called me right away."

"I did. I called from the hospital. The operator thought I was Kathy."

He jumped a little, as if from the shock of seeing someone he wasn't expecting, like the ghost of girlfriend present. He didn't meet her eye; instead he looked down at the fire burning hotly in the trash can. "Who set this?"

"It was burning when we got here," Ellen said. "Probably some wino around here looking to get warm."

"Ellen," Munch said.

"Oh all right, I set it."

"No, I set it," Munch said.

"Why?" Rico asked.

"Because I wanted to see the look on Fred Purcell's face when I burned the money he wanted so badly."

"This was evidence," he said.

"In the moment, it felt like the right thing to do." Munch looked into the flames where the pages of Elliot Dane's little black book curled in on themselves before igniting. She felt a deep satisfaction that proof of a father's disloyalty would never be used against his forsaken daughter.

Rico's brows came together in a frown. "Because you didn't want the money falling into the wrong hands?"

"Something like that. Do you want me to help you put it out?"

"We've got the fire department coming. They should be here in another couple minutes."

Becker walked over. "We're going to need some statements from you two." He took Ellen off to the side, leaving Munch and Rico alone.

"Who's Kathy?" she asked.

"I've been meaning to talk to you about that," Rico

said. "But this is not the time or the place." He looked behind her, toward the city. "What's taking that ambulance so long?" His arm was around her shoulders, holding her tightly.

She wanted the moment to go on, to feel safe in his arms. But in her heart she knew he was holding back. He hadn't said Kathy was his sister or a coworker.

"Just give it to me straight," she said. "Tell me now. I'm too tired for any more bullshit."

He sighed and then looked down into her eyes. "Kathy is a woman I've been seeing for a couple years. She's the third reason I moved to Los Angeles. Let's talk about this later," he said. "Right now we need to get you to a doctor."

"What about Ellen?" They both looked over and saw Becker seating Ellen in the backseat of a squad car. She wasn't in handcuffs. Becker had also draped a blanket around her shoulders and left the door open.

"We're going to take her statement and then see where we stand."

"Go easy on her. She's been through a lot."

"I know."

Becker joined them. "We're going to head down to the station now."

"Can I say good-bye to Ellen?"

"Yeah, c'mon." He walked her over to the squad car and opened the door. Munch slid in beside her friend.

Ellen was looking out her open door at the form of her dead father. The parking lot was filled with squad cars. Perimeter tapes had been strung. The fishermen Munch had seen earlier had abandoned their equipment and fled when the action started. A patrolman was asking questions of the bag lady. Munch knew they would question all possible witnesses. The truth was the best way to go and, in the long run, the easiest.

"Ellen?"

"I'm all alone now," she said. She looked terribly lost. Munch had never seen Ellen so deflated. She had hoped for this moment of vulnerability in her friend, but now that it had come it was more painful than she could have dreamed.

"I know he meant it when he said he loved you," Munch said.

"You do?"

"How couldn't he?"

Ellen leaned into her and Munch felt her exhaustion. "You think he would have come back after?"

"Of course he would. Remember that his last act was heroic. He went for Purcell, when he could have just waited it out. In the end, he chose you."

Ellen looked out past Munch where Rico was giving instructions to the crews of police personnel. "What's up with you and him?"

"I'm not sure yet." She put a hand on Ellen's shoulder. "I'm going to call a lawyer for you. His name is McManis. Jim McManis. After you're done with the cops, come over to my house. I'll leave a light on."

Chapter 33

"So it turned out that Elliot Dane was working with the Secret Service," Munch said to Rico. They were at the hospital. The doctor had cleaned and closed the wound on her arm, and she and Rico were seated in the foyer outside Admitting, waiting for her discharge instructions. "I can't believe a father would take a job that might mean turning in his own daughter."

"There was a lot at stake."

"Like what?"

"I've just heard rumors, and you can't repeat any of this."

"I can keep a secret."

"Yeah, I believe that about you."

"Anyway," she prompted.

"The money Ellen, uh, *found* was part of a much larger shipment. It was produced in the Middle East, Iran to be exact. President Reagan supplied the shah with a few of the Treasury Department's intaglio printing presses. You know what they are?"

"Sure," Munch said. "They're what the BEP use."

He looked at her a moment with one eyebrow cocked, shook his head, and then went on. "After the shah fell, the new regime used those presses to print millions in counterfeit U.S. currency. The purpose was to undermine the American economy."

"Leave it to Ellen to get herself mixed up in a caper of international proportions," Munch said. A woman with a swollen ankle sat down next to them and picked up a magazine. Munch lowered her voice and leaned close to Rico. "Is the Secret Service going to keep after her?"

"Let's just say she better not turn up with any more funny money."

"Oh, she won't."

"You did the smart thing, fixing her up with that lawyer."

She noticed he didn't say "the right thing."

"Just one question," she said.

"Yeah?"

"That anonymous tip you guys got about where Billy could be found . . ."

"What about it?"

"Was the caller a man or a woman?"

Rico hesitated a moment and then said, "It was a woman."

"Isn't it always?" Munch replied.

To Rico's credit, he didn't mindlessly agree.

"She probably won't cop to it," Munch said, "but it had to be Darlene."

"The woman scorned?"

"You know about that?" Munch asked.

"I know she bailed him out of jail a few times."

"Yeah, she had it pretty bad for him. Big mistake."

A paramedic walked past them, and somebody paged a Dr. Fenton over the hospital's loudspeaker. Munch figured it was time to take the plunge. She took a deep breath for courage and asked, "So you've been dating this Kathy chick for years. Do you live together?"

"No. We thought we might at one point, but it didn't work out. She has cats. I keep telling her that I'm allergic, but that isn't it. She travels a lot with her job. My hours are crazy. I told her it would be better for both of us to keep our own places."

"And she's cool with that?"

"She wants more. She wants to get married and have kids."

"Does she know you screw around?"

When he leaned in close to speak into her ear, she felt the warmth of his breath all the way to her knees. "It didn't feel like screwing around," he said.

She smoothed down a piece of surgical tape on her splinted finger. "Do you love her?"

"She's a good person," he said.

Munch relaxed a little, her question had been answered. That "you're a good person" line had been used on her a few times, and she knew what it meant.

"I was thinking you two would like each other," he said.

"That's not going to happen."

"No, I'm not saying I want you guys to meet."

"What are you saying?"

"I'm going to need a little time here," he said, rubbing his neck. "I feel things for you that I never have for her. Never could, I know now. I'd like to give us a chance."

"You would?"

"Why are you surprised?"

"I just thought . . . I mean, after how you acted at the station. You know, with my rap sheet and all."

"Who am I to judge you? I've done my share of shit too. Stuff I'm not proud of."

"Like what?" she asked.

"That's not important. What's important is who we are today. And all I know is that since I've met you, I can't stop thinking about you."

Munch wanted to take the happiness his words brought and package it. Another part of her warned her that there was another shoe waiting to drop. "So what's the problem? Break up with her."

"I don't want to hurt her if I can help it. She's been good to me and my daughter."

Munch couldn't figure where he was headed with this. She didn't want to see anyone hurt either, most of all her. Two attendants walked down the hallway with a gurney. Munch and Rico pulled their feet back to let it pass.

"Kathy's been offered a really good job in Boston," he said. "I'm going to tell her to take it."

"When would she leave?"

"Not until March. We can wait until then, can't we? I know this is a lot to ask of you, but it's how I need to handle this to feel good about it."

"March what?" she asked.

"I don't know yet," he said.

"Let me know when you do," she said. "You've got my number. You've got all my numbers."

At three the next morning, Munch woke up to the sound of her front door opening. Ellen was in the living room. "How'd it go?"

"Much better once my new best friend Jimbo got there."

"Jimbo?"

"Jim McManis, that lawyer guy. Thanks for calling him. He was great. The cops kept asking me the same questions over and over. I just hate when they do that, don't you? Like you wouldn't be smart enough to remember your own story."

"What about the feds?"

"Agents Carter and Long told me not to leave town. I told them I didn't have any immediate plans. The cops are going to want you to come back and swear out a formal complaint against Billy Vega."

"With pleasure."

Ellen pointed to Munch's hand. "I'm sorry that happened."

"I'll live."

"I know. But I screwed up getting you involved in all this. I was wrong."

"I don't think I've heard you say that before."

"I've been thinking about a lot of things differently lately."

"Maybe there's hope for you yet."

"You think you can still get me into a recovery house?"

"I'm sure I can." Munch hoped that somewhere Lila Mae was smiling down on them.

"So what's the deal with you and that cop?" Ellen asked.

Munch brought her up to speed.

Ellen listened, and when Munch was finished, she shook her head. "I can't believe you're screwing around with a cop."

"I told you they weren't all jerks."

"That remains to be seen," Ellen said. "Next time, you should give *him* the hickey."

"If there is a next time."

"I think you're a long way from being through with that one," Ellen said.

Munch knew her friend was right.

Epilogue

On Saturday, Mace and Caroline St. John sat on Munch's couch and made her go through the whole story one more time. Asia was in the backyard, throwing the ball for the dogs.

Mace shook his head in a gesture halfway between amusement and disgust. He looked at Munch long and hard before he spoke. "Darlene Tarrel is being charged with everything from felony assault to murder, although she's claiming to be just an accessory after the fact, that Purcell and Billy Vega handled all the rough stuff. We know Vega wasn't directly involved in the Summers's murders, and ballistics on the gun Purcell had at the pier match the bullet we recovered from Dwayne Summers's head."

"What an idiot," Munch said. "He should have tossed that gun immediately."

St. John smiled.

"Ba-Boom-Ba . . . Darlene . . . is not going to get away with Elliot Dane's murder either," Munch said.

"No, she's not, although she's trying to claim self-defense. Meanwhile, the DA has enough documented evidence to indict her on the other three murders. They're going for murder one with special circumstances in the case of Lila Mae Summers and Dwayne Summers."

"And Suki's?"

"Probably plead it down to murder two, depends on the physical evidence."

"Right," Munch said, wondering if Suki had family somewhere, and if they'd care enough to come to the trial.

"They're also ninety percent sure Lawrence Whitley killed Corinne Adams, believing she was ripping him off because of information supplied by Darlene Tarrel. Billy Vega, unaware of Darlene's instigation, killed Whitley in retaliation."

"So," Munch said, "all the bad guys are dead or in jail and the surviving good guys"—she held up her splinted finger—"are healing nicely."

"Does it hurt much?" Caroline asked.

"No, not really. I just have to remember to keep it elevated. I flushed the rest of my codeine yesterday. Probably a day too soon, but better that than taking one too many."

"And what's going to happen to Ellen?" Caroline asked.

"The DA and her attorney are working out a deal where she gets a deferment in exchange for her cooperation with their task force on organized crime. Meanwhile, she checked into a women's recovery house, and she's talking like she's going to stay."

Mace made a disgusted noise. Caroline patted his knee and said, "We hope so."

"But here's the real kicker," Munch said. "It turns out Ellen was her father's sole heir. So as usual, she's going to make out like a bandit. It'll pay for the lawyer anyway. I only hope she uses the probate period to get her head right."

"And the little girl? Lindsey?"

"She's back with her father. Noreen Ramsey is in Metro Hospital undergoing evaluation. Somebody called child welfare on them, so they've got a caseworker to answer to now. It's not a good situation. I just hope the father steps up to the plate and does what's right for his kid." She looked down at her hands. "Remember Garret?"

"The boring one?"

Munch smiled. "Yeah, he has a new girlfriend."

"Good for him."

"That's right."

"And what about this Rico?" Caroline asked.

"Well, he's not boring, that's for sure."

"I'm going to check on the dogs," Mace said, excusing himself.

Munch and Caroline waited until he had left the room, and then Munch told Caroline all the details.

"Quite some soap opera, huh?" Munch asked when she had finished.

Caroline waited for her to continue.

"Part of me knows I should tell him to call me after the girlfriend is really gone," Munch said.

Caroline nodded thoughtfully. "That sounds like the smart, safe path."

"Yeah, and it's the one I'd take if I were buying a car or something. You know, not work on the engine until the title is clear."

"So what are you going to do?"

"He wants to see me tomorrow."

"And will you?"

"I want to." Munch shook her head and smiled. "I read somewhere once that when you fall in love, your body produces a euphoria-inducing hormone. Why do you think they call it dopamine?"

"You're not being stupid," Caroline said. "Your ability to still trust and hope is one of the things that make you so special. Don't lose that."

"What do you think I should do?"

Caroline looked at the door Mace had walked out. "There are no easy answers, kiddo. I guess if I were you, and I really had strong feelings for the man, I'd wait until March and see if he was good to his word."

"I can't picture myself doing anything else," Munch said. "How about until then?"

"Be happy, joyous, and free."

Munch looked at Caroline and then threw her head back and laughed. She'd forgotten all about that part. As she laughed, she kept her middle finger up and extended as per doctor's orders.

Acknowledgments

I would like to thank in no particular order the following persons who provided me with valuable information and insights:

The big guy with the ponytail and walkie-talkie at Carolina Entertainment who didn't want to give me his name. Resident Special Agent for the U.S. Army Criminal Investigation Command, Anthony DeSiderio, who wanted me to use his name. Robert A. Jakucs, retired cop and private investigator, who taught me the art of interrogation. Officer Joe Flores, the nicest narc I've ever met and compared notes with. Lamborghini, the exotic dancer who would have comped me a lap dance if I hadn't looked so freaked out. Gary Bale, a wonderful consultant and truly exceptional cop. Charlie Sinatra, the correctional counselor at the California Institution for Women at Frontera who led me through the prison and answered all my questions. To the inmate who casually mentioned being there sixteen years, proudly showed us her little cell, and reminded me how lucky I was to not be in her place. Thanks. Private investigator and retired LAPD detective Don Long, who never answers a simple question without giving me a chapter's worth of material. Stan Lane of Internal Control, who taught me about lie detector tests. Gerry Petievich for his information regarding counterfeit currency and the Secret Service. Patricia McFall, teacher, author, friend. Martin J. Smith, another wonderful writer and traveling companion on this rocky road. Readers and friends, Barbara Eilert, Marie Reindorp, Kathleen Tumpane, and all the Fictionaires of Orange County.

Praise is also in order for my agent, Sandy Dijkstra, and my editor, Susanne Kirk, for seeing this book through to production.

Last, but not least, I want to thank my husband, Ron, who is my best friend.

Turn the page for a preview of
Unpaid Dues. . . .

The sixty-two-year-old groundskeeper of the exclusive Riviera Country Club spotted the bodies at first light. The corpses huddled against each other at the bottom of the concrete storm channel just before it disappeared downstream beneath the golf course. Wide enough to drive in, the storm channel had offered many surprises in the past—hubcaps, beach chairs, the broken shafts of misbehaving 7-irons, but never anything so horrific. Hector Granados had been hoping for treasure this Monday morning, especially after the heavy winter rain the previous weekend. Golf games had been canceled, and the typically barren storm drain that ran beneath the course had turned into a raging torrent. This amount of water, he knew, was capable of carrying and then depositing a vast range of large, sometimes valuable, refuse.

At first, he thought it was a bundle of clothing, then he saw the hands. The larger body, the female, clutched a baby to her bosom. He looked for a long time, and the baby never moved. Its little hand reached out stiffly from beneath the blanket swaddling it. The slow-moving current carried a branch. It tangled with the woman's hair, causing her head to pull back. Her gaping throat wound opened like a second mouth into a grotesque and silent scream. Her eyelids were purple and protruded from her face like two hideous grapes, and a small stream of foamy pink bubbles trickled from her lifeless mouth.

"Oh my God," Hector said, first in English, then several more times in his native Spanish. He used his two-way radio to contact the clubhouse. "The police," he told Pat, the starter. "We need the police."

"What's wrong?" Pat asked.

"It's terrible," he sobbed. *"Dios mío."*

"What?"

"Bodies, two of them," Hector said, his breath short, as if he had been running. "In the canal. *Ay, pobrecito bebé."*

"Oh, shit," Pat said, "and I just let the first foursome tee off ten minutes ago."

Mace St. John, the newly promoted homicide detective-three of LAPD's West Los Angeles Division, arrived to supervise the investigation. The groundskeeper opened the maintenance-yard gate at the end of Longworth Drive and allowed the police to set up a command post on the blacktop next to the country club's tennis courts. The other cops on the scene, including St. John's partner, Tony "the Tiger" Cassiletti, made themselves busy studying the surrounding houses and their yards, glancing only briefly below.

"C'mon, ladies," St. John said, feeling angry, wanting a living target to vent on. A lot of the officers with families had problems dealing with dead children. Hey, he didn't love it either, but the poor little kid was already dead and someone needed to figure out the who, why, and how of it.

The bodies were slumped against the south vertical wall of the large cement trough. At first glance, they appeared to be embracing, but that tender aspect was shattered when, after a moment's concentration, St. John made out the rope binding them together. It didn't seem likely that they had been dropped the twenty feet from the bank above. The woman's red shirt was scooted up her back, and her shoulder-length brown hair pointed downstream. They looked as if they had been dragged. Another ten yards and they would have been lost forever under the golf course.

Getting them out of there was going to be a trick. The storm channel was bordered by double rows of chain-link fence. There were narrow dirt easement roads in between the eight-foot chain-link fences, running parallel to the channel until it reached the perimeter of the country club. St. John learned that the entrances to those roads were off Allenford, across the street from Paul Revere Junior High School. The gates to the easements were padlocked, and signs posted by the Metropolitan Water District warned off trespassers. But St. John could see by the cigarette butts crushed into the dirt that those signs were regularly ignored, probably by students out sneaking a smoke. He was instantly grateful that kids hadn't been the ones to make this discovery. It was a difficult enough sight for even the most seasoned of cops.

St. John stared at the dark mouth of the tunnel and the rocky, muddy embankment above it. Climbing down from up above was out of the question. There were already piles of loose shale and scrub brush on the concrete floor of the storm channel—small-scale replicas of the Pacific Palisades' landslides that had recently narrowed the width of Pacific Coast Highway. All those hopeful idiots who'd built on the cliffs were now paying dearly for their ocean views.

St. John dragged a milk crate over to the fence and climbed atop it. White out-of-bounds markers stuck into sturdy kikuaya grass on the crest of the embankment defined the golf course's border. A low layer of fog hovered over the fairways. It reminded him of mornings in Vietnam and how the steam used to rise off the rice paddies.

His radio crackled to life. He lifted the Handie-Talkie from his belt and pushed the transmit button. "Go ahead."

"MWD is on the way."

St. John had had dispatch call the Metropolitan Water District flood maintenance people to bring a key and charts of the system. He studied the chain-link fence again before responding. The poles were anchored in cement at ten-foot intervals. There were no recent tire tracks on the easement. The backyards of the houses on either side of the easement fences were heavily shrubbed. Storm water, he decided, had carried the bodies to this resting place from farther upstream.

"We're gonna need a fire truck with a detachable twenty-foot ladder, winch, litter, and bolt cutters."

St. John called over one of the uniformed patrol

officers who had been guarding the scene since first responding to the call.

"Where does this feed from?" He looked at the cop's name tag and added, "Henderson."

Henderson pointed as he explained that the system originated at Sullivan Dam to the northwest, and Mandeville Canyon due north. Natural tributaries and storm drains came together just above Sunset Boulevard. Here the large concrete storm drain tunneled under Sunset then ran open alongside the school, following the curves of the boulevard. It also went under Allenford. On the other side of the golf course, the channel reemerged in Santa Monica Canyon and ultimately ran into the ocean.

"We're going to need to look upstream," St. John said.

Henderson nodded and seemed ready to get on the task immediately. "No," St. John said, "I need you here." He got back on the radio and ordered a chopper to fly the fence line.

The fire engine arrived within ten minutes of the yellow MWD truck. St. John approached the driver of the water district truck, introduced himself, and told the guy what he needed. Minutes later, the gate was unlocked, and the eighteen-wheeled hook-and-ladder rolled noisily down the dirt easement. School kids gawked as their buses turned in to the driveway of the school. St. John posted patrolmen at the gate to keep onlookers back. He sent Henderson to stand on the golf course.

"Should we call in divers?" Cassiletti asked.

"There's like an inch of water," St. John said as he snapped photographs with the Polaroid camera he always brought to crime scenes. "I think we can handle it."

Cassiletti cast a nervous eye downward. "That can change in an instant."

"We'll work fast."

To the dismay of the guy from MWD, St. John borrowed a pair of bolt cutters from one of the firemen and snipped the fence away from the pole twenty yards upstream from the bodies. He then asked the fireman to lower a ladder into the channel and was the first to climb down. The floor of the storm channel had its own weather system, colder and damper than topside.

St. John understood Cassiletti's concern. It was February sixteenth, still officially the rainy season which stretched from October to April. Five feet up from the concrete floor, a crust of lighter wood and floatable garbage marked the height the storm water had reached in the last few days. But today the sky was clear, in fact, it was a brilliant blue. The small grove of eucalyptus trees above them had put out small white tendriled blooms in response to the soaking of their roots. One of the houses nearby had a fire going, and the air carried the smell of wood smoke.

Up close, the bodies looked reasonably fresh, especially the child's, whose perfect little fingers were frozen in a reaching gesture. One small plump foot was bare. St. John looked closer and almost laughed out loud in his relief. The child wasn't a child at all, but a doll. No wonder it had yet to show the darkening signs of decomposition. He examined the real corpse, trying to get a fix on her age. She was either a teenager or a small woman. Her hands were withered from immersion and bore no rings. The face was unrecognizable, rendered into a pulpy ruin from repeated blows.

He walked past the body and shined his flashlight into the opening of the cement sleeve that ran beneath the golf course, built, he was told by the Metropolitan Water District's flood maintenance supervisor, thirteen years previously in 1972 at a cost of $1.7 million. The tab was happily picked up by the golf course in lieu of an ugly cement trough bordered by chain-link fence running through the barranca of the first and seventh fairways.

St. John treaded in increasingly smaller semicircles that brought him closer to the body, working with his eyes focused just ahead of his feet, pausing every now and then to squat and study the odd bit of flotsam that could possibly matter later. At last, he arrived back at the corpse. The distinct, oddly sweet, scent of decay rose to his nostrils. So maybe not so fresh. Seeping blood formed a halo on the wet cement around her head. In St. John's experience, the severity and abundance of the facial wounds was an indicator that the dead woman's attacker knew her. The slit throat was very personal.

Had the rains continued, the corpse would have been swept into the tunnel and never been discovered. St. John examined the cinder block that had been used to weigh down the body. It was the two-cell variety and had no clumps of dried cement clinging to it—the sort of thing college kids used to build shelves for their stereos. Not much in the way of a clue, but they would have to follow every lead, no matter how unpromising.

He hunkered down next to the body to wait for the Scientific Investigation Division criminalists. There was not much more to be done, but he didn't want the victim left alone any longer. She had the rest of eternity to be alone and forgotten.

The crime scene photographer arrived and took pictures, beginning with over-alls of the scene, then close-ups of the dead female before the scene was disturbed. The doll's face was buried in the woman's chest, nestled between her breasts. The two had been bound together with white cord, with the ends of the rope fastened by odd, looping knots to the cinder block.

Firemen, at St. John's direction, built a dam of sandbags upstream. Kids from the junior high school filtered over to the fence at Allenford, trying to get a peek at what was going on. St. John sent an officer to the admittance office with instructions that the school run a check on the whereabouts of any student who was absent, particularly the brown-haired girls.

Frank Shue from the coroner's office appeared at the top of the bank. As usual, he wore wrinkled, ill-fitting trousers, and his striped, long-sleeved dress shirt was half untucked. "What you got?" he called down.

"Body dump," St. John answered, his voice echoing against the steep walls. The worst. Smart killers who dump the bodies simultaneously eliminated the victim, the crime scene, and most, if not all, trails leading back to them.

"Oh, jeez," Shue said, eyeing the ladder and rubbing an open hand across his mouth.

"I'd like to transport the body as is." St. John heard the crack in his own voice and cleared his throat.

"You got it," Shue said. He returned five minutes later with a four-by-ten-foot opaque sheet of plastic and a roll of twine. He joined St. John, wading through the muck in a pair of weathered high-top tennis shoes. The men put on latex gloves and laid the plastic on the paved floor of the storm channel.

St. John used a sharp pocketknife to sever the rope where it threaded through the cinder block, thus preserving the nooselike knots. He grunted slightly as he climbed halfway up the ladder and handed the wet block to Cassiletti. The second, younger detective took the evidence in one of his big hands and lifted it easily, as if it were made of Styrofoam.

"You should be down here," St. John said.

Cassiletti said, "Oh, I'm sorry," in that high nervous voice of his and set down the cinder block on a sheet of white butcher paper he'd spread on the ground. St. John sighed as the big man climbed almost daintily down the side of the bank, taking his time, as if worried he'd break a fingernail.

Shue secured paper bags over the woman's hands to preserve possible evidence under her fingernails, and then searched her pockets. He found nothing by way of identification.

Overhead, a helicopter beat back ocean breezes. St. John caught himself listening for distant mortar fire.

"Let's get her out of here," he said, collecting his breath and feeling the ever present weight in his chest, a reminder of the heart attack he'd suffered four months ago at the tender age of forty-two. His hand strayed for a moment to his pocket as he assured himself that he had his nitroglycerin tablets with him. It was a gesture he repeated at least twenty times a day.

The body flopped a bit as Cassiletti and Shue rolled it onto the plastic. The woman was now on her back, her bagged hand fell to her side. Rigor mortis had come and gone, there would be no point in taking liver temperature readings to determine loss of live body temperature. She had been dead for over twenty-four hours, probably closer to thirty. St. John placed the woman's bag-encased hand over the doll's body, then Shue folded the tarp around the cadaver, burrito-like, and bound the macabre package with lengths of rope at the corpse's waist, ankles, and neck.

"Good thing she wasn't in the water that long," Shue said, "or you'd want to be real careful about tugging on any body parts."

St. John was also grateful the body hadn't been in salt water, where crabs and shrimp would nibble off the smaller extremities.

"See if you can plump up those fingers and get me some prints," he said, blinking into the sun. Her own mother wouldn't recognize her face, not with that much damage.

At St. John's signal, the boom of the fire engine swung over the canal. A litter attached to a heavy steel winch hook was lowered. The shrouded body was loaded onto the litter, lifted up the embankment, and then onto a gurney for transportation to the coroner's office.

The detectives and the coroner met up top for a

brief huddle. Shue told St. John he'd let him know as soon as he had any information on the identity of the deceased and left.

St. John removed his latex gloves, clamped a hand on Cassiletti's big shoulder, leaving an imprint of the white powder they put in the gloves to facilitate slippage over sweaty hands, and pointed at the cinder block. "Find out everything you can about this. I want to know where it's made, sold, and used. And I want that information today."

Cassiletti, ever anxious to please, said, "I'll become the world authority."

After the coroner left, St. John drove the tree-lined, curving canyon roads north of Sunset Boulevard. Large convex mirrors warned of oncoming traffic. Many beautiful homes were nestled in the rustic hillsides, some were under construction—signs of Reagan prosperity—many had stables. He drove slowly, attempting to trace the route of the storm drains, but after Sunset Boulevard, the channels weren't visible from the street. Riviera Ranch Road ended at a house that reminded him of the entrance to Disneyland's Frontierland, complete with a two-story outer wall made of logs and a wrought iron porch light the size of a chandelier.

He returned to Sunset Boulevard, where the channel split, and parked his car in a space between a wooden guardrail studded with orange reflectors and a six-foot-high redwood fence. The easement road here was no wider than a footpath but easily accessible. The chopper pilot had noticed a disturbance in the silt lining the bottom of the channel just before it turned under Sunset Boulevard.

The gate to the wooden fence was open so St. John peeked inside. He saw six horse stalls, all occupied. A bay mare in the first stall stuck her head over her railing to greet him. He took a moment to stroke her soft muzzle and look into one of her big brown eyes.

"See anybody suspicious lately?" he asked.

She twitched her ears and snorted softly. He wished he had a carrot.

Beyond her swishing tail, St. John noticed that someone had stacked several bales of hay on the narrow easement outside the stall and against the fence flanking the canal. He pushed the top bale aside, and saw where the chain link had been cut. The severed ends of steel were still shiny, showing no hint of oxidation. He also found the bend marks where a triangular flap of chain link had been bent outward and then straight again. Using his car radio, he requested that the Scientific Investigation Division send a unit. When they arrived, he told them what he wanted and how badly he wanted it.

Jane Doe 85-00248 was transported to the Los Angeles coroner's office downtown. There, workers unwrapped the plastic shroud and carefully delivered the plastic doll from the dead woman's unresisting arms. She was photographed again, X-rayed, weighed, washed, fingerprinted, and prepared for autopsy. Samplings of vegetation, fibers, and soil clinging to the body were also collected and cataloged; pubic hair was combed; debris under the fingernails was scraped into sterile white envelopes labeled with her case number. The life-size baby doll was put in a plain cardboard box, face up.

Results from the fingerprints of the Jane Doe came in within an hour, due to the lucky break that she had a police record. Her name was Jane Ferrar. She had been arrested for prostitution, petty theft, and under the influence. Most of her offenses were in neighboring Venice Beach, but one charge was listed as occurring in West Los Angeles—St. John's division.

He returned to the station and pulled the hard copy of her arrest report. He had to hunt a bit in the station's archives to find it. The arrest date was ten years earlier on June 10, 1975. The charge was driving under the influence. He brought the folder back to his desk and opened it. Before he got a chance to read the arresting officer's narrative, he spotted the black-and-white mug shot paperclipped to the 5.10 form.

"Oh, God," he said. His chest constricted. He picked up his telephone, but couldn't remember the number, digits kept transposing in his head. Still not breathing, he flipped through his Rolodex and stopped at M.

M for Mancini, for Munch, for mechanic, for mother of an eight-year-old daughter.

He punched in the telephone number of the Texaco station where she worked, her photograph gripped between his thumb and index finger. The telephone rang in his ear. Munch looked disheveled in the picture. Her light brown hair uncombed, a rebellious sneer on her face, not yet the smiling, sober young woman he'd come to know and—

"Bel Air Texaco," a man's voice answered.

St. John fought to calm his thoughts, trying not to superimpose Munch's face on the battered corpse. "Lou?"

"Yeah."

"It's Mace St. John."

"How's it going? Just a sec." Lou put down the phone and called out, "Munch, line one."

St. John exhaled, and by the time Munch picked up, his heart rate was back to normal.

"Hello?" she said.

"I need to talk to you," he said.

"Sure, what's up?"

"Not on the phone."

"This can't be good," she said.

"It could be worse. Trust me."